Praise for Karin Gillespie

LOVE LITERARY STYLE

"Witty and smart, entertaining and lyrical, in *Love Literary Style* author Karin Gillespie explores all facets of love and language through her evocative characters and charmingly delicious plot."

— Laura Spinella,
Bestselling Author of *Ghost Gifts*

"An intelligently written novel packed with Southern wit. This is a story book clubs will devour. It's warmly humorous, thought-provoking and shines with emotional depth."

— Amy Avanzino,
Author of *From the Sideline*

"Cheeky and charming, Gillespie's sweet, outlandish fable is as much a sendup of books, authors, and the publishing industry as it is a love letter to it all."

— Phoebe Fox,
Author of *Out of Practice*

GIRL MEETS CLASS

"Funny, empathetic, and wise. Gillespie shines a light into dark corners we need to examine, but somehow manages to entertain us at the same time. A fantastic read."

— Susan M. Boyer,
USA Today Bestselling Author of *Lowcountry Bordello*

"A delectable page-turner with twists and turns at every corner."
— *San Francisco Book Review*

"Filled with humor and a happy ending, I highly recommend this to anyone looking a humorous read with just a dash of romance!"
— *The Southern Bookworm*

"Gillespie knocks it out of the park...[her] humor is as tender as it is sharp. At first, Toni Lee's figures of speech zip by like jerky ducks in a shooting gallery; but as she orients herself her aim improves. By the time you fall in love with her, bells are ringing all over the place...It's got everything: gymnastic sex, moonlight and madness and love and romance."

– The Augusta Chronicle

THE BOTTOM DOLLAR SERIES

"With a flair for timing and a cheeky southern turn of phrase...Brace for a wild ride chock-full of Southern wit and down-home advice from a clutch of quirky characters you will hope to see again soon."

– Booklist

"A winner of a first novel, filled with Southern-style zingers and funny folks."

– Kirkus Reviews (starred review)

"The characters are the kind of steel magnolias who would make Scarlett O'Hara envious."

– The Atlanta Journal-Constitution

"Laugh-out-loud antics as...Gillespie continues her entertaining Bottom Dollar Girls series...Certain to please women's fiction fans of all ages."

– Romantic Times (Top Pick)

"As tart and delectable as lemon meringue pie...a pure delight."
– Jennifer Weiner,
Author of *Good in Bed* and *In Her Shoes*

"A fine romp of a book, well-written and thoroughly entertaining."
– The Winston-Salem Journal

Divinely Yours

Books by Karin Gillespie

GIRL MEETS CLASS
LOVE LITERARY STYLE
DIVINELY YOURS

The Bottom Dollar Series

BET YOUR BOTTOM DOLLAR (#1)
A DOLLAR SHORT (#2)
DOLLAR DAZE (#3)

Divinely Yours

Karin Gillespie

HENERY PRESS

DIVINELY YOURS
Part of the Henery Press Chick Lit Collection

First Edition | September 2017

Henery Press
www.henerypress.com

Trade Paperback ISBN-13: 978-1-63511-263-4
Digital epub ISBN-13: 978-1-63511-264-1
Kindle ISBN-13: 978-1-63511-265-8
Hardcover ISBN-13: 978-1-63511-266-5

Printed in the United States of America

To my husband, David Neches,
who consistently makes my life heavenly.

ACKNOWLEDGMENTS

Henery Press is an amazing, forward-thinking publisher. I'm so grateful to them for their helpfulness, accessibility, and accommodating nature. Thanks to Rachel Jackson whose editorial skills are some of the most honed in the business and whose cheerfulness is unflagging. Thanks to Kendel Lynn who is always optimistic and warm, and just an overall wonderful person. Thanks to Art Molinares who's always genial and always makes time to discuss any pressing business needs. Thanks to Erin George for her organization of those fun Facebook hops, and I'm also grateful to Amber Parker for her marketing abilities and flawless execution of group giveaways.

Thanks to Dr. Les Betrand for walking me through some of the orthopedic info I needed while writing this book.

One

The red light on Skye Sebring's computer blinked rapidly, announcing the arrival of her first client of the day. Within seconds a girl with darting eyes entered the cubicle. She wore a spiked leather wrist cuff and a t-shirt with the logo "Hustle or Die."

Skye barely made note of the vivid splash of red dripping down the front of the girl's shirt. In her line of work she saw more blood-soaked and broken bodies than an ER physician. Her main concern was the young age of her client. She didn't have a lot of experience processing teenagers, and this one looked like a handful.

"Welcome, Chelsea," Skye said. "My name's Skye Sebring. I hope you had a pleasant journey."

The teen swept a suspicious gaze around the cubicle, taking in the utilitarian wooden desk, the metal wastepaper basket, and the bare walls. Skye had just been reassigned to a new cubicle and hadn't done anything to fix it up yet. Usually she had a couple of cheerful posters hanging—photos of blue-eyed kittens or smiling dolphins seemed to have a calming effect—and she generally kept a dish of Hershey's Kisses on her desk.

"Where the hell am I?" the girl said.

"Not Hell, thank goodness. You've arrived in the Hospitality Sector of Heaven. Sorry it doesn't look very celestial around here."

Chelsea slouched against Skye's desk, her hands jammed into the pockets of a pair of scruffy blue jeans. "If this is heaven," she said in a low measured voice, "where's Morrison?"

"Morrison?" Skye shuffled through the papers on her desk. "Is Morrison a relative of yours, Chelsea?"

She jerked a corner of her mouth downward. "What about Hendrix or Cobain?"

Skye studied the girl's information sheet. "Sorry, Chelsea. I don't see any of those people in your record. There is, however, your great-aunt Ethel, who's very anxious to see you."

"Aunt Ethel?" Chelsea's hair had a severe part in the middle, and was so fine and pale it looked like sheets of cellophane. "The one who sent me a Little Mermaid sleeping bag for my last birthday? *That* Aunt Ethel?"

"The very one." Skye chuckled. "Unless you have more than one Aunt Ethel."

"What's so funny?" Chelsea said. "I'm taking a dirt nap, and you're laughing?"

"I apologize. I didn't mean to make light of your current situation. About your aunt Ethel—"

"I don't want to see her." Chelsea punctuated her statement with a stomp of her clunky tennis shoe.

"It's just that you died so young, there really isn't anyone else—"

"And whose fault was that?"

Actually, it was Chelsea's fault. According to her death report, the thirteen-year-old had been practicing skateboarding stunts in a church parking lot and had sailed over a brick wall, falling onto the blacktop below. Chelsea would almost certainly have avoided her fatal acute subdural hematoma had she been wearing the hundred-dollar helmet her mother bought for her. Instead, she'd filled the helmet with ice and used it to cool a half-liter bottle of Mountain Dew.

"Chelsea, I know you're upset—"

"No kidding. I'm worm food."

"Being dead isn't the end of the world, Chelsea. In fact, it's a wonderful new beginning. Heaven is very..." Skye cast around in her mind for some current teenage slang. "...epic?"

Chelsea shoved a balled fist in the crook of her waist. "So what's there to do here? Play harps?"

"That's a common fallacy, Chelsea. Let's go over this pamphlet, 'What to Expect When You're Expired.'"

Skye held out the pamphlet, but the girl ignored it. "Can't you just give me a straight answer? What are you hiding from me?"

"I'm not hiding anything."

The newly dead were a notoriously suspicious bunch, always half expecting Satan to leap from behind the desk like a rubber snake out of a can.

"You can do whatever you want in Heaven. It's surprisingly unstructured." Skye picked up the remote for the television. "I have a DVD that will answer—"

Chelsea startled Skye by snatching the remote from her hand and lobbing it across the cubicle. "I don't want to watch some stupid DVD." Her kohl-lined eyes glittered like chips of mica, daring Skye to challenge her.

Page seven, paragraph four of the *Hospitality Handbook* had several specific suggestions for dealing with belligerent clients:

1. Speak in soothing, even tones.

2. Validate your clients' feelings with active-listening techniques.

3. If a client cannot be calmed by other means, administer a dose of Tranquility In a Can. (Should be kept in right-hand desk drawer at all times.)

When faced with client insubordination, Skye generally skipped the first two directives and went right for the TIC. Why put up with unpleasantness when tranquility was so close at hand?

Skye eased open her desk drawer, but the canister was missing. She'd forgotten to stock the drawer when she'd switched cubicles. Now she was forced to reason with the girl.

"That wasn't very nice, Chelsea, but I understand this is a big change for you and—"

"Get me out of here *now*!"

"Chelsea, please, if you'll just—"

The girl's pale skin flushed crimson; spittle dotted her bottom lip.

"Shut up. I hate you!"

"I realize you're dead," Skye said calmly. "But I didn't kill you. Would you stop being such a pain in the ass and let's get on with this, please?"

The girl's eyes grew so wide Skye could see the gold flecks in her irises.

"You said ass," she whispered.

All traces of toughness drained from her body, leaving behind a wide-eyed child with a quivering lower lip and a nose on the verge of running.

"If the shoe fits."

"You're allowed to call me a name?"

Skye glanced at the ceiling. "I don't see any lightning bolts."

Chelsea tugged at her pimpled chin. "And people in heaven swear?"

"Damn straight we do."

"Thank God." She bit her knuckle and glanced around the cubicle. "Oops. Do you think He's eavesdropping?"

"He happens to be a She. And of course She's eavesdropping. They don't call Her omniscient for nothing." Skye opened Chelsea's file and made a brief notation. "Hopefully She won't hold this ugly little incident against you."

Chelsea dropped into a swivel chair in front of Skye's desk and twisted back and forth in it as if it were a piece of playground equipment. "I'd never fit into a place where everyone's a goody-two-shoes. You'd have to send me to you-know-where." She winced as she pointed at the floor.

"Nobody's perfect in Heaven. Well, maybe a few high-ranking angels in Headquarters, but they're not very much fun at cocktail parties." Skye laughed at her own joke. The teenager blinked blankly, the quip zooming over her shiny blonde head.

"You'll also be glad to know there isn't a 'you-know-where,'" Skye continued. "Just Heaven."

"No Hell?" Chelsea looked astonished. "Where do all the bad people go?"

Skye dreaded such questions. The Hospitality Sector functioned primarily as a welcome wagon. There wasn't time for lengthy discourses on complex theological issues.

"There's an FAQ in your orientation packet, which will answer your question better than I can," Skye said. "For now, let's just say that 'bad' people have a very hard time getting into trouble once they're in Heaven. Nobody to kill. Nothing to steal."

"I thought Heaven would be like church," Chelsea said. "I figured I'd have to hang out in a pew all day, singing hymns and saying prayers." She caught her fingers in her long hair. "Do girls get their periods here?"

"Absolutely not," Skye said. "You'll never have to worry about that bloody nuisance again."

Chelsea pouted.

"Oh. Did you *want* your period?"

The teen toed the carpet with the tip of her tennis shoe.

"I've been waiting for it since I was eleven, and I'm the only one of my friends who hasn't gotten it yet. I'd even picked out the tampons I wanted to use, Tampax Satin Teen in the pink and blue box."

"I'm sorry about that. I never imagined someone would actually *want*—"

"What about cute boys?"

Skye frowned. Teenage boys were surprisingly durable and didn't make frequent appearances in the Hospitality Sector.

"I may be able to scare up a couple of guys for you, but right now, let's stream your orientation video, shall we?"

She dimmed the lights and hit play. All orientation videos were customized for the client. The cubicle filled with a voice saying, "Chelsea, welcome. I know this is a scary time for you, my dear, but you're going to adore Heaven. It's a lovely place for little girls. In Heaven, all of your wishes can come true."

It was Chelsea's Aunt Ethel. She held up a device that looked like a BlackBerry and jabbed at the keys. In a flash, an oversized teddy bear appeared in her arms. "Isn't that a darling trick?"

Chelsea almost tumbled backward in surprise. "How did she do that?"

"She used a WishBerry." Skye handed Chelsea a similar device. "In Heaven, you can wish for anything you want, and, abracadabra, it appears."

"Go ahead, Chelsea. Give it a whirl," Aunt Ethel said from the screen. "Baby dolls, jacks, party dresses. Anything your heart desires."

Baby dolls? Skye raised an eyebrow. Aunt Ethel was going to have quite the shock when she reunited with her niece.

"Can I try?" Chelsea asked.

"Sure," Skye said. "Type in whatever you want in the box."

"I know exactly what I want. My dream skateboard. A Flip New Wave HKD Red deck with Grind King trucks and Pig wheels." Chelsea's fingers flew over the keyboard of the handheld computer, and in seconds, the skateboard appeared in all its glory.

"Snap!" Chelsea said, running a finger along the edge of the shiny deck. "Wait until I show it to my skating buddy Horsemouth. He'll have kittens."

It took a second for the reality of her situation to come crashing down upon her. Chelsea's eyes glazed over and a panicked look crossed her face. Skye knew the "look" only too well. It was when the newly dead realized they were not only dead; they were positively, absolutely, undeniably, and reliably dead.

"Horsemouth won't see it, because I'm...I'm..."

Skye appeared at her elbow with tissue in hand. "It's okay to say it aloud, Chelsea. Being dead is not as awful as you think."

Chelsea wrenched away from her. "Yes, it is. And I don't want to be—" She stopped for a moment and her lips twitched into a sly smile. Immediately she gritted her teeth and scrunched her eyelids closed. When she opened them, disappointment darkened her face. She banged the WishBerry with the palm of her hand as if it were defective.

"It didn't work," Chelsea said.

"Of course it didn't. Heaven is your home now. You can't go back to Earth."

"How did you know what I wished for?"

"I've been doing this job for a while now."

"What about my mom?" Chelsea said. "And my little brother, Andy. I can't see them either? They're lost to me forever?"

"Not forever. You can see them very soon on a special television channel we have in Heaven called Earthly Pleasures."

"Let's watch it now." Chelsea lunged for the remote on Skye's desk. "I want to see if they're okay."

"Not yet, Chelsea." Skye gently pried the remote from her fingers. "Newcomers are barred from watching Earthly Pleasures until they've been here for at least one week."

"Why?"

"We want to discourage unhealthy attachments to those left behind. You have to understand, Chelsea. You and your family are now on two separate planes of existence."

"In other words, I'm plant fertilizer and they're not," Chelsea said with a glum nod.

"I wouldn't put it exactly like that, but yes."

Chelsea's expression brightened. "Could I back home and do a little recreational haunting? Maybe put a little scare into my younger brother? Make his Matchbox cars float in midair?"

Oh, the newly dead and their preoccupation with ghosts. Truth was, there were no such things. What the living mistook for specters were just residual energy fields. The dead could only return to Earth under very special circumstances.

"I'm sorry. That won't be possible. Shall we finish watching the DVD?"

"Do we have to?" Chelsea said with a frown. "I'm kind of jetlagged from the trip."

"I suppose you can watch it later in your room. I'll take you there."

"Where exactly are we going?"

"Newcomer quarters, where you'll be able to relax. Counselors are on hand at all hours to assist you should you feel sad or start to miss loved ones."

Chelsea fiddled with a large shark's tooth hanging from her neck. "When am I going to be interrogated?"

"Never. Contrary to what you may have been taught in vacation Bible school, Heaven isn't a place of judgment."

"Are you sure?" Chelsea said. "Because there might have been a time or two on Earth when I accidentally broke one of the Commandments. None of the really important ones, but—"

"I'm positive."

"But if Heaven isn't about judgment, what is it about?"

"Contentment," Skye said with a smile. "Heaven is like that old Corona beer commercial—the one where the people on the beach toss their cell phones into the ocean without a care in the world."

"Are you trying to tell me there aren't any cell phones in Heaven?"

Skye suppressed a laugh. "Of course there are cell phones. There's just never any bad news or telemarketers on the other line."

Skye led Chelsea out of her cubicle, and the two of them stepped into a hall that contained a glass elevator. When they boarded, Joy, another Hospitality worker, was already inside, comforting a young woman garbed in a satin wedding dress with a long white train. Skye nodded a greeting as the bride sobbed into a bouquet of daffodils.

"Three hundred guests and not one of them knew the Heimlich," the bride said. "I told Arnold we should have ordered salmon for the wedding dinner."

"Chicken bone," Joy mouthed.

"Skateboard mishap," Skye mouthed back.

The elevator pinged when they reached the ground floor, and Skye and Chelsea exited and hopped onto a moving sidewalk.

"You are now entering the Newcomer Sector," said a soothing disembodied voice. "Average newcomer stay is from five to seven days, Earth time. Concierge is located on the ground floor and manned twenty-four hours a day. Join us for a mixer in the Divine Ballroom at seven p.m. with piano stylings provided by Ray Charles."

The sidewalk teemed with clients and their greeters. Some of the newly dead still looked pale and drawn from whatever ailment had claimed them. A group of high-school students in torn and bloodied formal wear rode the sidewalks in stunned silence.

Skye had forgotten it was prom season. Chelsea might meet some cute guys after all.

Chelsea scrutinized the knots of bedraggled people traveling with her on the sidewalks. She glanced at Skye with a questioning look. "Are all of these people...Are they all..." She made a cutting motion across her throat and emitted a gagging sound.

"Yes, Chelsea. They're all dead. And while they might look shell-shocked right now, they'll perk up soon enough. As your aunt Ethel said, Heaven is a fantastic place to be. It's a lot like Earth, but with all the kinks ironed out."

The sidewalk ended, and they entered a vast atrium that looked very much like the lobby of a luxury hotel. A black-suited bellhop, dressed in a white bow tie and gloves, greeted them and bowed at the waist.

"Welcome, Chelsea. You're in guest-room suite 302. I hope you enjoy your stay."

The elevator doors parted, and Skye and Chelsea boarded. There were more efficient ways to travel in Heaven, teleportation for instance, but many familiar elements of Earth were incorporated into the sector to make the newly dead feel at home.

They traveled to the third floor and strode down a lilac-scented hallway lined with several ornate gold mirrors and heavy wainscoting. When they arrived at room 302, Chelsea said, "We forgot to get the key."

"No keys necessary in Heaven," Skye said. Skye switched on the light in the bathroom. "This is a very special bathtub. It allows you to soak in anything from Perrier to rose petals to buttermilk. The controls are on the faucet."

Chelsea stood behind her, glancing around as if looking for something. "Excuse me, but where's the...you know?"

"A toilet is just one more thing you won't need in Heaven."

Skye stepped into the bedroom and drew the blinds to reveal the ocean lapping against an expanse of white sand.

"This is your view remote," she said, picking up the oblong device. "You can change your view with a click of a button. Mountain vista, Paris skyline, Bavarian village, or you can program in your own preferences."

She pointed to the four-poster king-sized bed covered with a down comforter, heaps of frilly pillows, and an assortment of stuffed animals.

"There's a turn-down service every night. You can also use your WishBerry computer to redecorate this room any way you like, or you can put the room into mood mode, and your outer world will reflect your inner world. Why don't you try it?"

Mood mode was a reliable way for Skye to gauge her client's state of mind. If paintings like Munch's *The Scream* suddenly appeared on the wall, she knew she should send up a grief counselor a.s.a.p.

She showed Chelsea the proper button to use, and as soon as the teen pushed it, loud punk music blared, posters of bare-chested teenage boys plastered the purple walls, and the smell of sausage pizza wafted through the air.

Skye covered her ears. "Your inner world is certainly lively."

"I'll save this for after you leave," Chelsea said, changing the room back to its former state. Then she stroked her chin and quickly drew back her hand as if she'd been burned.

"Something's weird." She hurried to stare into the gilded framed mirror above the dresser. "Holy crap! My zits are all gone."

Skye nodded. "That's just one of the many benefits of life in Heaven. Your body gradually loses all of its flaws."

"Wow," Chelsea said, continuing to admire her unblemished chin in the mirror. "Selena Gomez, watch your back."

"Are you going to be okay?" Skye asked. She felt slightly

uneasy leaving such a young girl to her own devices. "Your aunt will be here shortly to welcome you."

"I'll be fine. My mom always used to say I was an old soul. She said she could see it in my eyes." Chelsea frowned. "That's weird."

"What?"

"Five minutes ago I was really missing my mom, but all of the sudden she seems so far away now, like I'm looking at her from the wrong end of the binoculars. How can that be?"

"That's the way it's supposed to be. The longer people are in Heaven, the less they tend to pine for those they've left behind."

Chelsea kicked off her shoes, pushed aside a menagerie of plush toys, and flopped down on the bed. "How long ago did you die?"

"Actually, I've never died."

"I don't understand."

"It's simple. I'm a brand-new soul—only a year off the assembly line." Skye pretended to sniff her armpits. "Still have that new soul smell."

"So are you ever going to Earth?"

"Not for a while. New souls usually spend years in Heaven before they're selected to live their first life on Earth. Besides, I'm perfectly happy where I am." She paused. "But if I were to go to Earth, what words of advice would you have for me?"

Chelsea wrinkled her brow. "Obviously you should wear a helmet when you try an ollie."

"An ollie?"

"Skateboard talk. And be sure and learn how to fall, 'cause you're going to spend a lot of time on your butt."

Skye laughed. "I'll try and remember that." She reached for the doorknob. "I better scoot. You sure you're okay?"

Chelsea smothered a yawn. "I'm just a little tired. Death takes a lot out of you." She plumped her pillow and sunk her head in the middle. "One more thing. I know there's a turn-down service—"

"All you have to do is pick up the phone beside your bed."

"I don't suppose there's also a tuck-in service? My mom still insisted on tucking me in even though I told her I was way too old. But now—"

"Now you wish she was here to do it?"

Chelsea nodded.

Skye tucked the blanket under her chin and brushed her lips across Chelsea's broad forehead.

"Sweet dreams," she whispered.

Skye switched off the bedside lamp and tiptoed out of the room. She rode the elevator down to the lobby and boarded the moving sidewalks. Saturday was always a brisk day in the Hospitality Sector. People on Earth had more time to drown, wreck their cars, or fall off roofs. The only day busier than Saturday was Monday, which ushered in the cardiac arrest and stroke victims. Apparently the prospect of facing another long workweek eked the life out of many people on Earth.

A Muzak version of "Stairway to Heaven" competed with the thrum of the monorail as it wove its way around the building, delivering the newly deceased to various destinations throughout the area. There were an average of 146,000 deaths per day on Earth; thus, the Hospitality Sector was a mammoth operation. The monorail never stopped running, and the enormous glass structure always bustled with the comings and goings of greeters and their clients.

Skye closed her eyes and let the sidewalk transport her throughout the sector. "Stairway to Heaven" was replaced by Ella Fitzgerald singing, "Heaven, I'm in Heaven. And my heart beats so that I can hardly speak."

She'd heard the song so many times before it barely made a blip in her consciousness. The Fitzgerald tune, along with "Pennies from Heaven," "Tears in Heaven," and "Thank Heaven for Little Girls," played continuously throughout the sector.

"Skye!"

Her best friend Rhianna was behind her. Skye waved.

"What're your after-work plans?" Rhianna said.

"Nothing in particular," Skye said.

"Why don't we go in the Live A Little Lounge for a quickie?" Rhianna pointed at the bar, which was near the exit of the sector and only for greeters. "Glory and Joy said they were stopping by."

Skye shook her head. "I feel like being outdoors." Ever since she'd started dating her new boyfriend, Brock, she had much less interest in nightclubbing.

Two Hospitality workers staggered out of the bar. Obviously the evening's festivities were already underway. Greeters were a notoriously wild bunch, and no wonder. In Heaven, there were no hangovers.

"Big birds, five o'clock," Rhianna whispered.

Two guardian angels traveled on the adjacent sidewalk. They wore diaphanous white uniforms with gold wing-shaped pins fastened to their bodices. The two angels' heads were nearly touching as they spoke in low tones.

"Who do you think will get promoted this year?" Rhianna said.

"Probably Joy," Skye said. "She's been nominated for Who's Who in the Hereafter two years running."

Greeters were evaluated each year. According to their performance, they either stayed in their positions or were promoted to guardian angels. Every once in a great while a greeter was selected to go to Earth—an incredibly rare honor. It indicated a new soul had developed, in a short time, the fortitude to live his or her very first life.

"I hear there are surprises every year," Rhianna said. "Who knows? Maybe *you'll* be promoted."

Skye laughed, knowing Rhianna was teasing. There were a handful of fiercely competitive greeters who desperately tried to distinguish themselves by taking continuing-education courses or volunteering for overtime after earthquakes and other natural disasters. Skye wasn't among their numbers and was perfectly happy to put in her eight hours and toddle on home.

Rhianna and Skye exited the main entrance of the building.

"What do you feel like doing, Ms. Skye?" Rhianna said. She

wore a gold ring on each one of her fingers and a silver hoop in her navel.

Navel rings weren't regulation for greeters, but there was nothing regulation about Rhianna's appearance. Her hair was a riot of red snarls and curls, and she'd woven various colors of shiny ribbons through them. She was frequently cited for violating the Hospitality Sector dress code. Once she even fashioned a little skirt out of all of her reprimands and wore it to work, earning yet another one.

"I'm open to suggestions."

"Cloud art? I'm feeling creative." Rhianna waved her hands through the air as if swiping at a canvas on an easel.

"Okay. But I'm not very good at it. All my clouds look like fluffy blobs."

"Don't be so hard on yourself. They're very artful blobs," Rhianna said. "I think I'm in a Chagall mood today."

They passed under an awning of oak trees and headed toward a park. Rhianna scampered in front of Skye, jingling merrily from all her bangles and chains. The waistband of her hospitality skirt had fallen down her hips, revealing a narrow strip of hot-pink underwear.

"On second thought, I'm not feeling ethereal enough for Chagall," Rhianna said, dropping to the ground. "I want something with a touch of whimsy. Maybe Klee."

Cloud art was a popular pastime in Heaven, and involved the use of a brush, pencil, or even a finger as an instrument to render objects in the sky.

"What's it going to be today?"

"A goat maybe?" Skye dipped her finger into an imaginary inkwell.

"Boring." Rhianna brayed like a goat.

"What can I say? Water vapor isn't my preferred medium."

Rhianna's tongue peeped out of the corner of her mouth and as she began to draw Klee's round-headed man, one of her favorites.

"Can I tell you a secret?" Rhianna asked.

"Fire away."

"I'd really like to be chosen to go to Earth."

"Why?"

"Lots of reasons. Body surfing in the ocean for one."

"Why go to Earth when you can body surf right here in Heaven?"

"Not the same," Rhianna said. She uprooted a dandelion and blew the fluff into the air.

"That's right." Skye caught one of the errant seeds with her thumb. "Surfing here is safe. No jellyfish, no undertow, and no sharks who like to snack on redheaded girls."

"I happen to like jellyfish. They look like the ghosts of flowers. So pretty." Rhianna wriggled her fingers to suggest tentacles.

"And pretty painful if they sting you."

"A little pain never killed anyone."

"What do you know about pain?" Skye said. Like Skye, Rhianna was a new soul and had never been to Earth. Physical pain was as foreign to her as the prick of a cactus needle was to a goldfish.

"The threat of pain or danger is exactly what makes surfing interesting on Earth."

Skye had heard other greeters express similar desires. They seemed oddly attracted to the ceaseless drama of Earth life. Not Skye. Why should she ever want to leave a place that was so completely perfect?

"Earth is an extremely hazardous planet," Skye said. "Babies should be born with hard hats and knee guards."

Skye gazed at the pristine blue sky. The weather in Heaven was continuously mild and sunny. If a person longed for rain or snow, there were places in Heaven with diverse weather conditions, but Skye never had any desire to visit them.

"The most frightening thing on Earth is the threat of death." Rhianna wound a fiery curl around her finger. "And we already know what happens when you die, so what's there to be scared of?"

"Maybe there are worse things on Earth than death."

"Like what? Potted meat? Disco music? A *Brady Bunch* reunion show?"

Skye didn't know why she'd said such a thing. It's not like she knew anything about Earth. She stood and dusted off stray blades of grass from the back of her uniform. Her interest in cloud art was waning.

"You know what fascinates me the most about Earth?" Rhianna said.

"What?"

"Hardly anyone wants to leave."

Very true, Skye thought. The first hours in Heaven were the most trying for the newly dead. They mourned the existence they'd left behind, not knowing the life ahead of them was far superior.

"Why are we even talking about this?" Skye said with a yawn. "Neither of us will be chosen to go to Earth anytime soon. Our lives will continue on just as they always have. Blissfully uncomplicated. Who could ask for anything more?"

Two

Caroline Brodie was watching *General Hospital* in her room at Magnolia Manor Nursing Home. The door opened and Mona Scales, the director, burst in without knocking. Two orderlies followed her, wheeling a sheet-covered gurney.

"Guess who has a new roomie?" she said.

"Not me, I hope," Caroline said.

"Now, Mrs. Brodie, don't be a sourpuss. Surely you can use the company. And this roommate will be very quiet. Emily's from the Verandah Wing."

"Then what's she doing here?"

Magnolia Manor Nursing Home in Birmingham, Alabama, had two wings, the Terrace and the Verandah. The Terrace Wing was for residents who still had enough vinegar left in them to play Parcheesi in the parlor or take their bland meals in the dining room. The Verandah Wing, on the other hand, was the dying wing of the facility. Patients there were bedridden or spent their last days strapped into chairs in the hallways, staring at blank walls.

"The Verandah Wing is a bit overcrowded right now. You won't even know Emily is here."

Caroline turned her attention back to her television program; she had no interest in Emily, whoever she was.

"I don't know why you keep it so dark in here." Mona adjusted the blinds. "It's so gloomy."

"And what's wrong with gloom?" Caroline shielded her eyes from the sunlight trickling through the slats, causing a glare on the television screen. Her attention was drawn to the bed near the window, where Mona and the orderlies was situating her new roommate.

She'd expected someone gray and shriveled, ten breaths away from a toe tag. Instead, her roommate looked to be in her mid twenties. Her eyes were a bright blue and stared straight ahead; her brow was pale and unwrinkled.

"What's she doing here?" Caroline said.

Mona made a minor adjustment to the thermostat. "Emily's been with us for almost a year now. She's a Jane Doe."

"Pretty white lady like that and nobody claiming her? Doesn't seem normal."

"Emily is a special case," Mona said. "Poor thing was found badly beaten in an alley, and so far, nobody has come to claim her. Supposedly she had a bit of a drug problem. Crack is what I was told. Some even say she used to stand in front of a pawnshop on First Avenue...soliciting."

Both the words "crack" and "soliciting" were said with a hushed voice.

Caroline pointed a finger at her new roommate. "Why is she staring like that?"

"Emily is in a persistent vegetative state," Mona said. "She's always asleep, which makes her the ideal roommate."

"Ain't no such thing," Caroline said.

"You'll be nice to Emily, won't you, Caroline?"

What was she going to do? Ask the zombie to play a game of gin rummy? Caroline decided Mona's question was too silly to merit an answer and pretended to be deeply engrossed in a commercial for Swiffer mops.

For an entire week Caroline kept a wide berth from Emily. She didn't adjust the blinds (even though they sometimes allowed in too much sun), nor did she water the African violets on the windowsill even though they were wilting.

Both were on her roommate's side of the room. The woman never made a sound, no moans in the night or snores. She just kept staring at the tea-colored stain on the ceiling, eyes welled with fat, wet tears that never evaporated. Caroline discovered they weren't real tears; a nurse's aide squirted liquid from a bottle into Emily's eyes every day so they wouldn't dry out.

She considered asking to be moved next door to share quarters with Hilda Castello. She wondered which would be worse, hearing the occasional shrieks from Hilda—an eighty-nine-year-old Alzheimer's patient who always clutched a soiled Raggedy Ann doll—or sharing her space with a silent sheet-covered mound.

But as time wore on, curiosity gradually replaced her fears. Caroline started sitting beside Emily, watching the blanket rise and fall with her breath and gazing into her empty eyes. She kept testing her, not quite believing someone could sleep so soundly with her eyes wide open. She waved a hand close to her face to see if Emily would blink, and she dropped books on the floor to see if she'd startle. Sometimes, when Caroline felt especially brazen, she'd come nose to nose with her roommate, observing every pore in Emily's face as well as the fine little hairs in her nostrils. Now and then she would jump back in fright, imagining Emily jerking her arms straight out and seizing Caroline's neck like a creature in a fright flick.

Emily's eyes were as electric blue as window cleaner. Her hair, cut ragged by the nurse's aide, was wheat-colored and wavy. Her skin had been out of the sun so long it was bluish white, like milk out of a cow's udder.

"You don't look like a streetwalker," Caroline said.

Maybe if Emily were wearing stiletto heels and crushed-velvet hot pants, she'd look *exactly* like a streetwalker, but in her flannel nightgown and long white elastic stockings she looked more like a sleeping princess.

Caroline decided to reject Emily's whoring history and invent more glamorous backgrounds for her. One day she imagined Emily as a missing heiress; the next, a silver-scaled mermaid fished from the sea. Sometimes she was a beautiful alien from another planet whose spacecraft had made a crash landing on Earth.

She also started talking regularly to Emily. Every evening at midnight, Caroline turned her clock radio to *Minerva,* her favorite show, and she began to direct her comments to her roommate.

"I'm in a terrible fix, Minerva," the first caller said.

A smile flitted across Caroline's face, and she rocked faster in her chair in anticipation of the caller's miserable tale. Most of the callers on Minerva's show were suffering from some heartache or another. The sorrier the story, the more Caroline lapped it up.

"What's the trouble, sweetie?" Minerva said. She always so sounded sugary sweet.

"I'm seven months pregnant," the caller said. "And my baby's daddy, Robbie, is dating my best friend."

"'My baby's daddy,'" Caroline said with a frown. "They didn't have that expression in my day. When I was a girl, if a woman had a baby, the baby's daddy was her husband."

The caller went on about how much she loved Robbie, even though it sounded as if the boy deserved to be tied to the back of a pickup truck and drug around town. Minerva made a few sympathetic clucking sounds and asked the caller what song she wanted to hear.

"'Hit the Road, Jack' is what she should be requesting," Caroline said. She tossed a glance at Emily. "Ain't that right, Sleeping Beauty?"

Emily, of course, didn't say a word; she just kept staring at the ceiling.

The next caller used the moniker "Alone in Atlanta."

"Are you there, caller?" Minerva said.

"Yeah, I'm here," Alone said in a faltering baritone. There was a clattering noise and the musical sound of phone buttons being pressed.

"Alone, are you still with us?" Minerva said.

"I just dropped the phone in the ficus plant," said the caller. "I don't know what I'm doing anymore. This is crazy."

"What's crazy?" Minerva asked.

"This show. I mean...the show isn't crazy. Me calling the show is what's crazy. I feel like Tom Hanks in that movie..." There was more fumbling with the phone.

"*Sleepless in Seattle*? With Megan Ryan?" Minerva said. She seemed amused by the clumsy caller.

"I guess so. Truth is I don't go so much for love stories, Meredith. I'm more of a James Bond kind of guy."

"What's on your mind tonight, Alone?" Minerva asked, her tone more businesslike after having been called the wrong name by Alone in Atlanta.

Alone's voice got softer and more tentative. "I've experienced a...What I mean to say is I've lost..." He cleared his throat noisily. "Someone important to me. It's been over a year now."

"Would you like to tell us what happened?" Minerva asked.

"It's complicated. I don't know why I'm calling. I happened to catch the show last night when I was looking for the ball game and I thought, geez, that Meredith sounds like a good egg. Here she is listening to complete strangers while they go on and on about their—"

"Minerva, Alone. My name is Minerva."

"Minerva! See, I'm usually good with names, but I can't seem to think straight lately. It's been over a year and you'd guess after all that time...I just wanted to talk with somebody about how much I...miss her." He paused. "Listen to me. Spilling my guts on the radio."

'That's what we're here for," Minerva said. She seemed to have forgiven the caller for mixing up her name. "Is there a special request you'd like to hear tonight? A song to help you get through this difficult time?"

"Let me think for a...I'm not up on all the pop songs. I'm more of a jazz fan. John Coltrane, that sort of thing. Tell you what. Is there a song about going back in time? That's what I want. I just wish I could turn back the clock a year and go back to the best time in my life."

Best for you, maybe, but not for her, Caroline thought. Otherwise why did she leave? Caroline knew a thing or two about no-good men driving women away.

"I'm sorry about your troubles, Alone," Minerva said. "I hope this song helps." After a moment, Cher started singing "If I Could Turn Back Time."

"Sentimental claptrap," Caroline grumbled.

After the radio show was over she gabbed to Emily until she was cross-eyed with exhaustion. Caroline had never encountered such a willing listener.

"Did I ever tell you what that pitiful excuse for a husband of mine did the day our son was born? Well, maybe I did, but it bears repeating. Went to a pit-bull fight. While I bled and moaned in agony, he lost two hundred dollars on a dog named Dirty Harry."

It got to the point where Caroline told Emily things she'd never told another living soul. Like how the baby, whom she'd named Russell, had been a stillborn, and she'd held on to him until he was stiff and cold, refusing to let go until one of the nurses begged her. Or how she didn't shed one single tear for her husband, Max, when he died, and instead drank an entire bottle of Muscatel after she'd gotten home from his funeral. Talking to Emily was like airing out a room that had been shut tight for years.

As Caroline's attachment to Emily grew, so did her concern for her health. One afternoon when Poppy, the physical therapist, came in, Caroline quizzed her about her roommate's condition.

"Look here. There must be something you can do to wake that gal up. What does her doctor say?"

"Don't you worry yourself about her, ma'am," Poppy said brusquely. "She's not your concern."

She moved Emily's right foot back and forth and didn't bother to turn her head to address Caroline.

Caroline expected as much. Poppy was a snappish girl whose personality didn't match her cheery name. Cruella or Brumhilda would have been a better fit.

Mona, the nursing home director, was more helpful. When

Caroline mentioned she wanted to learn about Emily's disorder, Mona taught her how to Google for information on the computer in the activity room.

Caroline spent several sessions at the slow-as-molasses PC, learning what she could about vegetative states and traumatic brain injuries. While the aging machine clicked and whirred, she read several articles that claimed the longer a person stayed unconscious, the less likely he or she would ever wake up. There was scant hope held out for those who had been trapped in unresponsive states for more than a few weeks.

She scrolled past the gloom-and-doom information and nosed around for some encouraging news. There was a woman in Albuquerque, New Mexico, who'd gone into a vegetative state after a difficult childbirth. Sixteen years passed, and she finally woke up and spoke to the nurses who were changing her bed sheets.

Most medical professionals gave up on patients who were unresponsive for long periods of time, but after hours of searching, Caroline found an article by a Dr. Irving Frost, who believed stimulating the five senses of his patients helped to rouse them from their vegetative states.

Frost said that health practitioners should try clapping two blocks of wood near a patient's ear or touching the patient's fingers and toes with ice cubes.

Finally there was something she could do for Emily— something that might actually help her. As soon as Caroline returned to her room, she threw herself into a program designed to awaken her sleeping roommate.

She'd learned hearing was the first sense to return in unconscious patients, so she talked to Emily until her throat ached—giving a running commentary on TV shows and reading to her from the latest *Soap Opera Digest* or *Reader's Digest*. She also shook a bottle of calcium tablets near Emily's ear before she took a dose each morning, and then sprayed the room with witch hazel and Secret deodorant. After meals, she smuggled lemon slices from her iced tea back to the room so she could dribble the juice on

Emily's parched lips. In the evenings, she'd run the bristles of her hairbrush lightly along Emily's arms and legs and then she'd massage them until the ache in her arthritic fingers grew too sharp to ignore and damp patches of nightdress clung to her skin.

"I like a good sweat," she said after a rigorous session of kneading her roommate's floppy extremities. "It's a sign of being alive."

As she settled back into her chair, a low moan rumbled from her bowels.

"Another sign of life," Caroline said. She flapped the air with a corner of her gown. "Good thing you sleep so soundly."

The last thing she did every night was sing: "Inky Dinky *parlez vous*." It was a song the kids used to sing when Caroline worked in the lunchroom of Harriet Tubman Middle School, taught to them by the French teacher. The middle-school students would often change the words, substituting "potty poo" for *parlez vous*.

Caroline sang off-key and entirely too loud, reasoning such terrible caterwauling would penetrate Emily's skull and possibly jar something loose. She could only hope and pray.

Three

"Flowers," Brock said. He brandished a bouquet of a dozen long-stemmed red roses and sprays of baby's breath wrapped in green tissue paper.

"Candies." He handed Skye an enormous heart-shaped box of assorted chocolates festooned with a satin bow.

"And finally, kisses," he said, leaning in to give her a gentle smack on the lips.

"You know, Brock," Skye said with a half-smile as she pulled away from his embrace, "you don't have to give me gifts every time we go out on a date." She stood on tiptoe to reach a vase atop an armoire in her living room. "Every other time will suffice."

Brock laughed, revealing a spectacular set of white teeth. Smiles in Heaven were unmarred by cavities or overbites, but Brock's teeth were particularly stunning, a trait that served him well as anchorman for the news show *Today in Heaven*.

"Did you catch the program?" he asked. His hazel eyes were set in an aggressively chiseled face. He was so handsome he made George Clooney look like an old piece of shoe leather.

"How could I miss it? And it was comforting to see that, as usual, all the news was good."

"Is there any other kind in Heaven?" Brock said in his rumbling newsman's voice. "Did you notice this?" He pointed to his blue and white striped tie.

Every day at sign-off, Brock tugged on the knot of his tie, a secret signal to Skye, letting her know he was thinking about her.

"I certainly did. If you're not careful, you're going to end up winning the Best Boyfriend in the World award."

"I hope so. I've been campaigning for it ever since I met you." He extended a well-muscled arm. "Are you ready for your big night?"

"It won't be so big for me," Skye said. "I'm not getting promoted." She glanced at her watch, a diamond-studded Chanel that Brock had given her to mark their three-month anniversary. "We'd better be off or we're going to be late."

The Valhalla Hotel, site of the annual Hospitality banquet, was located in the heart of Celestial Center, an arts-and-entertainment zone similar to Broadway in New York. Rows of performance houses lined the streets, their lit marquees advertising a dazzling variety of diversions. That week Zero Mostel was starring in *Fiddler on the Roof*, Andy Kaufman was performing stand-up at the Laugh Zone, and Anna Pavlova was dancing the lead in *Swan Lake*.

Skye and Brock strolled past an outdoor Lynyrd Skynrd concert, featuring Ronnie Van Zant, who shouted in a hoarse voice, "What song do you want to hear?" The first moody strains of "Freebird" followed his question to the crowd and the amphitheater lit up with the flickering flames of thousands of Bic lighters.

A riot of lit-up billboards competed for the attention of passersby. One, a jumbo-sized photo of a man gazing imperiously down at the sidewalk below and straddling a Harley, caught Skye's notice.

"He looks familiar," she said, pausing for a more careful inspection. The caption beneath the billboard said "Red-Hot Right Now! Ryan Blaine."

"Handsome fellow for an Earthling," Brock remarked after taking a perfunctory look at the sign. "How would you like to go dancing after the banquet?"

"I'd love to." She lifted Brock's arm and twirled beneath it.

They entered the hotel lobby and Rhianna greeted them. She wore a pink long-waisted flapper-style dress, which clashed aggressively with her orange-red hair.

"Ready?" she said.

"Have you ever heard of an Earthling named Ryan Blaine?" Skye asked, still thinking about the insouciant-looking motorcycle man on the billboard outside. "He reminds of me of someone."

Rhianna clicked her tongue. "Where have you been? Ryan Blaine is the son of Richard Blaine, a former president of the United States. He's currently *the* most succulent morsel on Earthly Pleasures. Didn't you see it last night? There was a brand-new episode."

"Oh, Earth," Skye said with a dismissive flick of her wrist. People in Heaven fixated their attentions on select earthlings, gossiping about them and eavesdropping on their lives via the TV channel Earthly Pleasures. It was like reality TV for Heaven dwellers. Obviously, Ryan Blaine was the hunk du jour.

"Ryan's fiancée, Susan, had a terrible car accident about a year ago, and when it looked as if Susan might not make it, they had a bedside wedding ceremony. Now Susan has miraculously recovered, and they can finally live a normal life," Rhianna continued, oblivious that Skye had long since tuned her out.

"Let's go." Skye gestured toward the ballroom. "Professional glory awaits us."

The three of them strolled to the Cerulean banquet room and found seats together near the stage just as Doris Fain, the Hospitality Sector supervisor, crossed to the podium to begin the program. She tapped the microphone in an effort to get the audience's attention.

"A boss asked one of his employees, 'Do you believe in life after death?'" Doris said. "'Yes, sir,'" the new recruit replied. 'Good,' said the boss. 'Because after you left early yesterday to go to your grandmother's funeral, she stopped in to see you.'"

The crowd responded with a polite smattering of laughter. Skye shifted in her straight-backed chair. It was probably going to be a long drawn-out event.

"I'm pleased to welcome all of you to the Hospitality annual awards banquet," Doris said. "Every day the young men and women of this sector welcome thousands of the newly deceased to Heaven and convince them there is, indeed, life after death. Tonight some of them will be honored with promotions to guardian angel. This is also a very special year because one of our own, an extremely talented and evolved greeter, has been chosen to go down to Earth."

Rhianna gasped and pinched Skye's elbow. "Did you hear that? I was told it's been three years since a greeter's been chosen for Earth duty. I'm dying to know who it is."

Skye shrugged and used her WishBerry to hustle up a dirty martini, extra olives. Likely the person they were going to choose wouldn't be anyone she knew.

The ceremony wore on, beginning with all the first-year greeters trotting up to the stage for certificates of service. Brock whistled and clapped vigorously when Skye went up to retrieve her plaque for tidiest cubicle. After all the frivolous awards were given out, Doris started on the promotion announcements. Skye yawned, wondering if they could risk sneaking out early.

"Our final candidate for promotion to guardian angel is Rhianna Roe," Doris said.

Rhianna was sucking down a White Russian. When she heard her name called, her lips froze on the straw.

"Go on, Rhianna," Skye said. "Get your wings."

Rhianna wandered to the stage in a daze, a foamy line of milk still clinging to her upper lip. The room hummed with the announcement. Rhianna Roe promoted? The redheaded rebel? They'd been told surprises occasionally happened at the annual banquet, and Rhianna's appointment as a guardian angel trainee had been the biggest one of the night. People would be dishing about it around the Hospitality water cooler for weeks.

After an astonished Rhianna returned to the table, Doris once again approached the microphone. "And now, the moment you've all been waiting for."

"Obviously you've been brown-nosing behind everybody's back," Skye said in a teasing voice. She poured champagne into a flute and handed it to Rhianna.

"I don't even look good in white. It washes me out," Rhianna said. She stared at her promotion certificate with an incredulous expression. "You think these wings are real gold, or will they turn my uniform green?"

"Sweetie." Brock nudged Skye's shoulder.

"Don't tell me you're not excited," Skye said, ignoring Brock for the moment. "Think of all the perks. Partial omniscience, access to classified secrets of the universe, not to mention the occasional breakfast meeting with the Supreme Being."

"Grits with God." Rhianna nodded. "Could be interesting."

"Skye," Brock said, this time louder.

"Hush, Brock," Skye said. "Can't you see I'm congratulating Rhianna?" She lowered her voice to speak to Rhianna. "Handsome men are such a needy breed. Like pedigreed poodles." She lifted her glass in a toast. "Who would have guessed my closest friend—"

"But, darling," Brock continued, "they're calling your name."

"Huh?" Skye slowly turned her head. A hush had settled over the room and everyone in the ballroom was gawking at her.

"Yoo-hoo! Skye Sebring," Doris said, fluttering her handkerchief. "Come on up here. Don't be shy."

Skye rose tentatively from her seat and shot Rhianna and Brock a dumbfounded look as she hustled to the front of the room.

"Every once in a great while a greeter shows such extraordinary promise she or he is selected to live their very first life on Earth," Doris said to Skye once she'd arrived onstage. "You are that greeter, Skye Sebring. You've been chosen to be born on Earth. What an honor. We're so proud of you." She flung herself at Skye, enveloping her into a bosom-crushing embrace.

The room thundered with an applause that seemed to have no end. People sprang from their seats, rushing the stage. In moments Skye was swallowed up by dozens of well-wishers. Rhianna fought her way through the crowd and sidled up to Skye, whispering in her ear, "What's this you were saying earlier about brown-nosing?"

Four

Ryan Blaine gingerly eased out of bed so as not to wake his wife. She wore a black satin sleeping mask and was plugged into a machine that played the sound of the rain forest. She'd swallowed a Lunesta before retiring. Most likely a twenty-gun salute wouldn't rouse her, but it didn't pay to take chances. Not if he didn't want to get caught.

He tiptoed toward the door, failing to see his twenty-pound free weights in the darkness, and stubbed his big toe as he tripped over them.

"Cheese and rice!" he screamed. Ryan's mother had taught her children never to take the Lord's name in vain, so he'd developed a couple of replacement phrases over the years. "Cheese and rice," he hollered once more before clapping a hand over his mouth and freezing in place as his toe throbbed.

He stood motionless for a couple of minutes, alert for the slightest stirring from the bed. As soon as he was satisfied his wife was still sawing logs, he crept down the hall to his office and locked it. He listened intently for a moment until he felt safe enough to pick up the receiver.

"It's not like it's phone sex," he whispered to himself as he punched in the number from memory. Although frankly, he'd probably prefer that Susan catch him talking dirty to someone named Naughty Nina. Phone sex he could explain; this he couldn't.

"Hello. Welcome to the *Minerva* show," said the now-familiar honeyed voice.

"Hi, Minerva. It's Alone in Atlanta...again."

"Good evening, Alone," Minerva said warmly. She didn't seem to mind him calling several times a week. "Having trouble sleeping?"

"'Fraid so," Ryan said as he relaxed into his easy chair. Her voice was soothing, like Zoloft for the ears. "Tonight was a tough one. I got a little choked up, which isn't like me."

"Why don't you tell me what happened, Alone?" He liked her use of the word "me." It made him feel as if they were enjoying a private conversation over a nice glass of Merlot, instead of one shared with thousands of her listeners.

"The fireflies came out for the first time this year. I never used to notice, but she did," Ryan began. "Last summer when she spotted the first firefly, she made popcorn, set out some chairs, and invited me out to the lawn. We sat outside, just listening and watching bugs light up the night."

"That's a lovely memory, Alone."

"Tonight when I saw my first firefly of the year, I rushed into the house to find her, but then I remembered I can't tell her, because she isn't...She..."

"You okay, Alone?"

"I'm okay. Perfectly fine."

Not that he was fooling anyone, least of all himse1lf.

"Thanks for sharing, Alone. I know how difficult it can be to get over the loss of a love. Sometimes it takes years. Did you have a song in mind tonight?"

"You pick one, Minerva. You know I'm lousy at that."

"How about 'Baby Come Back'?" Minerva said. "I've got my fingers crossed. Maybe she'll return one day. Here's your song. And don't forget. You're not really alone anymore. Minerva is right here rooting for you."

"Thanks for listening."

Ryan hung up the phone and turned on his radio so he could hear his request. His back shook and the features of his face contorted, but he didn't make a sound. Just as the song finished, he thought he heard footsteps in the hall. He watched the doorknob, tensed like a cat, expecting any moment for it to rattle as his wife demanded entry.

If she ever did catch him, Ryan wouldn't be able to explain his actions since he didn't always understand them himself.

But he had no intention of giving up the calls. Talking to Minerva provided much-needed relief after a bone-wearying day of playing the role of loving husband. And sometimes, even though he knew it was impossible, he almost believed the woman he'd lost was actually hearing him.

Five

"I need more greeters," Doris Fain said to the person on the other end of the phone line as she motioned Skye to sit. "An epidemic's brewing in the Congo. Newcomers will be stacking up like cordwood."

While Doris talked, Skye smothered a yawn. She'd always been a poor sleeper, but last night she'd tossed and turned so fretfully she'd woken up wrapped in her bedclothes like a mummy. And she'd experienced the same peculiar dream again, the one she could never quite recall.

After a few minutes of grumbling about her staffing woes, Doris hung up the phone and pushed aside a foot-high stack of papers. "Here she is, the woman of the hour. My phone hasn't stopped ringing with calls of congratulations. Have you heard from the *Divine Digest* yet?"

"No."

"You will. A reporter called me, and they want to do an article. Possibly a cover piece. What do you think about that?" Doris asked. Although she had no wrinkles, Doris still managed a grandmotherly look. Whorls of tight curls covered her scalp, and her faded blue eyes begged for a pair of wire-rimmed spectacles.

"Well, I—"

"Don't wear prints. Solids photograph better. They're very anxious to interview the young woman who's causing such a stir. Did you know it's been three years since a greeter's been chosen to go to Earth?"

"Yes, I'd heard, but—"

"And to top it off, you're only a first-year greeter. I don't remember a first-year greeter being chosen ever. Most people have been in Heaven twenty years or more before they go to Earth. You're truly an exceptional case."

Skye scooted her chair closer to Doris's desk. "You see, that's precisely why I came to talk to you this morning. You claim I'm exceptional—"

"Extremely so," Doris said with a nod.

"But I'm having a little trouble understanding why. After all, what have I done to merit being sent to Earth? I could list at least a half-dozen people who are more deserving."

Doris shook a finger at her. "Don't be so hard on yourself, Skye. You're a top-notch greeter or you wouldn't have been chosen to go. Everyone in the sector is proud of you."

"Well, that's lovely, of course, and I appreciate their support but...they shouldn't be proud of me," Skye said abruptly. "I don't deserve it."

"Why do you say that?"

"I've done bad things."

"Such as?"

"Remember that time someone piped in 'Highway to Hell' through the Hospitality Sector sound system, practically causing a riot among the newly dead?"

Doris frowned. "I certainly do."

"That was me! I did it on a dare after tying one on at the Live a Little Lounge."

"Good Lord. What a mess that was."

"Exactly. And now you understand why someone who is capable of such a heinous prank can't possibly accept this honor." Skye gazed shamefully at her shoes.

"Agreed."

Skye stood. "So, if there's nothing else—"

"Only one problem. You didn't do it."

"Yes. I did."

"No, you didn't. Don't you think I know who the perpetrators were? This is Heaven. You can't get away with anything here, my dear."

"Well, maybe I didn't actually do it," Skye said. "But I wished I'd thought of it. Honestly, Mrs. Fain, if you send me down to Earth I'd probably end up being a menace to society, maybe even a sociopath. I have no inkling why you chose me."

"I didn't choose you."

"You had to. You're my direct supervisor. Who else would have chosen me?"

Doris jabbed her pen skyward. "The SB Sector."

"Supreme Being?" Skye said with a reverent whisper. "She's the one who wants me to go to Earth?"

"Precisely. And naturally, nobody ever questions the infinite wisdom of the decisions from the SB."

"Isn't it possible She made a mistake?"

"What...did...you...say?"

"Well, personally, she's not infallible. What about the platypus? And hail? Is it really necessary to have balls of ice falling from the sky? What possible purpose—"

"The SB does *not* make mistakes. We may not always understand why She does what She does, but I can assure you it's all part of a divine plan."

Skye had heard the "divine plan" explanation before. Sounded like a convenient way of covering up any number of blunders.

"So basically you're saying I don't have a choice? That I have to go to Earth?"

"It's an honor!"

Skye snorted. "That's what they used to say to the virgins they hurled into volcanoes."

"No need to get dramatic. I think you'll enjoy it. Now your first step is to enroll in Earth Orientation classes."

"And afterwards I'll be born in some strange women's uterus?"

"Well, yes, but—"

"I don't want to go. Please don't make me! I'm very happy in

Heaven." She was being flooded with an unfamiliar and extremely unpleasant emotion.

"Good gracious, Skye. No need to work yourself into a state. There's nothing to be afraid of."

Fear. That was the emotion she was experiencing, and it felt horrible. It made her hands quiver and her thoughts gallop in a half-dozen different direction.

"Get the SB on the phone," Skye pleaded. "I know She's supposed to be infallible, but I'm not ready for Earth. I know I'm not! I won't go."

Fear had taken her hostage; tears gushed from her eyes and the shaking in her hands spread to her entire body. Her supervisor eased open her desk drawer. Skye assumed she was reaching for a box of Kleenex until she saw the familiar aerosol can.

"What are you doing?" Skye said.

"I think you know." Doris took aim with Tranquility In a Can and hit Skye between the eyes.

"Stop it!"

But it was too late. Her face was covered with the fine mist.

"You're not thinking rationally," Doris said. "This wasn't some careless selection from an SB Sector pencil pusher. This came directly from Her office. The orders were stamped with Her seal."

Skye responded with a dreamy nod.

"Chin up, Skye," Doris said. "Earth isn't such a dreadful place. I've been there myself. Eleven times."

"You're right, I'll love it there. What a glorious planet." Skye floated around the cubicle, singing, "For the beauty of the Earth! For the beauty of the skies!"

Doris examined the label on the can. "I hope I didn't give you an overdose."

"Not at all," Skye said. She snapped her fingers and shimmied her hips. "I feel the Earth move under my feet. I feel the sky tumbling down."

"That's lovely, Skye. Would you stop singing for a moment, please? I have a favor to ask you."

"My wish is your command," Skye said.

"Early this morning, I received a call from an Ethel Long. Her niece Chelsea was one of your clients, and the girl's having a hard time adjusting to Heaven. Her aunt would appreciate it if you'd take her under your wing and spend a day with her next week. Turns out the girl really took a shine to you. How's that sound?"

"Divine," Skye said. She kissed Doris on both cheeks. "I'm delighted to assist. Thrilled. Elated. Whatever you want!"

An hour Skye was coming down hard from the dose of TIC as she entered the Hospitality break room to grab a cup of coffee before her shift.

Two of her coworkers, Glory and Joy, were sunk down on the sofa, so engrossed in whatever program was on the big-screen television they didn't even look up to greet her. That suited Skye. She didn't feel like talking to anyone at the moment.

"Now that's what I call biceps," Glory said.

Skye stirred sugar into her coffee, her gaze skimming her coworkers.

"Look at him," Joy said, fanning herself with a napkin. "The heat is rising from the TV in waves."

Skye, who'd been half listening to their conversation, glanced at the TV to see what the two women were getting all worked up about.

"Not him again," Skye muttered as she watched the now-familiar billboard man extricate himself from an embrace with a woman wearing a Grace Kelly-style head scarf and sunglasses. Then he mounted his motorcycle, gave the woman one last smoldering look, revved his motor, and sped off, his tires kicking up a spray of gravel.

"Your boy is definitely a looker, but he's also careless," Skye mused, turning away from the television. "Where's his helmet?"

At the sound of Skye's voice, Glory bounded from the couch, upending her Cracker Jack box. "Skye! Way to go," Glory said.

"Kudos," Joy said bitterly. She'd been Greeter of the Month three months running and hadn't even been promoted to guardian angel.

Skye knew she was the talk of the sector. No doubt everyone was wondering why an undistinguished greeter like herself had been singled out when there were so many better candidates to choose from.

"It still hasn't sunk in yet," Skye said quickly. She left the break room and hurried to her office, nearly spilling her coffee. Her mood wasn't helped when she sat at her desk, checked her email, and read one from Doris:

Earth Orientation class begins tomorrow evening at 7 p.m. after your shift. Book list is attached, as well as important information. Please read carefully.

She closed the email program and scrounged around in her desk drawer for a Hershey's Kiss, flattening it between her tongue and the roof of her mouth. The light on her computer blinked red, ushering in the first client of the day. Skye touched ENTER on her keyboard and brought up the data screen, reading quickly. Ryan Blaine, age twenty-five. At first she couldn't understand why her client's name sounded so familiar. She scanned his statistics: Attorney from Atlanta, Georgia. Motorcycle accident. Then she remembered. He was the Earthly Pleasures guy! The one she'd just seen on television.

Before she had time to gather her thoughts, Ryan Blaine stood in front of her, looking utterly baffled.

"Where am I?" He rubbed his eyes and squinted. "Everything's blurry. My contact lenses must have popped out."

For a moment, Skye was speechless from the shock of seeing the once alive and healthy Ryan Blaine now literally coming through death's door.

"Your vision will clear up in a few minutes, Mr. Blaine," she finally managed.

"Who are you?" he said.

Bits of glass fragments glittered on his chin, and one of his jeans legs was torn, exposing a gashed knee. But there weren't any bones poking out of his clothes or cuts coursing with blood. He looked relatively unscathed for a dead person.

"My name is Skye, and I'm your greeter," she said. Studying his face, she could understand why Joy and Glory were such devoted fans. Mr. Blaine was exceedingly easy on the eyes. His only discernible flaw was a slightly crooked nose. "You're in Sector Seven, the Hospitality Department of Heaven."

"Heaven?" He shook his head and a forelock of gold-brown hair fell into his eyes. "You're kidding me, right? I'm dead?"

"You had a motorcycle accident, Mr. Blaine," Skye said, rising from her chair. "Have a seat, and I'll try and explain—"

"No, no, no," Ryan said, shrinking away from her. "I'm not dead. That spill took the wind out of me, but it didn't kill me."

That's what they all say, Skye thought. Denial is a dead person's middle name.

"Mr. Blaine, one's own death is always a hard to accept, but you *are* in Heaven, so logically, that means—"

"Ridiculous," he said. "Look at me." He pounded his chest with his fists like King Kong. "I'm fine." He threw himself to the ground and launched into a set of one-arm push-ups. "You ever see a dead guy do this?" He stood up and tucked one hand under his arm and flapped it, making an obnoxious sound. "Or how about this?" He flung himself into a handstand.

Ryan's hair brushed the floor like a broom and his shirt rode up so Skye could catch a glimpse of his well-toned abdominal muscles. He finally righted himself and flashed a lopsided grin. "I think you would agree—" He tapped his chin with his index finger and squinted at her once again. "What was your name?"

"Skye."

"S-K-Y?" He laughed. "Your name is Sky and you live in Heaven?"

"It's Skye with an 'e,'" she said primly.

"Forgive me. Skye, I think you would agree that a serious error has been made. I've never felt better in my life."

"How you feel is immaterial, Mr. Blaine. Everyone in Heaven feels fantastic. The thing is—"

"Don't make me ask to speak to your supervisor, Skye." He approached her desk with his hip cocked, waving a finger at her in a playful manner. He tripped over his feet and nearly fell.

"Are you all right, Mr. Blaine?" she asked.

"Fine and dandy. Just having a little trouble keeping my moorings. Where were we? Oh, yes, you were about to clear up this silly mistake."

He was so disarming she'd forgotten her spiel. What was next? Oh yeah, the tiresome orientation DVD.

Ryan cast a puzzled glance around the cubicle. "Wait a minute. Something's going on." He stared at her desk calendar and gradually backed away from it until he bumped into the wall. "Whoa. I can see without my contacts. Everything's getting crystal clear. It's like I've had LASIK or something."

"I told you your vision would sharpen. You'll never have to wear contact lenses again. That's just one of the numerous fringe benefits of being..." She stopped short when she realized Ryan Blaine was gaping at her.

"Do I have spinach in my teeth, Mr. Blaine?"

"You...I..." His words were stuck in his throat.

"Can I get you a drink of water, a cold compress, a shot of tequila?"

"Who...are...you?" he finally managed, gasping out each syllable.

"Skye, your Hospitality greeter," she repeated.

He took a tentative step toward her. "It *is* you." His voice was reverent. "I thought I'd never see you again."

"Are you okay, Mr. Blaine?" Skye said. She hadn't been looked at this intently since the last wet t-shirt contest at the Live a Little Lounge.

"I don't know. This is so confusing. How can you...? What's your favorite chocolate?"

What a strange question. "Hershey's Kisses. The original ones.

Not those ones in the gold foil with almonds or the Hugs. They're terrible."

"Cheese and rice!" His hands frantically worked through the thicket of his hair. "I knew it."

"Jesus Christ," Skye said. "Is that what you're trying to say? He's not here at the moment, but..."

"I hurt you. Terribly," he said, with eyes that were now far more contrite than cocky. "That's why you went away. You always said you would."

"You haven't hurt me, Mr. Blaine," she replied.

The poor man was suffering from residual brain damage. Luckily it would be repaired in a few minutes.

"Mr. Blaine, I think you're—"

As soon as she spoke his name, his image blurred and stretched like a scrambled television signal and then he was gone.

"Mr. Blaine," she repeated several times, knowing she was wasting her breath. He couldn't hear or see her anymore; her cubicle was empty. Clearly he'd returned to Earth. This wasn't the first time she'd lost a client. Every now and then the newly dead would disappear from her cubicle without warning. Sometimes the shock of defibrillation paddles or the compression of CPR jolted souls back into their bodies. Other times they'd fade away more slowly, coaxed back to Earth by the prayers or sobs of loved ones.

Skye consulted the computer monitor. Ryan's information had disappeared and the screen blinked with the words "intake aborted."

She fumbled with the television remote, tuning it to the Earthly Pleasures station. Skye had never watched it before, so she didn't know exactly how to proceed. She pressed the menu button and one of the options was "This Week's Most Popular Earthlings." Fortunately, Ryan was featured prominently on the list between Brad Pitt and Angelina Jolie. She highlighted his name and was offered another set of options.

Ryan and Susan: Their Latest Romantic Dinner
The Best of Ryan and Susan: A Compilation

Ryan and Susan's Bedside Wedding Bloopers and Blunders
The Funniest Moments from Ryan's Life
Ryan Flexing His Muscles in the Mirror
There were about twenty-five different options.

Obviously the lives of people on Earthly Pleasures were edited and compiled to provide the most entertainment value for viewers in Heaven. But Skye wanted to see what was happening with Ryan right now. She used the remote to scroll down until she got to the end of the list. There, at the bottom in small letters, was an option called *Real Time*. She selected it.

The following message appeared:

Warning: Real Time is not recommended. It's slow-paced and lacking in any entertainment value. Since the content is completely unedited, the producers of Earthly Pleasures cannot be responsible for any disturbing images. Do you wish to proceed?

Skye eagerly pressed YES.

Are you sure? Ninety-eight percent of all viewers prefer to watch edited versions of Earthly Pleasures.

Skye frowned and impatiently pressed YES again. The picture flickered and wobbled until it showed a shot of her former client being loaded onto a stretcher.

"I'm fine, I tell you,'" Ryan Blaine said. He was addressing two EMTs who were preparing him for transport as the red lights of the ambulance flashed in the background.

"I'm sure you are, sir," said one of the EMTs, a burly mustached man who squatted to lift the stretcher. "We just want to get you checked out at the hospital."

"Where is she? You saw her, didn't you? The pretty blonde who was standing here only a minute ago? What happened to her?"

Skye turned up the volume. Ryan Blaine was talking about her! Here I am, she wanted to shout, but, of course, he wouldn't be able to hear her.

"Whoever she is, she's probably at the hospital," one EMT said. He and his partner loaded Ryan onto the ambulance. "Waiting for you there."

"She was just..." Ryan's eyelids drooped as he struggled against passing out. "I...don't want to...lose...her again," he said in a whisper, and then his eyes closed and did not reopen. The EMTs looked unconcerned. They didn't pound his chest or begin mouth-to-mouth resuscitation. Instead, the EMT who was monitoring Ryan's vital signs asked the driver if he thought the Braves would make it to the Series this year.

Skye would have liked to watch Ryan's safe delivery to the hospital and overhear the doctors' conversations, but the light on her desk was blinking. She cut off the television and prepared to greet her next client.

As soon as it was time for her morning break, Skye retrieved the remote from her desk drawer and tuned in to Earthly Pleasures again. Ryan, thank God, was not in an ICU plugged into a collection of blinking machines, but was instead asleep in a regular hospital room tethered to a simple IV. A woman, who was reading *The National Enquirer*, sat beside his bed.

"Sweet Jesus! What's wrong with Ryan?" Glory stood just outside the door of Skye's cubicle, staring at the television. She barreled inside and dropped her backside on the corner of Skye's desk.

"He was in a motorcycle accident," Skye said, "but it looks as if his injuries aren't too serious."

"You're kidding." Glory's eyes were fastened to the television screen and her jaw worked furiously on a piece of gum. She tossed Skye a quizzical look. "I didn't know you were an Earthly Pleasures fan."

"I'm not usually," Skye said. "But—and you're not going to believe this—Ryan Blaine was right here. I was about to show him the orientation DVD and then, *poof*. He checked out."

"Get out of town," Glory said. "Ryan was here in the Hospitality Sector?"

Skye nodded.

"Aren't you the lucky one?" She punctuated her statement with a cuff to Skye's forearm. "What did he say?"

"Denial as usual. You know how some clients can be, men especially, always assuming they're immortal. But then something peculiar happened. He started talking to me like he knew me."

"Hmmm. Maybe he was confused and thought you were his wife. You kind of favor her."

"Wife?"

"Hey, is this Real Time? I've never selected that option before."

"Wife?" Skye repeated, this time with more urgency.

"There she is." Glory pointed at a woman whose nose was deep in her magazine. "Her name is Susan."

"Come to think of it, you mentioned he was married earlier," Skye said, her shoulders sagging. "I completely forgot."

The jingle of a cell phone was heard from the screen, and Ryan's wife dropped her magazine and pawed through her purse. Skye was finally able to see her face. At first she didn't notice much of a resemblance. Skye had long curly locks that spilled over her shoulders, and Susan wore a pixie hairstyle. Susan's nose was also thinner than Skye's and her cheekbones, marred by several scars, looked sharper. But the more she studied Ryan's wife, the more she discerned distinct traces of herself in the woman.

"The eyes are the same, and you both have heart-shaped faces," Glory said.

Ryan's wife had finally located her phone. "Hello," she said to whoever was on the other end. "He's fine, thank God," she said to her caller with a pronounced lisp. "He's fine" came out as "heth fine." "He escaped with a broken ankle, but also had the wind knocked out of him."

Not just the wind, Skye thought. His life was knocked out of him, at least for a little while.

"What kind of wife are you?" Skye shouted to the television. "Letting him roar off on his motorcycle without a helmet?"

Glory shot her an odd look.

"And what does Ryan see in her? Look at her choice of reading material, for starters."

"Hey now, go easy on Susan. She was injured in a car accident last year, and Ryan took a leave of absence from his law practice just to be near her."

"Is that why her face is scarred?"

"Yup. Took her almost a whole year to recover. I heard Ryan used to be a big-time ladies' man, but now he's as tame as a lamb." Glory transferred her gaze from the television to Skye. "I told you Earthly Pleasures was addicting. Although, I guess soon you'll be living it instead of watching it."

Skye continued to glare at Susan. Her dress was a shade of green only tree lizards should be sporting, and she wore more accessories than a home-shopping hostess. As Skye's catty thoughts spawned kittens, she wondered: Was she jealous? Impossible. Why should she get green-eyed over a woman who was married to a man who, from now on, would always be just an image on the screen?

"This Real Time stuff moves way too slow for me," Glory said, hopping off Skye's desk. "Guess I'll go back to work. Dead people await."

Six

"Ryan. Are you awake?"

The voice sounded tinny, as if it were coming from the inside of an empty soup can. Lemme sleep one more minute, he wanted to say, but his lips were so dried out they couldn't form the words. All that came out was a *psst* sound, like a tire slowly losing air.

He recognized the voice. Any moment, he'd smell freshly shampooed hair, a mixture of pomegranate, persimmon, and passion fruit. He knew the ingredients of her shampoo because the last time she was out of town he'd read the label, uncapped the bottle, and waved it under his nose as if the scent would conjure her up.

Soon he'd feel the weight of the mattress shift as she sat on the edge of the bed. Without opening his eyes, he knew she'd be wearing a white chenille bathrobe, her wet hair slicked back like a seal's, and in her hand she'd be holding a tall glass of freshly squeezed orange juice. Very softly she would start singing that old Allman Brothers song. "You're my blue sky. You're my sunny day."

"Ryan, are you awake?"

He wanted her to sing. Then he'd sit up and bask in her smile as she handed him the glass. Maybe after he'd quenched his thirst, he would coax her back into the bed with him as he'd done so many other mornings before.

"Ryan!" The voice was sharp, like a hook yanking him from the cozy nook of his memories. His eyes flew open, and he saw her standing over him, wearing a blinding lime-green dress. There wasn't a glass of orange juice in sight.

"You're awake," Susan said. "I'm so relieved. You were scaring me."

Ryan heard the sound of Susan's lisp ("scaring" sounded like "tharing") and it all came rushing back to him. He'd been on his motorcycle, worrying about their relationship. Likely he'd been so consumed by his thoughts he hadn't paid proper attention to the road. No telling what caused him to crash his bike. He didn't remember the moment of impact.

He made a quick inventory of his extremities. Toes wiggled; fingers bent; legs and arms were stiff but still in good working order.

"Do you know what month it is? What year?" Susan asked.

Yes, he did. It was June 2017, but if she'd asked him the same question just a few seconds ago he would have said June 2016. Trump wasn't president, nobody had ever heard of Brexit, and Susan had yet to slam into that embankment on 1-285.

He forced himself up on his elbows, but the sudden motion made his head feel swimmy as if it were housed in an old-fashioned diving helmet. Slowly, he eased his torso back down on the mattress.

"You do recognize me, don't you?" Susan asked.

He gazed at her, taking in the short haircut, the concerned, blinking blue eyes, the scarred cheeks.

Who are you? he wanted to say, or more accurately, *Who have you become?* She wasn't the same woman who used to bring him orange juice each morning. Everything had changed between then and now.

"What's your favorite chocolate?" he whispered.

She ran her tongue over her upper lip. It was one of the nervous habits she'd picked up since her accident.

"Maybe I should get the doctor."

"Just answer the question," he said with a gruffness he hadn't intended.

Her eyes flickered, as if she were looking for an avenue of escape. *Why are you afraid?* he wanted to ask.

"M&M's?"

Wrong answer. Not a surprise. She rarely gave the right answer.

"The day is June 25, 2017," Ryan said quickly, pretending as if he hadn't just gone against the grain of their everyday interactions.

"Are you sure you're okay, hon? You look like you're in pain."

"Just some soreness, sweetie," Ryan said, gifting her a grin.

"You're such a tough guy."

She was obviously relieved they were once again playing their customary vacuous roles. To her, the meaningless banter they exchanged daily was their relationship.

"I don't feel so tough right now."

"Reporters have been calling the hospital," she said, her color high with excitement. "There's a security guard stationed outside your door to keep the media out."

Ryan had been dogged by the press most of his life. When he'd been a student at Columbia University, he was featured in the gossip rags at least once a week and earned the moniker "Bad Boy Blaine" after having dated practically every debutante in New York City. His hound-dog lifestyle slowed somewhat when his father, former U.S. president Richard Blaine, died of a heart attack just before his graduation and Ryan moved back home to Atlanta to be near his mother and sister.

"I'm beat," Ryan said to Susan, wanting to blot out all his worries, especially the one foremost in his mind, the one he could never discuss with her.

"Rest then, Ryan." She nervously twisted the serpentine strand of her heavy gold necklace. He could tell something was bothering her.

"What is it, Susan?"

She bit the cuticle of her thumb and a pinprick of blood appeared. "While you were sleeping, you kept saying something over and over...sky. Does that mean anything to you?"

Skye with an "E." The image of a small cubicle and a blurred blonde figure standing behind a desk flashed in his mind. He saw himself squinting at the woman's features until they came into focus, and remembered how he'd gasped in recognition. She'd been a dead ringer for the pre-accident Susan. Was it any wonder his mind had returned to the past a few minutes earlier?

"I must have been disoriented after my spill. I had no idea what I was saying." He winced. "I could use some pain medication. Will you get the nurse?"

"Right away," Susan said, probably anxious for an excuse to leave the room. Most of their encounters were marked with awkwardness. He wasn't really in pain; he just wanted some privacy so he could be alone with his memories for a minute. His dream after his accident had been so real. It transported him back to the earliest days of his relationship with Susan.

The first time he'd laid eyes on her she'd worn a stained lab coat and reeked of cat pee. She was holding her nose as she entered the waiting room of the vet's office, where Ryan stood with his golden retriever, Liberty, on a leash.

"Eau de Cat Piss is not my usual fragrance of choice, but I just got sprayed by Lex Luthor, a tabby with aggression issues," she said, explaining the odor. She pushed a loose strand of hair behind her ear and extended a hand. "Hi, I'm Susan Sims, and I promise not to stand too close."

Her handshake was energetic, as if she were plunging a toilet. She didn't have a lisp then. That came after the accident.

Ryan was staying at the Blaine beach home on Devon's Island, South Carolina. His mother had died six months before, and he wanted to spend one last summer at his childhood vacation home before he put it up for sale.

"My name's Ryan Blaine, and this is Liberty," he said, giving a short tug to the dog, who was sniffing a potted peace lily in the corner of the office.

"What's wrong with you, girl?" Susan wore a ponytail holder with plastic red balls, something Ryan had only seen on little girls. Everything else about her said robust small-town girl. Not his type at all.

"Lib has an earache," he said. "At least I think she does. She keeps shaking her head."

Susan crouched down to address Lib. "Cripes. I bet that hurts, doesn't it, Lib?" She scratched the dog between the shoulder blades, which was Lib's sweet spot.

Ryan could have sworn Lib nodded solemnly in response. She also nuzzled Susan's ear, a gesture she usually reserved for people she knew.

"A tick?" the vet said in mock horror, as if Lib had confided in her. "Let's take a look-see." She inspected Lib's ear and let out a low whistle. "Look at the size of this thing. It's the Vampire Lestat of ticks. No wonder you've been trying to shake him. Don't you worry, Lib, he's history."

Ryan laughed. Maybe he'd discounted Susan too quickly. She was kind of cute in a quirky way.

"Glad you found the trouble." He flashed her the infamous Blaine grin—the one that guaranteed consent to a dinner date or at the very least an eagerly scrawled phone number. "Lib's been keeping me up at night."

"Sorry to hear it."

He was used to getting some sort of response from women when he smiled—a sharp intake of breath, a smile, a flirty little hair toss—but from Susan he got nothing His eyes dropped to her left hand. No ring, so she probably wasn't married.

"Could you check her for fleas too?" he said, glancing around the small waiting area as he strategized. There were only two things hanging on the wall: a chart depicting the life cycle of the heartworm and a framed diploma.

"Applied animal behaviorist," he read aloud as he examined her credentials. "I've never heard of that before."

"I'm a trained veterinarian," she explained as she checked

Lib's coat for other parasites. "But I'm also certified to work with troubled pets. I like to think of myself as a pet whisperer. I speak their language."

"So you're a pet psychologist?"

"Yup."

"So where's your couch?"

"Where's the couch?" She clutched her stomach as she laughed. "You're slaying me. Has anyone ever told you you're a real funny guy, Mr. Blaine?"

He was caught off guard. Was she making fun of him? But no, she was gazing at him in such an innocent way it didn't seem possible. He couldn't quite figure what the heck was tumbling around inside that blonde head of hers. No dinner invitation, he decided. He'd start with something more casual.

"Would you like to have coffee with me sometime?"

"Nope," she said, not even looking up.

"No?"

"Nope."

He laughed nervously. "Woman usually qualify a 'no' answer, saying 'no, I have a boyfriend' or 'no, I have to wash my hair.' They don't just say no."

"You want an explanation?"

"Well, I—"

"Even though explanations are usually full of bull?"

"I'm just saying—"

"All right, you asked for it." She paused for a moment and looked him full in the face. "Your nose is crooked. That's why I won't have coffee with you." She gestured toward an open door. "You want to bring Lib into the back room? I'm going to need to dip her."

Ryan touched the tip of his nose. He'd broken it several years ago in a game of touch football. One former girlfriend said his nose lent a welcome ruggedness to his Ken-doll looks.

"Isn't that kind of shallow?" he demanded. "To judge someone solely by a part of their body?"

She shrugged.

Her rejection of him was a powerful aphrodisiac, like thigh-high boots, garter belts, and Spanish fly rolled into one irresistible package. Over the next week, Susan Sims entered Ryan's daily thoughts with the persistence of a pop-up ad.

After she declined his coffee invitation, he brought Liberty into her office every few days, each time with a new mysterious ailment. "Liberty coughed last night," he'd claim, or "She was limping on the beach yesterday." Lib was as boneless as an amoeba in Susan's presence, yielding to all of her probing and prodding with dark-eyed devotion. One afternoon when Ryan brought Liberty in, claiming her tongue color looked funky, Susan summoned him into her private office.

"I'll be frank with you, Mr. Blaine," she said. "I think we're dealing with some very serious psychological issues here."

Clearly she was going to try to sell him on therapy for Liberty. Not a problem. He was rapidly running out of physical symptoms to report on. Let her shrink Liberty's brain if she wanted. It would give him an excuse to keep coming into the office.

"Libby has seemed kind of depressed lately," Ryan said, expelling a worried sigh.

"I didn't mean Liberty," she said in an exasperated voice. "I'm talking about you. Are you familiar with Munchausen syndrome by proxy?"

"What?"

"It's when a parent fabricates medical symptoms in their child, often making them undergo unnecessary treatment. I never heard of it occurring with an owner and his dog before, but after seeing you and Libby—"

"You think I have this munch thing?"

"Yup."

He couldn't tell if she was serious or just working him over.

"I'll make you a deal," he said. "I'll quit inventing symptoms for Lib if you agree to have coffee with me after work."

"Nope," she said, her usual answer.

Ryan felt like banging his head against her desk. In the last few days he'd shelled out over five hundred bucks in vet bills and had worked so hard at being gallant he was exhausted. The woman simply wasn't going to go out with him. End of story. Time for him to tuck his tail between his legs and trudge home. He rose dejectedly from his chair and headed to the door.

"It'll have to be a beer instead," she said.

"What?"

"Coffee keeps me up at night. Pick me up at six and we'll grab a cold one."

"The nurse is on her way. She says she has to check the—" Susan skidded into the hospital room on a pair of needle-sharp heels. She stopped in mid-sentence. "You're smiling. Are you feeling better?"

"A little," Ryan said. He pondered her face, searching for a trace of the woman who'd charmed him on Devon's Island. Susan's hand flew to her cheek, her finger tracing a two-inch vertical scar. "What's wrong? Why are you staring?"

That was another thing about the post-accident Susan. She was as jittery as a squirrel.

"Nothing. Everything's fine," he fibbed, his usual response. He'd done enough fibbing in the past year, his nose should be as long as a yardstick.

Seven

Skye paused by a wooden bench on the Earth University campus and retrieved the class reading list from her purse, consulting it for the first time. Most of the Earth's major religious works were there: the Torah, the Bible, the Koran, and the Bhagavad-Gita. Several weighty philosophical works, like Plato's *Symposium* and Aristotle's *Ethics*, were also included, along with less daunting titles such as *Jonathan Livingston Seagull Life's Little Instruction Book* and *Everything I Needed to Know I Learned in Kindergarten*.

Two female students, one tall and willowy, the other short and curvy, strolled by, creating a female Laurel and Hardy tableau.

"Can you believe this thing?" said the slender one, waving the reading list. "Do you think there's *Cliffs Notes*?"

"I don't know why we have to read this nonsense anyway," said the other, who wore a tight t-shirt that said "Salt of the Earth." "I plan on being a supermodel."

"Really? I was thinking I might be an heiress or a pop singer," replied her companion.

"Why not be both?" said the short one with a shrug.

"Excuse me," Skye said, turning to address them. "How do you know you won't be a subsistence farmer in Nigeria? Or end up in a sweatshop in Honduras?"

Skye had been researching her future domicile, and frankly, the more she learned, the more fretful she'd become.

"Is a sweatshop like a sauna?" the slender woman asked, twisting a strand of hair around her finger.

"Not exactly," Skye said. Unlike her, these weren't new souls. How could they be so naive? "What I'm trying to say is not everyone on Earth can be a celebrity."

"If we don't go to class now we'll be late," the short woman said in a huff. She obviously didn't appreciate Skye dumping buckets of rain on her parade.

Skye tucked the reading list into her purse and was heading toward the main building when she heard the word "Boo!"

She wheeled around. A grinning Rhianna, wearing a plaid skirt, navy knee socks, and a white blouse tied at the midriff stood in front of her. Her wild auburn hair was tamed into looped sprouts on each side of her head, making her resemble an oversized mouse.

"Don't I look scholarly?" she said, doing a quarter turn in front of Skye.

"Why are you here?" Skye asked. "Shouldn't you be at guardian angel orientation classes?"

"Class doesn't start for another hour. Besides, somebody had to accompany you on your first day of school." Rhianna unzipped a Power Puff Girls book bag and inventoried the items inside.

"Glitter pens, holograph notebooks, glue sticks, Trapper Keeper, and a Red Delicious apple to bribe the teacher." Rhianna handed the book bag to Skye. "Everything you could possibly need for the new school year."

"I've always been a fool for glitter," Skye said, pulling her friend into a hug. "And since you're feeling so generous, I have a small favor to ask."

"Fire away."

"I was wondering if you could nose around and find out why the Supreme Being chose me to go to Earth." She related what she'd learned in Doris's office. "I have no idea why She singled me out, and I'm not so sure I like being on Her radar screen."

"Sweetie. Everyone's on Her radar screen."

"You know what I mean. Could you poke around? I've heard you guardian angels are privy to all kinds of juicy information."

"Rooting around in confidential records is strictly forbidden. I signed a sacred oath vowing I wouldn't engage in such nefarious activities." She smiled. "Lucky for you I don't consider anything to be sacred."

Skye laughed. "Thanks, Rhianna."

The two of them crossed under the shadow of Terrestrial Hall, an ivy-covered stone structure with a buttressed tower. In the spirit of academia, it was continuously autumn on the EU campus, and all the trees on the school's grounds flared with vivid golds and reds.

As they entered the building, Skye said, "Earth 101 is held in room 17. The sign says it's to the left."

The pair traveled down a long narrow hallway, and on their way, Rhianna paused to point at a sign posted outside one of the classrooms.

"Advanced Martyrdom is canceled this semester due to lack of enrollment. Ha! I can guess why."

"Where's the Charmed Life class? That's the one I want to sign up for," Skye said nervously.

The bell rang just as the two women located room 17. Skye jumped at the sound.

"This is it," Rhianna said. "Be a dutiful student, okay? I don't want to peek in the classroom and see you standing in the corner with a dunce cap on your head."

"I'll try," Skye said with a weak smile.

Rhianna pressed her cheek against Skye's face for a brief moment and sauntered down the hall toward the exit. Skye took a deep breath and slunk down the aisle through the middle of the classroom, glancing to the left and the right, looking for a place to sit. Most students had already claimed their seats, and the only unoccupied desks left were in the first two rows. Skye was disappointed; she was hoping to hole up in the very back of the room. She selected a place next to a female student with shiny dark hair that skimmed the pockets of her blue jeans. The student punched data into a WishBerry, and just as a latte with whipped cream appeared on her desk, a voice thundered from the back of the room.

"We'll have none of *that* in this classroom."

Everyone stopped their chatter and turned to see a spindly limbed man with a graying beard stride down the middle aisle to the front of the room. He paused beside the desk of the woman with the latte, picked it up, helped himself to a large swig, and wiped a trace of cream from his mustache with the back of his hand. Then he tossed the drink in a wastepaper basket, brushing his hands together as if they were soiled.

"Hey," the girl protested, "why did you—"

"What is the name of this class?" he barked.

"Earth 101," the girl responded.

"And on Earth is it possible to indulge our whims with a couple of keystrokes?" demanded the professor.

"Well, no," began the girl. "But—"

"It is if you're on Amazon," called out a smart aleck from the back.

The entire class tensed, no doubt expecting a strong admonition from the professor. Instead he considered the comment for a moment and then let loose a loud chortle.

"Amazon," he said, with a nod. "I suppose you're right. Amazon, indeed." Then he took his place behind the podium and surveyed the class. Skye slid down the back of her chair, hoping to disappear.

"I'm your professor, Dr. Mullins."

A sullen-looking fellow in the front row waved a piece of paper at the professor. "About this reading list—"

Dr. Mullins snatched the paper from the student and proceeded to tear it into tiny pieces that floated to the floor like snowflakes. "That's what I think of the recommended reading list for this class. Make a paper airplane from it or use it as a cocktail napkin. Better yet, throw it away. You'll have no use for it this semester."

His final comments were met by whoops and applause from the class. The girl next to Skye folded her reading list into an expertly rendered origami bird.

"I've studied all the texts on the list and quite frankly most of them say the same thing," the professor said. "Therefore, I've decided to simplify matters considerably. I've boiled down all of the world's greatest philosophies into five easy lessons. Once you commit these lessons to memory, you'll be prepared for your very first life on Earth."

He reached behind his podium and produced an iPhone, which he set atop an empty desk in the first row.

"It's a proven fact people learn and remember information more efficiently when it's paired with music," he continued as he fiddled with the iPhone. "Therefore each lesson will be contained within a Beatles song. The Fab Four, as it turns out, were quite the philosophers. Please listen carefully. We'll be covering two lessons today."

"I get by with a little help from my friends," harmonized The Beatles from the speakers. After the first stanza finished, a chorus of lilting soprano voices sounded from the back of the room. Every head in the classroom turned to see a white wave of guardian angels flow inside, clapping and singing as they made their way down the aisle to the front.

The angels reached Dr. Mullins and then pivoted to face the students, encouraging them to join in. Soon everyone was singing along.

When the song was over, a beaming Dr. Mullins shouted, "Bravo! I'm so delighted you could take time from your busy schedules to help teach my Earth 101 students," he said. "Now, I'd like to introduce one of the senior guardian angels, Davida Jones, who will say a few words to the class."

Davida was the picture of serenity with clear almond-shaped eyes and a smile that reached every feature of her face.

"Thomas Huxley was wrong when he said, 'The strongest man in the world is the man who stands alone,'" she began. "In fact, such a man is the weakest. On behalf of the sisterhood of guardian angels, we want you to know you'll never be alone on Earth. You have friends in Heaven to help you. Earth dwellers are assigned a guardian angel, who will be like their own private genie in a bottle. And that brings us to the second lesson of the day. Since the Supreme Being has given Earth dwellers free will, you must ask us for help, or we will be unable to intervene in your life."

"Help!" sang out the angels standing behind Davida, their faces aping comical expressions of alarm. "I need somebody! Help!"

This time everyone in the class joined in the tune without waiting for prompting. As the angels reached the last few stanzas of the song, they lined up and streamed from the classroom via the center aisle. After they departed, Dr. Mullins quieted his boisterous class by bringing a finger to his lips.

"Let me summarize," he said, once the room grew silent. "Lesson one. You're not alone on Earth. You have friends in Heaven looking after you and seeing to it you get everything you need. It's that old chestnut: Ask and ye shall receive. Lesson two: Seek out help if you need it. Sounds simple, but you'd be surprised how many Earthlings flounder about foolishly because they're too stubborn to request assistance. Any questions?" He looked around the class and when no one immediately replied he said, "Good. Class dismissed."

Well, at least that was quick and painless, Skye thought as she rose from her desk. Not that she had gotten much out of it. She was about to leave the classroom when Dr. Mullins said, "Skye Sebring. May I have a moment?"

What had she done to call attention to herself? Then she remembered the wad of Juicy Fruit in her mouth. She demurely removed it and tossed it in the trash can by his desk.

"Sorry," she said.

He smiled. "I didn't call you over because of your gum. I just wanted to make sure you were clear on today's lessons."

"Seemed pretty straightforward to me," Skye said. "Although frankly, I prefer the Stones over The Beatles."

"Hmmm," he said, rubbing his chin. "I'm not sure what kind of lessons I might have gotten out of 'Brown Sugar' or 'Honky-Tonk Woman.'" Then he touched her shoulder. "Ms. Sebring, if you have concerns, just call me. My number is in your course materials. I'm honored to have you in my class. You must be a very gifted soul to have been chosen to go to Earth at such a tender age. Most of your peers have been in Heaven for years."

"Lucky me," Skye said softly. Then a notion occurred to her. "Dr. Mullins, I don't suppose *you* know why I was picked. I have no idea why I've caught the notice of the SB."

"I'm not privy to that sort of information," Dr. Mullins said. Suddenly he was intent on stuffing materials into his already bulging satchel. "But pay attention, as I suspect you'll be needing these lessons. Maybe sooner than you expect."

After class she teleported home to her apartment and wished up her favorite snack, a bag of Hershey's Kisses. She'd sampled every delicacy Heaven had to offer—gold-foiled truffles from Belgium, dark semisweet squares of Venezuelan chocolate, and frothy mugs of liquid chocolate like the Aztec kings use to drink—but she always came back to her trusty Kisses.

Later that evening she peeked in on Ryan, hoping to take her mind off her impending journey to Earth. She snuggled against the arm of her sofa and turned on Earthly Pleasures. A dimly lit hospital room appeared on the television screen. Ryan was reading in bed, and the glow from an overhead lamp outlined his profile with a haloing light. Every aspect of him seemed endearing, from the cowlick springing out of the back of his scalp to his dangling foot, revealing a holey argyle sock and an exposed big toe.

Brock, flawless as he was, never had this kind of effect on her. In fact, it was Ryan's imperfections that most fascinated Skye: the crooked nose, the goofy smile, the tendency to trip over his two feet. Why was it that the one man who captivated her was married and living in an entirely different dimension?

A dimension you'll soon be visiting, she reminded herself. Not that going to Earth would improve her chances with Ryan Blaine. A drooling infant gnawing on a zwieback would hardly be an appropriate match for a grown man. And there was no telling where she'd end up on Earth—Ethiopia maybe, or a remote Polynesian island. The SB wasn't a travel agent. You couldn't book your destination ahead of time.

Skye continued to watch Ryan read. Maybe Earth wouldn't seem so bad if she were Susan and was able to cuddle up with Ryan every night.

Ryan put aside his book—it was the latest Nelson DeMille—and reached for the phone on the nightstand.

Skye touched the split-screen button on the remote in order to see the person he was calling. At this late hour she imagined it had to be his wife.

The right side of the screen revealed a middle-aged woman with white-blonde hair seated in a control room of a radio station. "You're on the air, caller. This is Minerva."

"Hello, Minerva. It's Alone in Atlanta."

"Well, hello, Alone," Minerva said. "Any news about your estranged girlfriend?"

"Still MIA, Minerva. The pain feels so fresh it's hard to believe it's been more than a year."

Girlfriend? Ryan was married. Who in the world was he talking about?

"What's on your mind tonight, Alone?" Minerva said.

"I recently had a dream about my girlfriend, and it was the most vivid dream of my life. I can't stop thinking about it."

"What happened in the dream?" Minerva asked.

"I'm sure it would give Freud a field day. I dreamed she was in Heaven."

Was he talking about her? Skye dropped down to the floor and knee-walked to the television until her nose was inches from the screen.

"Oh, Alone. You're not saying you think your girlfriend is—"

"No. It wasn't like that. She seemed very much alive. I've dreamed about her before, but this dream was so incredibly lucid. She glowed like some kind of angel, and looked exactly how I remembered her. I wonder what it could mean," Ryan mused.

"I truly hope for your sake she does come back," Minerva said, her voice thick with sympathy. "What song can I play for you tonight?"

"How about 'Get Out of My Dreams and into My Car'?"

Minerva chuckled. "I'm glad you still have your sense of humor. I'll play it for you right now."

Skye had never been so confused. Who was Ryan's girlfriend, and why did he mistake Skye for her? And why was he behaving as if he were in the perfect marriage when it was obvious his heart belonged to someone else?

Eight

Ryan was stretched out on his leather recliner in the den, a diamond-patterned afghan spread over his legs, listening to "Blue Sky" from the Allman Brothers' *Eat a Peach* album. His photo album was opened on his lap, and he lingered over a picture of Susan, her engagement ring winking on her finger. Convincing her to marry him was a Herculean feat. He'd practically had to walk barefoot on hot coals to get her to accept the darn thing.

Photography was his hobby, and while he dated Susan he took hundreds of images of her, documenting their every beach walk, sailboat trip, and moonlight picnic.

As their summer on Devon's Island neared an end, Ryan became anxious. He had to return to his law practice in Atlanta in a matter of days and wanted Susan to move there with him. Yet whenever he mentioned their future together, she flounced away from him.

One afternoon while Susan was at work, he drove to a jeweler in downtown Charleston and pored over the rings for hours. She'd once told him she wasn't crazy about diamonds ("cold and colorless stones," she said), so he selected a sapphire stone the exact shade of her eyes. After purchasing the engagement ring, he racked his brain for the most romantic way to propose. He briefly considered hiring a pilot to fly a plane trailing a banner that said "Will you marry me?" but then dismissed the idea as being too banal. His next plan was to rent a hot-air balloon. As he and Susan floated among wisps of clouds, he'd drop to one knee and ask (okay, beg) her to be his wife.

He continued to generate all manner of over-the-top schemes. One day he visited every grocery store within forty miles and bought out their entire stock of Hershey's Kisses. He intended to use the candy to spell out "Will you marry me?" on her front lawn.

Over a period of a week, he drove himself crazy with proposal ideas, so determined was he to find just the right one that would make her utter that simple three-letter word. (As opposed to the four-letter "nope," obviously Susan's favorite.)

He was never able to settle on a plan because he strongly suspected that even if he arranged for a hundred doves to swoop over her house, dropping "Will you marry me?" notes from their beaks while Julio Iglesias serenaded her, Susan would turn him down flat. He was convinced she had strong feelings for him, but she refused to acknowledge their relationship was the least bit serious, behaving instead as if they were two teenagers involved in a summer fling.

In the end, Ryan decided the old-fashioned way was the best. So he took her to Crabby Abby, a seafood restaurant, planning to propose there. After Susan had devoured two pounds of oysters—the woman had the appetite of a Teamster—he got down on one knee.

"What are you doing down there?" she asked, her chin shiny with melted butter. "You lose a contact?"

He reached in his pocket and produced a jewelry box. At the sight of it, her face paled. "Not the velvet box. Oh, hell no."

"Listen, Susan..."

"Nope, nope, nope," she said, shrinking away as if he were presenting her with a ticking bomb. Her elbow knocked over her Hurricane glass, spilling red liquid all over the table. She didn't seem to notice. "Get that thing away from me and promise me you'll never take it out again."

A gray-haired couple dining nearby shot him apprehensive looks.

"I can't do that, Susan—"

"Then I can't do this!" She bolted up from the table and bounded out of the restaurant.

After she left, Ryan ordered and quickly downed two Hurricanes. When he was thoroughly pie-eyed, he shambled home and rummaged in his pantry until he found a large trash bag, which he stuffed with Hershey's Kisses. At least the candy wasn't going to waste. He would use it to spell the word "why" in her yard in giant letters.

After the drunken candy incident, two days passed and he hadn't heard a word from Susan. He'd turned into a pathetic excuse of a man, sitting on his porch, chugalugging Michelobs and listening to Marshall Tucker while singing bitterly, "Can't you see, what that woman's been doin' to me?"

The next day he discovered a large manila envelope on his doorstep. It was stuffed with clippings from gossip columns and magazines from the past ten years, documenting his former relationships with assorted movie stars, heiresses, and party girls, the longest lasting a little over a month. There were at least fifty. An index card was enclosed that read, "You asked why. This is why. It's your past. I'd have to be a moron to marry you."

It was humbling and disturbing at the same time. He'd seen some of the photos and articles before, but never together in one damning pile. Not one of the women, gorgeous as they were, had ever prompted him to express himself via Hershey's Kisses.

He bought an oversized scrapbook and sat up all night mounting dozens of photos he'd taken of Susan over the summer: Susan with a shell to her ear, chattering into it as if it were a cell phone. Susan devouring her third tofu hot dog of the night (she refused to eat anything with a face) and sporting a trace of a mustard mustache. Susan strolling on the beach followed by a parade of adoring mutts.

He left the scrapbook on her stoop accompanied by his own note, which read, "That may have been my past, but you're the only woman I want in my future."

The next day he stepped out for a walk on the beach when Susan, her hair streaming in the wind, flew toward him like a wildfire. Before he could say another word, she raised a warning finger and pressed her mouth hard against his. They continued kissing until their lips were raw and Ryan was backed up against the front door, scarcely noticing the knob sinking into his lower back. Finally he scooped her up and carried her inside, his mouth never leaving hers.

Their lovemaking, which began with feral wildness, ended in silence and reverence. Ryan stroked her lightly freckled torso, marveling at each honey-dipped spot. His lips followed a trail of freckles to her long white neck, arched as if offering itself to him.

Susan's hands were tracing the terrain of his back muscles when her fingertips wandered to the top swelling of his buttocks and he felt his desire stir again. Ryan lifted up on his elbows to meet her eyes and was submerged in her gaze—a gaze that gradually blurred the borders between his existence and hers. He expelled a cry, one that started in the pit of his belly and rumbled through his body until it reached his tongue. How had he ever lived without her?

Hours later, after the light of an overcast morning had washed the bedclothes in muted grayness, they reclined on their backs, hips touching, calves entwined, both contained in private thoughts. Susan turned on her side to face him, hair spilling over shoulders.

He reached out, wanting to rub a strand of the silky gold between his fingers, but she caught his hand in mid-flight.

"There's something you need to know."

He could tell by her tone that their hour of oneness was officially over.

"From the start, I made up my mind not to get too involved with you," she said, her voice more emphatic with each word. "My father openly cheated on my mother and it completely ruined her life. I promised myself I'd never let something like that happen to me. But lo and behold, I find myself dating a man who thinks the female population is his own personal smorgasbord."

"Susan," he said, capturing her chin before she could duck away from him. "I promise you, I'm not that guy anymore."

"Shut up," she said, covering his mouth with her palm. "People only change in fairy tales. But none of that matters. Your diabolical plan worked."

"What plan?" His voice was muffled underneath her hand and she removed it.

"To make me fall in love with you. I tried not to. But you've lived up to your hype." She pushed on his chest with both hands "You're an amazing guy, even to someone as jaded as me."

"Susan..."

She scrambled to her knees, loomed over him, and roughly grabbed both of his ears. "No more words. I don't want to ever talk about this again. I'll go back to Atlanta with you and wear that engagement ring you bought for me. But if you *ever* decide to go back to your old sleazy ways..."

"I'm telling you, Susan—"

She tugged on his ears and her eyes looked as fierce as a timber wolf's. "I'll disappear from your life and never come back."

Ryan shook his head as he remembered those prophetic words. Susan had meant every syllable.

"Knock, knock," came his sister's voice from the back door.

"Come on in, Darce." Ryan tucked the photo back into the album and slipped it under his chair.

Darcy entered the den, carrying a couple of hardcover novels, the latest David Baldacci and a James Patterson.

"Hi, little brother," she said, depositing the books on the glass coffee table. "Thought you could catch up on some of your reading while you were recuperating. The bookstore clerk promised me both of these novels have ridiculously high body counts."

"How do you know I wasn't in the mood for Nicholas Sparks?"

"Please," Darcy said, hovering over him. "I know you all too well, little brother."

Not entirely, he thought. He wanted to confide in his sister but resisted because he could never predict how she'd react.

Darcy pressed her hand against his forehead, her long nails scratching him slightly. "So why did you check yourself out of the hospital against doctor's orders? Because you think you're indestructible?"

"My physician urged me to stay one more night, but as much as I was going to miss the runny Jell-O, I told him they'd just have to do without me," Ryan said, turning off the stereo with the remote. "And why should I stick around? There's not a single thing wrong with me."

Darcy wore a dress patchworked with eye-bleeding pinks and yellows. She was so thin her clavicle threatened to poke through her skin. All of her friends were similarly emaciated. How did so many affluent women manage to stay so skinny? Were they passing around Ex-Lax at their garden club meetings?

"Maybe you should take a nap," Darcy said, settling on the couch. "You seem cranky."

"I'm fine. Just frustrated." He softened his tone. "Thanks for the books."

"Where's Susan? She's the only reason I come here anyway," she teased.

"She has an appointment with her orthopedist. Just a follow-up."

"Those doctor's appointments are becoming less and less frequent. When I think of the condition she was in only a year ago..."

"Let's not talk about that, okay?"

"You're absolutely right." Darcy clasped her hands together and leaned forward. "Let's talk about happier things. Like the wedding." Her voice rose an octave. "Now that Susan's recovered we can start planning."

Ryan had married Susan at her hospital bedside, promising her a proper wedding as soon as she was up to it. Darcy was itching to be in charge of the affair.

"We're thinking of having it sometime during the Christmas season. Might keep away the media," Ryan said.

"It'll be a trick to have a ceremony with the press buzzing about, but I have some marvelous ideas—"

"Darcy," he said, holding up a hand to stop her. He'd have to swallow a half-dozen painkillers before he'd be in the mood to talk about the wedding. "There's something I want to discuss with you, but you have to promise to stay calm."

"I practice hot yoga, Ryan. You're looking at the poster child for calm. What is it? You can tell me."

He took a generous gulp of air and melded his hands on his lap. "Here's the thing. Susan and I are having...some problems."

"What kind of problems?" She leaned closer, eyes bright with curiosity.

"It has to do with me. I'm having serious doubts about our relationship."

She smiled and gave his knee an indulgent pat. "You know what this is all about, don't you? Pre-wedding jitters. Yes, I know you're already married, but this is a public declaration of your love. You should have seen me a month before my wedding to Ronnie. I drank Scotch like it was spring water."

"This is much more than jitters."

She stared at him hard, her cheek muscles twitching.

"Ryan Blaine, don't tell me you're going to break that poor girl's heart. Not after everything she's been through. Please don't tell me that."

"Would you listen to me? I've already decided divorce isn't an option. I'd never do that to her."

"So what, then? Oh, I see." She wrinkled her nose. "Well, you certainly won't be the first man of your stature to keep a mistress, and you won't be the last. Obviously there's someone else. You've always been so fickle, but I thought Susan cured you of that. Who is the little strumpet? That trampy paralegal in your office?"

There *was* someone else, the Susan he knew before her accident, but how could he begin to explain himself without appearing to be the world's most insensitive heel?

"I don't have a mistress, Darcy."

"Is this about Susan's scars? I know she doesn't look like the same woman because of all her surgeries, and *some* men—"

"Give me a little credit, Darce," Ryan interrupted. "It has nothing to do with the way Susan looks. She's still very attractive."

"I think you simply need to give the relationship time. It's only in the last couple of months or so that she's finally been able to function like a real person without having some operation hanging over her. Soon she'll go back to work—"

"She's not going back to work, Darcy."

Darcy made a *pfft* sound. "Come on. Susan adores furry and smelly creatures. Why do you think she was attracted to *you*, for God's sake?"

"I'm serious, Darce. She told me she's through being a vet. She doesn't even seem interested in our pets anymore. Liberty barked at her when she first came home from the hospital, and Susan's been anxious around her ever since. Whenever Mutsy puts his muzzle on her lap she pushes him off. You know how she used to dote on that dog of hers, and—"

"So she wants a career change. Did you expect her to fraternize with four-legged fur balls all her life? I think I read the average American changes careers four times, and—"

"It's not just that," Ryan said, rubbing his temples. It likely had been a mistake to tell his sister. There simply wasn't a good way of explaining how he felt. "It's as if she's a completely different woman since the accident."

He could cite hundreds of new Susan/old Susan contradictions, but the most wrenching difference was one he couldn't bring himself to discuss with anyone. Before the accident, his and Susan's lovemaking had become even deeper and more intense than their first extraordinary encounter. It was the one time he felt that she was completely giving herself to him. However, when he and the "new" Susan had their first sexual encounter, Ryan had to excuse himself to the bathroom afterward so she wouldn't sense how upset he was. There hadn't been a trace of their former connection, and for Ryan, that was the most painful difference of all. He'd kept trying, sometimes faking a desperate sort of passion, but their couplings never came close to those of the past.

"You know what Dr. Ambrose said," Darcy said. "Patients with traumatic brain surgery often experience personality changes—"

"That's an understatement," he said, shaking his head. "It's like *Invasion of the Body Snatchers.*"

He realized he sounded like a jerk. He knew Susan couldn't help it that her brain was damaged to the extent that she no longer seemed remotely like the woman she was before the accident. But he couldn't help how he felt about her changes either. If he didn't talk about it he'd go insane.

Darcy crossed her arms over her chest. "Well, if you're going to get married and you're not going to keep a mistress, what *do* you intend to do?"

"I have no idea," he said, tugging at the yarn of the afghan. He was considering having a sexless marriage with Susan but didn't want to discuss it with Darcy. "I wish I knew. I need—"

"A counselor. I know a woman who is a true miracle worker. Helped me work through my OCD three years ago and I still drop in for the occasional tune-up. I'm going to give you her card and I want you to call her today," Darcy said. She rooted through her purse until she found it.

"A shrink?" he said, recoiling. In his experience, counselors were often more screwed up than their patients.

"Call her," Darcy said, wagging the card in front of his face. "Jennifer Carr is a miracle worker."

Ryan took the card and dropped it on his lap. "I'll look into it."

"It'll be the best thing. Both of you have been through the wringer this year. It's natural that there'd be some adjustment problems."

This was far more than an "adjustment" problem. His sister still didn't get it.

"She's still recovering," Darcy said. "Every day she seems more and more like her old—"

"No, she doesn't!" Ryan hadn't meant to shout, but the situation was eating him alive. He paused for a moment to slow his breathing. "She's *nothing* like she used to be...but I'm going to try and deal with that."

"She is a little different. I've noticed it too. Coarser, somehow. And I'll try to have a word with her about her wardrobe. But considering what she's been through—"

"She's been through hell." Ryan shook a couple of Darvocets into his open palm and swallowed them dry. "Don't you think I'm ashamed of myself for feeling this way?"

"She tries so hard to please you."

"I know that," Ryan said, which made him feel even worse. Last week Susan had stood in front of her bookshelf and pulled down some of her favorite Anne Tyler novels. He suspected that she'd only done it for his benefit. These days it was hard to tell what her motives were.

Darcy stood and hitched a bulky leather bag on her shoulder. "Gotta run." She leaned down to kiss him on the cheek. "I know this year's been hard on you, and I'm not trying to make you out to be as bad as Bluebeard, but promise me you'll call Jennifer."

He looked down at the raised lettering on the counselor's card, not really seeing it. Maybe he would call. Not that he thought it would help. But at least he'd have someone to talk to other than his sister and a voice on the radio.

Nine

"Hi Minerva. It's Alone in Atlanta.'"

Caroline made a fake snoring sound. Not him again. The man probably had B.O. or halitosis. Maybe that's why he was "alone" in Atlanta.

"She's not coming back, Romeo," Caroline said. "Go find yourself another little chippy at the Waffle House."

"Hello, Alone," Minerva said. "So good to hear from you again. What's on your mind tonight?" Clearly she wasn't tired of the caller. Alone in Atlanta's sultry voice suggested a full head of hair and big biceps, but Caroline wouldn't be surprised if he sported a liver-spotted pate and a potbelly.

"I've gotten very discouraged over the last few days," he said. "She's not coming back. It's been too long."

"You *still* haven't heard a word?" Minerva said.

"No."

"Was there a disagreement?"

Alone paused. "I'm not ready to talk about it," he finally said.

"Maybe she's gone because he hit her over the head and buried her in the backyard," Caroline said. "Ever think about that, Minerva? Maybe that's why he's always shilly-shallying whenever you ask him what happened."

"Perhaps it is time to move on," Minerva said gently.

"I loved her so much," said the caller, his voice thickening. "And I had her with me for only a year. It seems so unjust to finally find the person you've been looking for your entire life and then—"

"Enough of that whining." Caroline switched off the radio and reached out to take Emily's hand, struck, as always, by the contrast between the two of them. Her own hand was a gnarled claw—mapped with eighty-five years of lines and blemishes. Emily's hand was small and pink, like something newly born. Caroline's fingers curled protectively around it.

"What should I sing to you tonight?" she asked, staring out the window. The sky was a moody dark blue, and a sliver of moon cut through a bank of clouds like a sickle.

This morning she sang "Seventy-six Trombones." Today before a lunch of beef patties she sang "Whoopie Ti Yi Yo. Git Along Little Doggies." Caroline decided to go with her old standard, "Inky Dinky *parlez vous*."

As Caroline began singing, her voice scratched in protest.

Her eyes watered after the first verse, so she decided to pack it in.

"Tomorrow's another day," she said, hefting herself out of the chair. She let out a groan when she noticed her door was ajar. It seemed like such a long trek across the room, and she was more than ready to crawl under the covers and slip into oblivion.

Caroline's slippers whispered over the carpet as she headed in the direction of the light slanting in from the hall. She grunted when she saw the "Welcome Friends" plaque lying on the floor. Mona had given it to her after Caroline had been living at Magnolia Manor for two months and hadn't yet decorated her door. Apparently there was some unwritten law that people in nursing homes were required to display a silly doodad on their door.

She put a hand to her waist and bent over to pick up the plaque.

"Welcome friends, my foot," Caroline said. "Have you ever seen a friend darken this door?" She glanced at Emily over her shoulder. "All my friends are dead, and I don't remember—"

She stopped in mid-sentence. It almost looked as if the girl was eyeballing her!

"Emily?" she called out softly. The bedside lamp poured light on the girl's face. Caroline blinked, took off her glasses, and rubbed them with a corner of her nightdress. Then she squinted at Emily again. She hadn't been mistaken; the girl's eyes were trained on her. Caroline took a step forward and then another. She was wide awake now, her heart beating as fast as a hummingbird's. She counted out ten steps before she reached Emily's bedside and then, with a slow and deliberate pace, she crossed back to the door.

She repeated her actions five times more, just to be absolutely certain that what she was witnessing wasn't a trick of the shadows or an invention of her imagination. Every single time Emily's eyes followed her path across the carpet, tracking her every movement.

"Katy bar the door! I think you can see me." She stared into Emily's blue orbs. This time Emily stared right back.

Caroline spent the rest of the night talking to her roommate until her voice cracked and she was left with a labored whisper.

"I can't believe it. You're finally coming out of your spell," she said for what must have been the hundredth time. The surge of adrenaline she'd gained earlier had petered away and sleep tugged at her eyelids. Emily was still staring at her as if taking in every word, and Caroline didn't want the experience to end. A few robins had made their first feeble morning calls, and the sky outside the window had lightened to the pearly gray of earliest morning.

"Never in my entire life..." Caroline began, but sleep cloaked her mind before she could finish the sentence.

"Mrs. Brodie, are you all right?"

Strong hands gripped her shoulders and gave them a brisk shake.

It was full light out now, and Caroline's gritty eyes were stung by the brightness. Gertie Haynes, a nurse's aide, loomed over her, a frown on her face. "You feeling punk, Mrs. Brodie? You slept through breakfast."

Caroline twisted her neck to glance at Emily, expecting the blue irises to still be cast in her direction. Instead, Emily's stare was fastened to the same stain on the ceiling, as if nothing had changed since last night.

"Emily looked at me," Caroline said, her voice still hoarse from overuse. "Her eyes followed me around the room. And I'm the one who made it happen."

"Did you?" Gertie said. She lumbered over to Emily and made a small adjustment to her feeding tube. "Looks to me like she's still counting the cracks in the ceiling."

"She is *now*," Caroline said, flinging her covers away and dangling her bare feet over the side of the bed. "But last night she was looking right at me. Listening to me. It was like there was finally a light in the window."

"Is that so?" Gertie's big square form blocked Emily from Caroline's view.

"We should call the doctor. Make him run some tests. He could see if—"

Gertie turned around to face Caroline, her uniform a series of straining white bulges like those of the Michelin Man.

"Coma patients are always doing strange things, Miz Brodie," she said. "They got electricity running in their body and every now and then it goes ka-flooey." She twirled a finger near her ear. "If you hooked this girl's brain up to a machine, I promise, all you'd see is a flat line." She jerked her head in the direction of the door. "You oughta get dressed. They probably got some danishes or bagels left over from breakfast."

Caroline punched her mattress. "There's been a miracle right here in this room and you're going on about bagels."

"Oh, Miz Brodie, I don't have no time for miracles. I got work to do."

"Never mind," Caroline muttered, deciding not to waste any more breath on the ignorant country girl. Gertie had probably gotten her nursing aide's certificate from the back of a matchbox. Caroline likely knew more about Emily's condition than she did. Nor would she say boo to Poppy, Emily's physical therapist, whose lips were permanently pursed into a sour pucker. No. She needed to talk with Mona, the nursing home's director. Mona would listen to Caroline and have a doctor run over to take a look at Emily. Yes.

That's what she'd do, Caroline thought to herself, feeling a sense of purpose, even though she was still groggy from her short night's sleep. She'd put on some clothes, have a little bite, and then pop by Mona's office. An hour later, after she was showered, dressed, and powdered, she headed toward the administration suite.

"You're going to flip your wig, Miss Mona," she whispered as she strode pass the cafeteria, the aroma of corned beef hash drifting into the hall. She'd been rehearsing her speech all morning. About how she'd been conducting research on the computer about Emily's condition. How she'd embarked on a regular regime to help the poor lamb wake up. How her labor of love had finally paid off.

The suite was located just off the front foyer of Magnolia Manor. It had a fake fireplace and fussy, overly formal furniture, which were all for show and never used by the residents. Caroline stuck her head into the small glass outer cubicle and saw Dixie Waters, Mona's niece, sitting at her desk eating a microwave burrito. Mona had recently hired Dixie on as the assistant director.

"Hey, Mrs. Brodie. You sure look pretty today. What can I do ya for?" Dixie's voice was loud enough to carry across a football field. She assumed all the residents were deaf as tree stumps.

"Where's Miss Mona?" Caroline asked.

Dixie looked like Betty Boop come to life with big round eyes, jet-black hair, and red baby-doll lips. Looked sweet, but had a mean streak longer than the tail of a comet.

"She'll be gone for two weeks." Dixie was chasing down an errant bean, which left a brown stain on the paperwork in front of her. "That's fourteen days! Her daughter had twin babies, and she flew out to Oregon to lend a hand."

I can hear you, Caroline wanted to say, but she held her tongue. She wouldn't bother telling Dixie about Emily's progress. The woman wasn't any brighter than Gertie.

"Is there something I can do, Mrs. Brodie?"

"No, no," Caroline said, lingering outside the office, wondering what she should do next. She was like a seed pod, bursting with Emily's news. What a shame there wasn't a single soul to tell.

"The craft lady will be in the activity room at one thirty. That's two hours! A little bit after lunch! She's having a *bead blitz!*"

"I'd like to blitz your bead," Caroline mumbled as she meandered down, the hall to the activity room, where the only "activity" going on was a speckled geezer snoring in front of *The 700 Club* on TV. That suited her just fine. She was grateful to have the computer all to herself so she could do some more research on Emily.

A while back, Mona had taught her how to conduct a Boolean search, so Caroline typed "eye-tracking" and "persistent vegetative state" in the Google box. She was tickled silly when she pulled up an article from a medical journal that said, "Eye-tracking can be the earliest sign of recovery from a persistent vegetative state."

The article also warned that many patient responses, such as eye-tracking, hand-grasping, and smiling, were reflexive and not necessarily an indication of increased awareness. It continued to say that patients who'd been in vegetative states for more than six months had about a one percent chance of recovery. Caroline paid no mind to such doom-saying. She knew Emily was coming out of her deep freeze as well as she knew her middle name was Topeka. She had a sixth sense about it.

However, much later that evening, Caroline wasn't nearly as optimistic. She turned the radio dial to *Minerva* and listened to the entire show. Then she sang three songs, rubbed Emily's legs until her fingers tingled, and shook her tin of Christmas nuts near her ear like a tambourine player, but her roommate's gaze was still stubbornly fixed on the ceiling.

She yawned and looked at the clock. It was one a.m. No wonder she was so tired.

"Don't know what's so interesting about that water spot," Caroline finally said, her weariness making her cross. "Doesn't even look like anything. Not a country, not an animal. It's just a big fat nothing."

She scowled at Emily, who still hadn't moved a smidgen. "Well, I'm fed up," Caroline said, rising stiff-legged from her rocker.

"Be standoffish if you want. I'll just talk to the plastic plant on the windowsill over yonder. It'll be better company."

Caroline reached over to pull the lamp cord when she noticed something gleaming on Emily's face.

"Good God Almighty," Caroline said as her eyes blinked in disbelief. She squinted and looked again. There was no mistaking what she saw. Those weren't bottled tears slipping down her roommate's cheek like a string of seed pearls; they were genuine tears made by Emily's own ducts.

"My precious child." Caroline grasped Emily's hand and gave it a gentle squeeze. "I'm so sorry I got crabby with you."

Caroline's knees went weak when she received an ever-so-faint hand squeeze as an answer.

Ten

Skye's alarm clock rang louder than an air-raid siren. She seized the machine with both hands and fumbled with the buttons to make it stop beeping. When that failed, she smothered it with her pillows.

"It can't be morning," she moaned to herself, but the sun screaming through the windows and the cardinals scolding on the oak tree outside contradicted her statement.

Last evening was her worst night yet. Skye heard angels and other high-level souls needed only an hour or two of rejuvenation, and that some people working in the Supreme Being Sector functioned with no shut-eye at all. But as a brand-new soul, she required at least five hours of sleep or she'd have concentration problems.

Skye gave her head a cobweb-clearing shake. Last night she'd stayed up late watching scenes from Ryan's life. She witnessed his conversation with Darcy. Then she heard his phone call to Minerva saying he was thinking of giving up on his mystery woman. The man was a complete paradox and yet she couldn't stop obsessing over him.

No time to sort it out. It was Monday—a heavy traffic day in the Hospitality Sector. But maybe she could afford to steal a minute to look in on Ryan Blaine before she left for work.

The remote was on her bedside table, and she aimed it at the television. The screen filled with Ryan soaping his nude body in the shower. She watched mesmerized for a moment until her conscience caught up with her. It was bad enough she spied on him with his clothes on, but to gawk at him in the buff made her as bad as a common peeping Tom.

I have to stop watching, she thought. It was ridiculous to get so attached to someone she would never see again in the flesh.

Skye arrived at work early and stopped by the break room to relax before her shift. Joy and Glory were hunkered down on the couch, staring at the television screen.

"Not Earthly Pleasures," Skye said, covering her eyes with her hand. "I promised myself I wouldn't watch it anymore." After a moment her willpower wilted and she parted two of her fingers. "So what's he up to now?"

"Kissing some starlet," Glory said, watching intently. "Dang. You think those two will ever come up for air?"

"What?" Skye said, dropping her hand. The screen showed an unfamiliar man kissing a tall leggy blonde.

"Where's Ryan?" she demanded.

"Oh. Him," Glory said with a shrug. "Ryan's pretty much run his course. Time for some new blood. Everyone's watching Lars Landers and his latest fling."

"Yes. They bicker a lot," Joy said, reaching into a box of Jujubes. "Then they make up. It's nonstop drama."

"Skye Sebring. You have a guest in your office," said a voice over the intercom system.

Skye hurried down the hall to her cubicle. When she arrived, a busty black woman spilling out of a red latex dress greeted her.

"May I help you?" Skye said. The woman was draped seductively in a chair.

"Yo, shorty. What do you think of the new me?" The voice was childish and didn't match the mature body.

"Chelsea? Is that you?"

The woman stood. She wore thigh-high vinyl boots and a too-tight dress that barely contained her curves.

"I'm Lil Kim, a.k.a. Queen Bee, a.k.a. Miss Brooklyn, a.k.a.—"

"Looks to me like someone has paid a visit to the Total Makeover Salon."

"I went yesterday. What do you think of my new pimped-out body?" Chelsea thrust her breasts and cupped them with the palms of her hands. "Aren't these awesome?"

"They definitely make a statement," Skye said. Total Makeover Salon allowed Heaven dwellers to customize their appearance through the use of holographs. The attraction was very popular with newcomers, and it wasn't unusual to see three or four Megan Foxes and a couple of Ryan Goslings strolling around ND quarters. The effect was temporary, lasting only about twelve hours. Even now, Chelsea's provocative look was beginning to blur around the edges.

"Looks like you're fading, Lil Gem," Skye remarked.

"Kim," Chelsea said with a snicker. She was smiling, and Skye could see a few freckles through the disappearing holograph.

"What are you doing here, Chelsea? Our outing isn't until tomorrow." Skye consulted her watch. "I'm due to get my first client any minute now."

"I want to watch you work. I thought maybe I could be a greeter like you someday."

"I don't know, Chelsea. It might confuse my clients, and they're already pretty confused as it is. Besides, how would I explain your presence?"

"Say I'm a trainee. I see that in restaurants all the time where the new waitress shadows the more experienced one. Please?" Lil Kim had disappeared completely and Chelsea was sitting in Skye's chair, wearing faded jeans and a Jeff Beck t-shirt. The red light had already started flashing on Skye's computer. There really wasn't time to argue with the teenager.

"Okay, but I don't want to hear a peep out of you." Skye opened her desk drawer and handed Chelsea a pocket computer. "Key in a Hospitality uniform. Quickly. And get your butt out of my chair."

Chelsea made some hasty entries into the computer, and in a flash, a navy-blue uniform replaced her clothes. "Boring," she said as she frowned down at her flared skirt and crepe-soled shoes.

"Hush," Skye said, pulling up the incoming file on her desk computer. "Mr. Barkowski is on his way, and he's had a nasty accident with a power drill."

During the arrival of the first several clients, Chelsea was congenial and helpful. She curtsied when introduced as a trainee, and she handed clients their bags of orientation materials with the flourish of a game-show hostess.

But after they'd finished with the fifth client of the day and were on their way to lunch, the teenager had a bug-eyed stunned look about her. Skye decided it was time she went home.

"I see dead people," Chelsea said in an eerie voice as they traveled on the moving sidewalks crowded with newcomers.

"Stop it," Skye said with a gruff whisper. "They might hear."

"They know they're dead," Chelsea said as they passed a man riddled with bullet wounds.

"Yes, but some of them are still sensitive about it."

"Did you know they have death-acceptance support meetings in the ND quarters? 'Hello, my name is Chelsea, and I'm dead,'" Chelsea said. She stuck a finger in her mouth as if she were about to gag.

"Have you been attending them?"

"Just one." Chelsea scrunched up her face. "Who wants to sit around talking about that dumb kind of junk? I prefer the nightly live chats with God. The Newly Dead can ask Her any question on the computer and She'll answer."

"Did you ask anything?"

"Yup. I asked her if Elvis was really dead."

"And?"

"Yeah. He is. My aunt Bernice will be disappointed to hear that. She could have sworn she saw him buying a bag of pork rinds at the Circle K."

They passed a sign in front of a corridor that read "Special Cases Department: Authorized Personnel Only."

"What's that?" Chelsea asked.

"It's a place for newcomers who can't easily be processed by a Hospitality greeter."

"Like who?"

"People whose bodies were severely damaged, very young children, people who are temporarily stuck in both dimensions."

"Creepy," Chelsea said with a shudder. She eyed a frail elderly man who was hobbling across the sidewalk in the other direction.

"All of the guys here are feebs. Doesn't anyone cute ever die?"

They'd reached the end of the moving sidewalk, exited the building, and headed toward an outdoor lunch area frequented by Hospitality Sector employees.

"You're still in the newcomers' quarters," Skye said. "Once you get into Heaven proper, you'll probably see some younger—"

She stopped short when she spied the billboard across the street. Ryan's photograph had been replaced with the pop star named Lars Landers.

"What are you gaping at?" Chelsea asked, following Skye's line of sight.

Skye averted her eyes from the billboard. "Nothing."

"Are you hot for Lars?"

"No," Skye said quickly. "It's pointless to have crushes on Earthlings."

"Do you have a boyfriend?"

"In theory," Skye said, with a bob of her chin. She'd been avoiding Brock's calls ever since Ryan Blaine had zipped in and out of her life. They reached the picnic area and took seats at one of the umbrella tables.

"What's his name?" Chelsea said.

"His name is Brock."

"Will I ever get to meet him?"

"I don't know," Skye said. Suddenly she felt a little wistful about good old Brock. Everything was so uncomplicated with him. Perhaps if the two of them got together again, he'd take her mind off Ryan.

"Maybe you will meet him," Skye said. "I'll invite him to join us tomorrow, at least for part of the day. We could go to the zoo."

"The zoo?" Chelsea said, rolling her eyes upward so only the whites showed. "I hate to break this to you, but I'm a little too old to get worked up over a bunch of monkeys."

"This isn't an ordinary zoo. They have every animal that's ever lived on Earth, even dinosaurs. It's one of my favorite places in Heaven."

"Dinosaurs? We could check it out, I suppose."

After lunch, Skye returned to her cubicle and left a message on Brock's voicemail inviting him to their outing.

Eleven

"Welcome," Dr. Mullins said, traversing the Earth 101 classroom in several long strides. He caught Skye's eye and smiled as he made his way to the blackboard. "We'll be covering two more lessons this period."

A television and DVD player were situated on a cart near the podium in front, and Dr. Mullins slipped a silver disc into the player. His limbs were a study in angles, elbows so sharp they looked like they'd pierce through the patches of his jacket.

"I visited guardian angel headquarters a few days ago, and they granted me permission to film a few of the things I saw while I was there."

Skye put down her pencil and leaned over her desk with interest. Guardian angels were shrouded in mystery, and few people in Heaven knew anything about their methods of helping Earth dwellers. She always imagined it involved hours of pious praying and spiritual contemplation.

Dr. Mullins turned on the television and the camera zeroed in on the face of a white-gowned angel who looked anything but serene. Her lovely features were tensed, and her tone was pleading as she spoke into a gold hands-free telephone mouthpiece. "If I have told you once, I've told you a thousand times, don't tease the kitty."

The camera panned backward and showed hundreds of angels speaking into similar mouthpieces, some of them shouting.

"Go back! You left the burner on."

"Slow down! There's a bridge out ahead."

"Stay clear of that cheese tray. You know it gives you gas."

Skye had never heard such a roar of voices in one place. It reminded her of footage she'd seen of the New York Stock Exchange.

Professor Mullins turned down the volume and faced the class. "On Earth, people talk about the 'little voice in their head' that helps them to make decisions. Some call it intuition," he said. "But as you witnessed, it's hardly a little voice. Most of the angels are screaming at the top of their lungs so as to be heard over their clients' ceaseless internal dialogue. They're competing with thoughts of self-doubt, worry, and judgment. When you're on Earth, you must distinguish between your self-talk, which is generally a lot of harmful nonsense, and the wise, persistent voice of your guardian angel, who's there to guide you through life."

"What's the song that goes with the lesson?" called out a dark-haired girl who was hunched over her desk, scribbling down every word.

"Glad you asked," Dr. Mullins said. "Are you ready for it?"

Everyone in the class shouted "yes" and Dr. Mullins nodded and pulled up the boom box from behind the podium.

"This will help you to remember to listen..." Dr. Mullins cupped a hand to his ear. "And pay attention to your intuition."

He adjusted a few buttons, and George Harrison started singing in a clear confident voice: "Listen. Do you want to know a secret?"

Once the song ended, Dr. Mullins pointed to the television screen again. Several angels were seated around a table, watching a PowerPoint presentation.

"This leads us to the second lesson of the day," Dr. Mullins said. "Sometimes on Earth you'll face dilemmas that seem insurmountable. You'll find yourself not knowing what to do or where to turn. When this happens, just release your troubles to the angels, and they'll devise a plan to help you. The key to this lesson is trust. You have to get out of the way so the angels have free rein to work their miracles. Here is some valuable advice from the greatest musicians to ever walk the Earth." He hit the button on the boom box again, and a song began. "Let it be. Whispered words of wisdom…"

The class sang along, some of them swaying and waving their arms as if they were at a rock concert. After the number ended, Dr. Mullins switched off the boom box and said, "That's all for today."

Twelve

"It's lunchtime, dearie."

Caroline heard the singsong voice inches from her ear. Her eyes snapped open and for a minute she had no idea where she was. A gently wrinkled face loomed over her, accompanied by the scent of rose water.

"Mrs. Taylor," Caroline said, blinking away the residue of sleep from her eyes. Her mouth tasted like the bottom of a terrarium, and the wing chair she'd dozed in was damp from her drool. "Lunch already?"

It had been eight a.m. when she'd decided to sit in the activity room and steal a catnap. The morning got away from her while she slept.

"Yes, dear."

Mrs. Taylor was all snowy-white hair, blue eyes, and porcelain skin. She was eighty-nine and had been crowned Miss Magnolia Manor three years running. Caroline was amazed at the tenacity of her beauty enduring through wrinkles, jowls, and age spots.

Caroline had been pretty once—for about ten minutes. A no-good husband and thirty-five years of feeding middle-school kids meat-loaf surprise had worn the good looks right out of her.

"I'll get up in a minute," Caroline said. The aroma of pork chops reached her nose, mingled with the unpleasant undertone that always accompanied institutional cooking. The smell reminded her of burned Brillo pads, and it clung to the cafeteria no matter what was being prepared in the kitchen that day.

The call of sleep was stronger than that of food, and Caroline was tugged back to her dreams. Such a pleasant place. She and Emily strolled along a sugary beach, strewn with shells pink as a baby's ear. Emily smiled, and Caroline realized she'd never seen her roommate's teeth before. They were white and strong, the one part of her untouched by illness.

"I'm coming back," Emily said. "Soon." Suddenly she was far away, a speck in the distance waving to Caroline. Emily shouted something over the rush of the surf, and her voice had an unexpected querulous tone.

"You've been in that chair all day," it said. "And yesterday too."

It took Caroline a minute to realize the voice didn't belong to her lovely dream world. It was gratingly real and accompanied by a sour odor.

"I want that chair," continued the voice, whining like a horsefly.

The voice belonged to Hettie Phipps. Caroline tried to stand, but her body had been plastered to the bottom of the chair so long she felt like she was part of it.

"Hold your water," Caroline mumbled. She was still wedged in the gauzy world between sleep and wakefulness.

Hettie wasn't inclined to wait. "I need that chair," she said loudly. She thrust her face closer, and Caroline could see gray whiskers sprouting from her chin.

"Take the darn thing, then." Caroline eased herself up, pins and needles pricking her backside as she surrendered the chair to Hettie.

The evening news blared on the television, jarring her into full consciousness. Not only had she slept through lunch; she'd missed dinner too. Caroline walked stiff-legged to the dining room, knowing she looked a fright. Her dress was wrinkled and strands of hair had loosened from her bun and hung limply in her face. But her hunger pains were sharp, like a cat trying to claw its way out of a croaker sack.

The dining room was empty; the dishes had been cleared away

and the tables were already set for breakfast. Cardboard flower cutouts hung on the walls. In July there'd be American flags; Thanksgiving would bring Pilgrims and horns of plenty. The decorations were meant to be cheerful, but Caroline found them patronizing, more appropriate for an elementary school than an assisted-living center.

She poked her head in the kitchen, hoping to get a sandwich. The bare stainless-steel counters gleamed, and the place smelled more like Comet than food.

Beulah, a big black woman, was rinsing a ten-gallon pot in the industrial-sized sink. She wore a hair net that sat like a blue mushroom cap on her bullet-shaped head. Caroline was all too familiar with the weariness in the woman's wide round back and knew the cook wouldn't be happy to open her refrigerator, dirty a knife, and sully her clean counters with crumbs.

She didn't speak to Beulah, but instead headed to her room, remembering the Christmas nuts on the top shelf of her closet. A handful of cashews should quiet the beast in her belly.

The nursing home was winding down for the evening just as Caroline was perking up. For the past three nights, she'd been as nocturnal as an owl, staying up until dawn. Emily was only active after midnight. Something was definitely stirring within the girl. Her eyes constantly followed Caroline, and she squeezed her hand several times each evening. Caroline couldn't wait to see what Emily would do next.

She ate a handful of nuts, licked the salt from her fingers, and tuned to the *Minerva* show on the radio. Alone in Atlanta was hogging the airwaves again; he and Minerva were in the middle of a conversation.

"We *did* have a terrible argument before she left, Minerva," Alone in Atlanta said. There was an uncomfortably long pause. "She believed I'd betrayed her by sleeping with another woman."

"Aha!" Caroline said. "The truth finally rears its ugly head."

"And had you?" Minerva asked, her voice breathless with interest.

"No. It was a misunderstanding."

"Well, Alone, maybe she's out there listening," said Minerva. "Maybe she's forgiven you and is ready to come back."

"I doubt it, Minerva. I've come to accept she's gone from my life for good, just like she promised she'd be. I've decided this is my last call to the show. But I wanted you to know it really helped me to talk to you. Thank you so much. Believe me, there wasn't anyone I could discuss this with."

"We'll miss you, Alone. There are legions of listeners out there who've been rooting for you, but I understand your decision. You've never once mentioned your girlfriend's name. Would you like to say it now? Maybe you could appeal to her one final time."

"I guess it won't hurt to tell you." He lowered his voice a decibel. "Her name is Susan."

"Susan? Okay, Susan, Alone in Atlanta hopes you'll come back to him. Here's a song just for you. Maybe you'll wake up and realize how much you're missed."

"Wake up, Little Susie. Wake up." Caroline hummed along with the song until she noticed Emily shifting her gaze from the water stain on the ceiling to Caroline's face.

Caroline turned off the radio and smiled. "So you're with me now, are you?" She reached for Emily's hand and gave it a small squeeze. Caroline was thrilled but not surprised when Emily returned her greeting. "We're going to let someone in on our secret."

Caroline knew Lydia Chance, the night attendant, would be making her rounds soon, and she'd decided to tell her about Emily. She'd been foolish to confide in Gertie, who only saw Emily during the day and wasn't very bright to boot. Miss Chance would be able to see Emily's progress for herself.

At a quarter of one, the door creaked opened, and Miss Chance padded into Caroline's room for her nightly check.

"Mrs. Brodie, don't tell me you're still awake? That's three nights in a row now," she whispered. "Do I need to give you a little something to help you sleep?"

Caroline ignored the woman's question. She was far too excited.

"Look at Emily," she said quickly, pointing at her roommate. "She's staring at me. Do you see? And watch this." She eased out of her rocking chair and crossed to the middle of the room, where Miss Chance stood. She was delighted the girl's eyes were still on her. Caroline had been a little afraid Emily wouldn't perform for an audience. "She's tracking me wherever I go."

Miss Chance didn't look a bit surprised. She nodded and said, "Like the eyes of a painting in a haunted house. Gave me the creeps the first time it happened to me."

"What do you mean?"

"Emily's been watching me on and off now for months. She started it in January."

"Months?" Caroline said, scarcely able to find her voice. "Land's sakes."

"You used to always be asleep when I came in, Mrs. Brodie." Miss Chance was a woman in her fifties with a ghostly complexion and nearly invisible eyebrows and lips. The only color on her face was the red rims of her eyes.

"She's also been squeezing my hand," Caroline said, frantically trying to save the situation. "Has she ever done *that* before?"

"Can't say that I've ever taken her hand," Miss Chance said, facing Caroline as she stood by Emily's bed. "But if she squeezed your hand it was likely just reflexes. Now if you told me Emily's been reciting the Gettysburg Address, I would sit up and take notice."

"It has to be more than just reflexes." Caroline's voice trembled with disappointment.

"I know exactly how you feel, Mrs. Brodie," Miss Chance said gently. "A long time ago, I was a home health aide for a little boy who nearly drowned in a bucket of mop water. Peter had eyes big as half-dollars, and he'd watch me every time I came into the room. Sometimes he laughed right out loud, and I would have sworn on my mother's grave he had some idea of what was going on around him. But after caring for him a few months, I realized everything he did was just a reflex. Sometimes he'd cry real tears, but not because he was sad. It was just something his poor empty little body did."

"I'm sure there are times when it's not reflexes, when someone *is* inside, trying to get out," Caroline said with an adamant whisper. "I think that's what's happening with Emily."

"Supposing it is," Miss Chance said, resting a hand on Caroline's shoulder, "how far can we expect the poor dear to come after such a long time? It'd be a miracle if she regained even a tenth of her faculties. Would you want her to live a life where the only things she can do are track people with her eyes and squeeze their hands?"

She stole a fond glance at Emily, whose gaze was still focused on Caroline. "No, Mrs. Brodie. For Emily's sake, pray what you're seeing is just reflexes from a body whose soul was freed a long time ago."

Caroline felt as if a pair of icy fingers were walking down her back. Maybe she'd done a terrible thing by trying to rouse Emily from her nonresponsive state. Maybe Miss Chance was right, and Emily would never progress beyond the simplest of skills, and Caroline should have left well enough alone.

"Better hop into bed, Mrs. Brodie," Miss Chance said, heading toward the door. She paused when she saw the look of distress on Caroline's face. "You shouldn't fret over this. Emily might be too much for you. Maybe it's time you transferred to another room."

"No!" Caroline shouted. An alarmed expression darkened Miss Chance's face, causing Caroline to soften her tone. "This is where I want to be, where I need to be."

"All right," Miss Chance said. "But I hope I don't see the light under your door when I come back 'round this way."

After she left, Caroline returned to her chair, rocking in stunned silence. Her late husband had often accused her of meddling in other people's business. Had she gone too far this time? If she'd done something to make Emily's plight worse, she'd never forgive herself.

"You stupid old biddy," she said to herself as tears scoured her cheeks. "Should have minded my own business."

For a moment, Caroline thought she saw Emily's eyes widen in sympathy. The whole situation was obviously taking its toll. She should listen to Miss Chance and crawl between the covers. She could use a nice long snooze. She was getting into bed when she heard a whisper.

"She is..."

Caroline's chin fell to her chest. Could she trust her ears? Did the girl speak?

"Wrong." Emily gasped out the next word. Then her eyelids dropped like shades, as if the effort of speech had exhausted her.

Thirteen

Skye rode the elevator up to Chelsea's hotel room in a woozy fog. She'd endured another restless night and was so tired she could practically sleep standing up. There were many times last night when she'd been tempted to check in on Ryan Blaine but willed herself to stay away from Earthly Pleasures.

The teenager answered the door on the first knock, wearing an oversized Abercrombie & Fitch hoodie and blue jeans that threatened to shimmy down her slim hips.

"Heaven is so boring," was the first thing that came out of her mouth.

"Boring?" Skye said, stepping inside. Chelsea's bed was heaped with what looked like an entire Juniors department of clothes. An oversized flat-screen plasma television was tuned to a rap video, and there were dozens of CDs and DVDS piled on the dresser. A desktop computer blipped with the sound of an incoming instant message.

"Looks like you've made a friend," Skye said, eyeing the computer monitor. "There's a Facebook message here for you saying, 'Wassup?'"

"It's just a stupid message from the activity director on my floor," Chelsea said with a frown. "She sends me one almost every hour because she feels sorry for me. I hate it when old people try to be hip. They always get it wrong. Nobody says 'wassup' anymore."

"She just wants you to feel at home," Skye said. "I take it you still haven't met anyone your own age?"

Chelsea sighed. "There was this one girl who got here yesterday, but turns out she's a Justin Bieber fan. Can you believe it? She saw him in concert just before she croaked. That's all I needed to know about her."

Skye wanted to suggest to Chelsea that maybe she shouldn't be so picky, but she wasn't in the mood for an argument.

"Well, summer vacation is coming up," Skye said. "Sadly, that tends to bring in lots of bike accidents and drownings. You're liable to have company soon. Are you ready to go?"

The pair left Chelsea's room and teleported to the zoo as planned, appearing in front of the dinosaur complex. Skye watched in awe as a fifty-foot Brachiosaurus lumbered about, devouring the tops of yew trees. A flock of leathery-winged pterodactyls squawked as they soared overhead.

"Some pterodactyls have a wingspan of forty feet," Skye read on a plaque outside the dinosaur pen. "Their bones are hollow, and they favor a diet of—" She glanced at Chelsea, who wasn't listening or even looking at the dinosaurs. Instead, the teen was absorbed in manipulating a miniature machine.

"What are you doing?" Skye asked.

"Playing Tony Hawk Pro Skater on my phone," Chelsea said over the roar of a Tyrannosaurus rex. "Snap! You made me mess up my backside nose slide."

"What about all these incredible dinosaurs?" Skye pointed at the animals behind the fence.

"They looked more realistic in *Jurassic Park*," Chelsea said, her focus still on the game. "Besides, you've seen one triceratops, you've seen them all."

Skye chuckled to herself. "We should probably head over to the reptile house. I'm supposed to meet my boyfriend there in a half hour."

The game made an electronic dying sound and Chelsea glanced up. "Are you in love?"

"That's kind of a personal question, isn't it?"

"What's his name again?" Chelsea asked.

"Brock," Skye said.

"Rock? That's a weird name."

"It's Brock, and I think it's a very nice name." Skye pointed to a winding path that led to a circular building. "The reptile house is that way."

"What's he like?" Chelsea asked, trotting beside her.

"Brock is highly intelligent, thoughtful, and very nice."

"Boyfriends are supposed to be hot, not nice," Chelsea grumbled.

"I think you watch too many PG-13 movies. And besides, Brock *is* hot. Smoking hot, as the saying goes."

They crossed through the ancient gardens, lush with feathery ferns and horsetails, which brushed their bare arms as they passed.

"Can I tell you something?" Chelsea asked. "And will you swear you'll never tell a living soul?" She paused. "Or even a dead soul?"

"I swear," Skye said, crossing herself, amused by the seriousness of Chelsea's request.

"I'm a virgin," Chelsea whispered. "Can you believe it? I died so young I never got to have sex."

"That's hardly a shock," Skye said, waving away a gigantic dragonfly that buzzed her ear. "You were only thirteen when you died."

"I was the last virgin in my class," Chelsea insisted. "Sex starts early at my school. If you haven't popped your cherry by the time you're twelve, everyone thinks you're a lesbian."

"Don't you believe it," Skye said as they reached the edge of the gardens. "I'd be willing to bet most of the girls in your class are virgins. They just want people to think they've had sex."

"I don't know," Chelsea said, hands in pockets, tripping every few feet because the hems of her blue jeans were several inches too long. "I just wish I'd done it, but I was too busy skating. Now I'll be a virgin for all eternity. It's mortifying."

Skye stopped on the path. "Chelsea, you do know there's sex in Heaven, right?"

"There is?" She looked furtively behind her as if fearing somebody was listening in on their conversation. "Really?"

"Of course. It's Heaven, not Hell."

"I didn't know. I figured sex was too naughty for Heaven. What with God hanging around and all."

"Only Earth dwellers see sex as naughty, particularly Americans. In Heaven it's considered natural and beautiful."

Chelsea's eyes gleamed. "I guess that means you've had sex with your boyfriend?"

"Chelsea!" Skye said sharply.

"My bad," Chelsea said, flicking a section of her long blonde hair over her shoulder. "You were the one saying how natural it is."

"It is," Skye said, quickening her pace down the path. "I'm just not sure it's an appropriate topic for discussion with a young teenager."

"Let me just ask this," Chelsea said as she struggled to keep up. "If you had sex with your boyfriend, and I'm not saying you have, but if you did, was it so romantic you felt like your heart would explode?"

"The subject is closed," Skye said. They had walked through the gardens and were now a few feet from the zoo's arcade, which was next to the reptile house. "We have about twenty minutes before Brock gets here. Why don't we see what's inside?"

The arcade was deafening with the bings and bongs from a riot of flashing games lining the walls. Just by the entrance there was a virtual-reality attraction called "Be an Animal in the Zoo."

"Look, Chelsea," Skye said, studying the instructions on the machine. "This is fascinating. You can experience what it's like to be any animal you want, from a tarantula to a giraffe. Wouldn't it be a lot of fun to be an eagle?" She smothered a yawn. "Although right now I wouldn't mind being a sloth."

She was talking to herself, because Chelsea had pushed past her to stand on a device that looked like an upright scale.

"Past Life Detector," Skye said, reading the lit-up sign. "Find out what happened in your last three lives."

Chelsea pulled down the arm of the machine to start it. "I bet I did some really amazing things in my past lives."

People in Heaven could usually remember only their last life on Earth, but a detailed summation of all of their preceding lives was available to them from the Reincarnation Archives in the Supreme Being Sector. Skye explained all of this to Chelsea, saying, "This machine is a novelty. It probably just gives you the bare bones of each life."

Sure enough, when a summary of Chelsea's last life spit from the slot, the details were scant: "Middle-school student. Cause of death: head injury while skateboarding."

"Tell me something I didn't know," Chelsea said, balling up the piece of paper and sticking it in her jeans pocket. A second printout shot out of the slot and floated to the ground. Chelsea knelt to pick it up.

"Eighteen-year-old banana picker. Cause of death: fall from a tree," she read aloud, and then dropped the paper. "No wonder I've never liked banana bread. This is too freaky."

"Here comes the next one," Skye said, catching the printout and handing it to Chelsea.

"Sweet," Chelsea said with a big grin after she read it. "Nineteen-year-old surfing champion. Cause of death: drowning in twenty-five-foot wave." She let out a low whistle. "Now that's the way to go."

"Sounds to me like you need to be a little more careful."

"Your turn," Chelsea said, gesturing toward the machine. "Hop on."

"It's not going to work for me. I haven't had any past lives."

"I know, but maybe it will tell you what your future life will be like."

"I seriously doubt that, and furthermore, I don't think I necessarily want to know how my life will come to an end."

"Let's just see. Come on."

Deciding to humor her, Skye stepped on the platform and thrust down the arm. The machine jerked and started spitting out a printout. Skye laughed. "I wonder what kind of nonsense this thing will come up with."

Chelsea pulled out the slip of paper from the front and examined it. "Snap! There's something here."

"Let me see," Skye said. She took the printout from Chelsea and read it softly to herself.

"Twenty-five; unemployed. Cause of death: N/A." She shook her head in bewilderment. "That's silly. The machine must be broken."

"Another one is printing out," Chelsea said excitedly.

"Obviously it's giving me someone else's lives," Skye said, ignoring the piece of paper that came from the machine. "Let's go. Brock will be at the reptile house any minute."

"Are you sure you've never had a past life before?" Chelsea asked, tripping behind her.

"Don't you think I would know if I had one?" Skye said as she pushed open the exit door of the arcade. "There's something wrong with that machine. Maybe when a new soul steps on it, it prints out a lot of junk. I'm not surprised. It's a toy, after all."

"I'm a little confused about this new-soul business. Did you just appear in Heaven one day, or were you a baby, or what?"

"New souls are fully functional adults from the start," Skye explained. "I was created a little over a year ago."

"How? Were you hatched? Did you come by stork?"

"No," Skye said with a laugh. They'd arrived at the reptile house, a concrete circular building with a cartoon cutout of an alligator just outside the entrance. So far there was no sign of Brock.

"There's a place in the Supreme Being Sector where new souls are born," Skye said. "It's an enormously popular attraction. You should go there."

"Will you take me?"

"Sure. How about sometime this week?" she said just as she saw Brock approaching.

"Skye! You look beautiful as usual," Brock said with a

delighted smile. He wasn't looking too shabby himself. The man *was* catch-your-breath handsome. A thought occurred to her. Was it possible her encounter with Ryan had primed her well, so to speak, and she'd now overflow like a fountain with feelings for Brock?

"I'm so glad you could make it," Skye said, linking arms with him. "Brock, this is Chelsea. She's one of my clients, and she's been anxious to meet you."

"So you're the boyfriend?" Chelsea said. She folded her arms across her chest and scrutinized him with narrowed eyes. "What exactly is it that you do?"

"Brock's the anchorman for *Today in Heaven,*" Skye said, giving Brock's chest a covetous pat. "He interviews all sorts of saints and important angels. Recently he snagged an exclusive telephone interview with God, and he wasn't afraid to ask the hard questions."

"What kind of questions did you ask?" Chelsea said.

"My first one was a toughie. I asked Her, if You've created everything, who created You?" said Brock.

"What was her answer?"

"Well, it was really intriguing. She hemmed and hawed a bit, but then She said—" The ringing of his cell phone interrupted him. "Yes," he said, bringing the device to his ear. After a moment of listening, he returned the phone to his belt. "A last-minute press conference has been scheduled in the Supreme Being Sector. Apparently they have some extraordinarily good news to announce. I'm so sorry, Skye. I gotta go there right now." He brushed Skye's lips with his own. "Can we do this another time?"

"Sure," she said, touching her lips where he'd kissed her.

There was nothing there. He might as well have been a tree trunk she'd brushed up against.

After he sauntered off, Chelsea said, "Are you sure he's the guy for you? I didn't see any sparks flying."

"It was that noticeable?"

"Yeah. You looked kind of bored."

"It's funny. I always thought Brock was the one for me, but then I met this other guy and then..."

"What other guy?"

"Never mind," Skye said quickly.

Even someone as inexperienced as Chelsea would probably question her getting wobbly-kneed over a man living in another dimension.

"Come on. Tell me."

Skye decided to ignore her question. "Maybe I should take you back to newcomers' quarters. It's getting late."

"It is not," Chelsea protested. "You promised you'd spend the whole day with me." Her lower lip jutted out like an open drawer.

"You're right. I'm sorry. I did promise. What would you like to do?"

"Are there any malls here in Heaven?"

Skye and Chelsea spent the rest of the day at the universe's largest shopping complex, Retail Rapture. Despite the fact that Heaven-dwellers were able to order anything they wanted via their WishBerrys, many, like Chelsea, still enjoyed shopping as a pastime. After hours of scouring the mall for the perfect pair of blue jeans, the teen was reluctant to return to ND quarters and begged Skye to take her home with her.

"We can have a slumber party at your apartment."

"I suppose," Skye said, even though she had to go to work in the morning. The teenager would probably keep her up late, but it didn't much matter. Skye wasn't getting a lot of sleep these days anyway.

Chelsea managed to turn her visit into a chow fest, ordering up caramel popcorn, pepperoni pizza, and a bag of peanut M&M's. Skye got into the spirit of things by devouring a pint of fudge ice cream straight out of the carton. After eating their fill, they changed into pajamas and sprawled out in Skye's living room.

Chelsea wore oversized fluffy pink slippers on her feet and

propped them up on the arm of the sofa. "Dying wasn't at all what I expected," she said.

"Really?" Skye was digging out the last of the ice cream with her spoon. "What did you think it would be like?"

"I thought it would hurt, like a dentist drill times a hundred. But there wasn't any pain, just a dark tunnel. Then I saw a bright light at the end. I thought, wow, God's going to be at the end of the tunnel, and then I wished I'd paid more attention in church because I figured He was going to give me a pop quiz. Who would have guessed the light was just an ordinary fluorescent light and I was standing in your cubicle? I thought you were an angel. You looked like Britney Spears before she got skanky."

Skye raised an eyebrow. "Then why were you so mean to me?"

"Because you were an authority figure, and I don't like to be bossed around, especially not in Heaven. Back on Earth, I used to eat substitute teachers for lunch." Chelsea smiled, obviously proud of her hellion tendencies.

"I also think you might have been a little scared."

"Was not," Chelsea said, kicking off her slippers. "Well, maybe just a little."

Skye yawned. "I don't know about you, but I think it's time for bed."

"My mom sometimes used to sing to me just before bed. She sang more than anyone on the entire planet. Not too well either," Chelsea said. "And talk about your hokey stuff. She knew every song Debbie Gibson ever sang."

"Why don't you tell me more about your mother?"

"Maybe," Chelsea said, nibbling on her lower lip. "I could tell you a shocking secret about her, but then you'd have to tell me a secret in return."

"I don't have any shocking secrets."

"We'll see about that." Chelsea stuck out her hand. "So is it a deal?"

"Deal." Skye shook her hand, thinking it might be good for Chelsea to talk about her mother for a while.

Chelsea sat Indian-style on the couch, rocking back and forth. "First off, my mom dyes her hair, and she doesn't want anyone to know. She used to bury the L'Oreal box under a pile of newspapers in the trash can. Second, she's a Dr. Phil fanatic and is constantly quoting him. Thirdly—"

"Dr. Phil?"

"Thirdly," Chelsea said, holding up a hand, "since I died my mom plays all of my old Red Hot Chili Peppers CDs while she drives around in the car. Sometimes she wakes up at night and sits on my bed and smells my pillow for hours."

"How do you know that? It's too soon for you to have watched Earthly Pleasures."

"Yeah, there *was* some kind of block on that channel in my hotel room," Chelsea said. "As if that would stop me. At home, I got around the parental controls on the internet and the V-chip on the television."

"The block's there for a reason, Chelsea," Skye said gently. "You aren't supposed to watch Earthly Pleasures until you've been in Heaven a week. It can be very troubling if you watch it too soon after you've died."

"It was awful," Chelsea said, tugging at the fringe of a pillow. "I was so sad for my mom. I wanted her to know I was okay. That Heaven was a really cool place. I couldn't watch for very long; it made me want to go home too much."

"That's because you tuned in too soon. You haven't been in Heaven long enough to let go of the people you left behind. Give it a couple more days, and you'll no longer get upset when you see your mom. Instead you'll experience the pure joy of seeing her without being attached to her."

"Does that mean I won't love her anymore?"

"Of course not. The love never leaves, but once the attachment is gone, you'll perceive love in its purest, most sacred form," Skye said. She was not speaking from experience but merely parroting passages of the *Hospitality Handbook*.

"So being attached to people is a bad thing?"

"It's only our attachment to others that causes pain," said Skye, again rotely repeating what she'd learned in her training, when it occurred to her for the first time that she *was* speaking from experience. Wasn't she hopelessly attached to Ryan Blaine?

"Speaking of love..." Chelsea crawled to the end of the couch closer to Skye. "Who's that guy you were talking about earlier?"

Skye waved away Chelsea's question. "I should have kept my mouth shut."

"Your turn to tell a secret. I want to hear all about him."

"Ask another question."

"No fair." Chelsea banged her fist on the armrest of the sofa. "We had a deal."

"I don't understand why you're so interested in my love life. Or maybe I should say my lack of a love life."

Chelsea's eyes grew big as shot glasses. "You mean the person you love doesn't love you back?"

"Worse. He doesn't even know I exist."

The teenager clutched her pajama top as if suffering from excruciating chest pains.

"The exact same thing happened to me. Before I died, I was crushing on Josh Carradine. When I passed him in the halls at school, he never looked my way. Even when I dressed goth, and everybody else was gawking at me."

"Goth?"

"It's an Earth thing." Chelsea peeled her nail polish, causing little flecks of sparkle to dot the couch. "I wonder what you could do to make this guy notice you." She scrutinized Skye for a moment. "Do you own a push-up bra?"

"You don't understand." Skye picked up the remote and aimed it at the television. "This is my crush."

The screen showed Ryan Blaine walking his golden retriever. Skye was surprised to see him exercise so quickly after his motorcycle spill.

"You're in love with an Earth guy? I thought you said it was insane to lust after Earthlings," Chelsea said. "Whoa. Talk about your long-distance relationship." She continued to stare at the screen. "Nice butt. Cute dog."

A series of lines rumpled Ryan's forehead. *What is he thinking about?* Skye wondered as she turned off the television.

"What did you do that for?" Chelsea asked.

"I promised I wouldn't watch it anymore. Right now it's difficult for me to see him, since there's no possible way we can ever be together."

Chelsea slumped against the couch cushions. "It is kind of bleak. I guess you're star-crossed lovers."

"Enough talk about that," Skye yawned. "I should try and get some sleep."

Chelsea stretched her arms above her head. "I'm getting a little drowsy myself. Where do I crash?"

"I don't have a guest room, but there's an extra twin in my bedroom. Will that suit?"

"Sure," Chelsea said, clambering off the couch.

A few minutes later, when they were both under the covers in their beds and the lights were turned off, Chelsea said, "It's strange, but today was the first day Heaven started feeling a little bit like home. You know why?"

"Why?" Skye said, her eyelids closing under the weight of her exhaustion.

"Because of you, Skye. I like hanging out together."

"Thank you, Chelsea."

Skye closed her eyes, thinking how she'd enjoyed being with Chelsea as well.

Fourteen

Susan heard the back door slam and the sound of Liberty's nails skittering across the tiles.

"Hi, honey," she said, pulling her chair away from the dining room table. She stood up to greet Ryan, who had just come back from walking the slobbering beast. "Would you mind giving these invitations a look-see? This one has a double-beveled frame with a little chiffon bow. It's sweet, don't you think?"

"Sweet" came out "sthweet," and a peeved look crossed Ryan's face. He probably didn't think she picked up on it. She tried to control her lisp but couldn't always manage.

"Whatever invitation you pick is fine with me." He glanced down at the selection spread out on the table. "But do we really need this filmy jacket around it?"

"It's called vellum, and the woman at the printer says it adds an elegant finishing touch."

"It also adds an elegant finishing touch to the price," he said.

As if cost mattered one whit, Susan thought. The Blaine family had more money than God, for Pete's sake.

"We don't *have* to have it," Susan said quickly, making nice like always. "Plain will do."

"It's okay, Susan," he said. He smiled and pressed his lips to her cheek. "Go for the vellum if you want it."

"Thank you, honey," she said with a smile.

"But no monogrammed matches," he said. "Remember that

wedding we went to with pink matchbooks on every table? Even the wedding cake was pink."

Susan shot him a blank look. She loathed his jaunts down memory lane. They were like land mines, waiting to trip her up.

"I'm afraid I don't remember that, sweetie. I'm sure if you keep talking about it, some of it will come back."

"It wasn't the greatest wedding anyway," Ryan said softly. He clapped his hands together to indicate a change in subject. "I assume we're not having a pink cake."

"It's candlelight."

"What?"

"That's the color of our cake. It has five tiers and will be decorated with butter-cream rosettes. It looked stunning in the photograph."

"No chocolate?"

"Of course. The filling will be chocolate."

"I should have guessed." He jerked his head in the direction of the den. "I'm going to see if I can catch the beginning of the baseball game."

"Enjoy yourself," Susan said, in the fake voice she used when dealing with him. Things were going better with Ryan. She wasn't goofing up nearly as much. It was so hard for her to constantly pattern her actions after the woman he'd been engaged to before the accident. "Saint Susan" was what she called her.

Planning this wedding was going to be a pain for Susan because she was still fuzzy about some of Saint Susan's tastes. Would she have been happy with plain white invitations? What kind of dress would she wear? At least she knew enough to pick a chocolate cake. Saint Susan's love of the cocoa bean was the stuff of legend. According to Ryan, she used to call chocolate her dark lord.

Susan gathered up the invitations and headed into the alcove off the kitchen, which she used as an office. Saint Susan had written poetry in the room, and when she was in the hospital Ryan had once convinced her to read some of the poetry. ("It might help you reconnect with your life before the accident.") Instead, it had nearly put her to sleep. Saint Susan's poetry was hard to follow, boring, and none of it rhymed.

"Isn't poetry supposed to rhyme?" she'd asked Ryan at the time.

He flinched as if she'd dropped a couple of ice cubes down his boxer shorts, and she knew she'd said the wrong thing. He tried hard to cover up his disappointment in her, but Susan wasn't a dummy. She knew he thought she was worthless since the accident, and as it turned out, poetry did not always rhyme.

The poetry incident had been months ago. Now she was a whole lot more careful about what she said. She was like a Christian with one of those "What Would Jesus Do?" wristbands, but hers would ask the question "What Would Saint Susan Do?" God, it was tiring and so easy to screw up. One night Ryan had taken her out for dinner and she'd ordered strawberry shortcake.

"But you're allergic to strawberries!" he had said, getting all choked up as if he were going to cry. "Don't you remember?"

Their relationship was like a gorgeous Oriental rug spread over a layer of dust and crud. The situation had gotten unbearable and he'd been giving her creepy looks as if he knew the truth.

Ryan never talked about it, but she could see it bubbling behind his eyes. He couldn't, of course, actually know the truth; the truth was rotting away, God-only-knows where.

But since he'd been home from the hospital, Ryan had turned into Mr. Nice Guy. His expression had lost that dangerous probing quality. He seemed like a person who'd finally accepted lies as truth, which would make life easier for both of them.

She closed the door of her office. While she was in the bedroom or den she felt that she had to pretend to read Saint Susan's long-winded books or listen to her Edith Piaf records. Her office was the only place in the house she felt free to be herself. Susan sat down at her desk and blew a kiss to her framed Johnny Cash poster. "Country is king and you are the prince," she said. Her entire office was covered in Johnny Cash memorabilia, from coffee cups to concert posters to ticket stubs. She'd even bought a pair of his custom-made knee-high alligator boots on eBay. They had pocketknife marks on the soles where he'd scuffed them up so he wouldn't slip onstage. Ryan didn't know what to make of her "newfound" devotion to Johnny Cash, and Susan didn't give a damn. She needed at least a shred of her old life to remind herself of who she really was.

The phone rang on her line, and Susan practically dove for it before Ryan could pick up. She was expecting a call.

"Susan Blaine?"

"Yes?" Susan said, her heart fluttering against her ribcage.

"I'm calling to confirm your appearance on *Talk to Me*. Everyone in America wants to hear your story. Did you speak with your husband?"

"Yes, I did," Susan lied. She kept meaning to bring it up with Ryan, but she hadn't yet worked up the nerve.

"Can we count on you?" the woman asked.

What would Saint Susan do? She would have turned the producer down because she respected Ryan's need for privacy. But Susan refused to let this opportunity slip by. She deserved a prize after more than a year of the worst suffering of her entire life. (Which was saying something, since her life had never been all that great.)

"I'll be there with bells on." Not to mention a fancy new designer dress.

Fifteen

When Caroline first woke up, she had no idea where she was. The wallpaper was striped, not flowered; the window was on the wrong side, and hers was the only bed in the room.

"Emily!" Caroline shouted as she sprang upright on the bed.

"Miz Brodie," Gertie said. The nursing assistant was stationed in front of the television, watching *Live with Kelly*. "You're awake. Finally."

Caroline touched her forehead, feeling a section of gauze taped to her skin. "What happened?"

"You were like Humpty Dumpty, Miz Brodie. You fell out of a chair and broke your crown. The doctor had to come by and put a few stitches in your head."

"Jack." Caroline experienced a wave of wooziness from sitting up so fast. "It was Jack who broke his crown. Not Humpty Dumpty."

Gertie turned off the television and now towered over Caroline's bed.

"What's that, Miz Brodie?"

Last night. Something extremely important happened. What was it, and why was she in such a daze?

"Emily!" Caroline said again.

Gertie tried to give Caroline a severe glance, but she ended up looking about as scary as a Kewpie doll. "I hope you're not planning to go off again, Miz Brodie."

Emily had spoken to her last night. Three words. Clear as the pluck of a harp. That much Caroline remembered, but why was she so foggy about everything else?

"Have I been drugged?" she asked.

"Yup." Gertie took a Snicker's bar from the pocket of her smock and unwrapped it. "They gave you something to calm your nerves. You were out of your head."

A memory took shape in her mind. She was shouting in the semidarkness as hands tried to subdue her.

"Maybe you should tell me what happened."

"Miss Chance came in late at night to check on you and you were on the floor. She told me this morning it looked like there'd been a bloodbath in your room. You'd hit your head. Head cuts bleed the worst, ya know."

Caroline didn't remember anything beyond Emily speaking. She must have been so startled she'd fallen out of her rocking chair.

"Turned out you had a cut in your scalp as long as a paper clip," Gertie said, measuring the length with her fingers. "When Miss Chance tried to help you up, you started screaming and thrashing around, saying something about Emily. She said she'd never seen anything like it. Your eyes were open and you were hollering, but you were still asleep. Miss Chance finally gave you something to calm you down."

"Why am I here instead of my own room?"

Gertie made a choking sound as if she'd gotten a peanut stuck in her throat. She avoided looking at Caroline as she got up from her chair.

"I better fetch Ms. Waters. She can explain everything to you."

"You know why I hit my head, don't you? It was because of Emily. She spoke to me. I'd like to hear someone tell me *that* was just reflexes."

"I'm getting Ms. Waters," Gertie said, hurrying toward the door.

Caroline had no intention of waiting around for that horrible Betty Boop woman. She was going to get out of bed and go back to her room and check on Emily. Then she intended to find the name of the doctor who'd given her stitches and speak with him about Emily directly. She should have talked to a doctor in the first place. Best to go straight to the experts instead of dealing with all these aides and their misinformed opinions.

Caroline was about to get out of the bed when she noticed a set of familiar clothes hanging in the open closet. They were hers. What were they doing there? She scanned the room and spotted more of her things: her blue ceramic pillbox, her back issues of large-print *Reader's Digest,* and her clock radio.

They'd moved her. They'd come in like thieves, packed up her things, and plunked them down in this strange room without her say-so.

"Hello, Mrs. Brodie," said Betty Boop, a.k.a. Dixie Waters, entering the room with Gertie trotting behind her. "How are you? Is there some kind of *problem* I can help you with?"

"Yes." Caroline raised her chin in a regal manner despite the fact that she wore pajamas and her hair was probably sticking out from her head in nappy tufts. Fortunately, whatever drugs they'd given her were wearing off and she was finally feeling clearheaded. "There is a serious problem. Why am I in this room? I don't want a change."

"For your own *good*, Mrs. Brodie," Dixie said, standing at the foot of Caroline's bed. "It wasn't healthy for you to room with that vegetable anymore. I'm surprised Mona let it go on so long. Miss Mona is the *nursing home director*, Mrs. Brodie. *Remember*?"

"I'm not senile or deaf, Ms. Waters," Caroline said. "And Emily is not a vegetable. She spoke to me."

Dixie and Gertie exchanged a look.

"Mrs. Brodie," Dixie began. "Emily's in a *coma*. That's like a *long sleep*, only you never *wake up*. People in comas don't *talk*. You must have been *hearing* things."

There was no point in reasoning with this woman; she was dumber than a dinner roll.

"All right, Ms. Waters," Caroline said. "Maybe I was imagining things. I won't argue with you, but I still want my old room back. It's where I belong."

"This is your *new room*, Mrs. Brodie. *Room 206*," she said, pointing to the door. "I've already moved Mrs. Kale into your old room."

"With Emily?" Caroline asked.

"Yes, indeed," said Dixie. Her eyes were so round and glassy they looked as if they belonged in the head of a ventriloquist's dummy.

Caroline was horrified. At one hundred and two years of age, Mrs. Kale was deaf and dumb and had just enough gray matter left in her shrunken skull to spit at people as they walked by. The nurse's aides claimed it wasn't deliberate, but the old biddy had excellent aim for someone who wasn't doing it on purpose.

"Mrs. Kale can't room with Emily. I'm the one who's been looking after her." Caroline imagined Emily waking up at midnight as usual, and instead of seeing Caroline next to her in the rocking chair, she'd see the cloudy-eyed Mrs. Kale, her pruney lips slick with saliva.

"She can't *miss* you, Mrs. Brodie, because she's in a *coma*. That's a *deep sleep* that—"

"I'm done with you, Ms. Waters," Caroline said, putting a foot on the floor. "If you won't move me back, I'll just have to move myself."

"Mrs. Brodie," Dixie said. An ugly note had entered her voice and the foolish round eyes now looked hooded. "You will *not* be moving. *Do you understand?*"

Caroline ignored her, looking under the bed for her shoes. "I'll be speaking about Emily with that doctor who treated me, and as soon as Miss Mona comes back she'll get an earful too."

Dixie nodded to Gertie, an ominous gesture. The nod of one Klansman to another just before they ignite a cross. The nod of a plantation owner to his overseer, prior to the flogging of a slave.

Big clumsy Gertie lumbered toward Caroline wielding a hypodermic needle she'd been hiding behind her back. At least she had the decency to look shameful. It was the last thought she had before the nurse's aide plunged the needle into the cheek of Caroline's left buttock.

Sixteen

Skye woke up with someone's hot breath on her face. "Yow!" she screamed, throwing off her bedclothes and sitting up straight.

"Calm down. It's just me."

Chelsea was sitting cross-legged on the bed, wearing a nightshirt that skimmed her knees. She nibbled on a Pop-Tart.

Skye blinked several times to clear her head. How long had she slept last night? Five, ten minutes? Her head felt stuffed with wads of cotton. "Did you have a nightmare?"

"Did *I* have a nightmare?" Chelsea said with a giggle. She broke the frosted Pop-Tart in half, revealing an oozing strawberry interior. "Want some?" she asked. Her blue fingernail polish contrasted brashly with the red filling.

Skye shook her head. "No thanks. Why were you on the bed then?"

"I was checking on you," Chelsea said. "Who's Lynn?"

"Lynn? I don't think I know anybody named Lynn."

Chelsea crawled along the length of the bed to lie beside Skye. "You were talking in your sleep, saying, 'Call Lynn,' or maybe it was 'call in'? Or how about 'Colin'? Do you know a Colin?"

"No," Skye said. "I was talking in my sleep?"

"Practically all night. But in the last few minutes you were shouting."

Skye ran her fingers through her tangled curls. "I have this strange dream every night, but I can never quite remember it…Good Lord, would you look at the time? I'm going to be late for work."

Later that morning Skye sat at her desk, sipping on a tall mug of coffee and reading a brochure about the attractions she and Chelsea might visit in the Supreme Being Sector. She noticed an article for the Nocturnal Theater, a place that retrieved a person's dreams and projected them on a screen for viewing. It wouldn't hurt to pay the theater a visit. Maybe she'd finally be privy to the odd dreams that were plaguing her sleep every night.

"Hi-de-ho!" Rhianna said, sticking her head into the cubicle.

"Hi, Rhianna," Skye said.

For the first time ever, Rhianna was following the Hospitality Sector dress code to the letter. Her white shirt was pressed, her skirt was regulation length, and her knee socks were spotless.

"What's the occasion?" Skye asked, indicating Rhianna's uniform.

"It's my last day here,'" Rhianna said. "I wanted to go by the book."

Skye's eyes trailed to Rhianna's feet. She was wearing purple Converse tennis shoes.

Rhianna smiled. "Well, no sense in being anal about the whole thing."

"So it's official," Skye said. "The next time I see you, you'll be a guardian angel."

"I finally finished my orientation. That's why I haven't been around much. I'll be getting my first client any day now." Rhianna's glance fell on the brochure on Skye's desk. "Oooh, the Supreme Being Sector. I love it there. I've heard they opened a new amusement park. 'Watch Sodom and Gomorrah burn daily at three and seven p.m.' Sounds like fun."

"You're welcome to come with me," Skye said. "I'm taking Chelsea, one of my clients, on Saturday after lunch."

"I'd love it."

"Meet me in the newcomers' lobby." Skye paused. "I don't suppose you found out anything—"

Rhianna smacked her forehead. "That's why I came in here in the first place. I did find something. I used my password to look you up in the computer to see if your record would reveal anything. There wasn't an explanation about why you were chosen to go to Earth, but I did see something peculiar. Just under your name it said 'L' status, and it was blinking. When I clicked on it for more information, I got a message saying 'access denied.' I looked up a whole lot of other people and no one had that particular designation by their name."

"What does L stand for?" Skye asked. "Lazy? Loopy? Loveless?"

"No clue, and no one else seemed to know."

"That's so odd. I just wish—"

The red light on Skye's desk flashed. "Incoming," she said, summoning the appropriate file on her computer.

"See you on Saturday," Rhianna said as she dashed off to her own cubicle.

Seventeen

"This is my favorite lesson," Dr. Mullins said. "And I'm celebrating with treats for everyone."

Skye watched her teacher stroll down the center aisle. He had a basket on his arm and was passing out cupcakes. The blue and white frosting on the cupcakes was swirled to look like planet Earth. When he was finished, he returned to the front of the room and eagerly surveyed his students.

"This next lesson is the most powerful of all. Are you ready for it?"

"Ready," everyone said in unison like a class of kindergartners. Most of the students couldn't wait to live their first lives.

"We have a very special guest who will help us with our lesson today. She can't physically be here, but I have Her on speakerphone, direct from the SB Sector."

Dr. Mullins clapped his hands together several times as if he couldn't contain his glee and the class buzzed with excitement. He picked up the speakerphone set up on the table in front of the room and dialed.

"Office of the Supreme Being," a female voice answered. "How may I direct your call?"

"This is Dr. Mullins from over at the university. The SB is expecting my call."

"Please hold," the voice said. An interlude of Bob Dylan singing "Knockin' on Heaven's Door" emanated from the phone.

After a moment the music was interrupted by a female voice.

"Mullins, is that you? Testing, testing? Can you hear me?"

"Yes, SB, it's me, and you're coming in loud and clear," Dr. Mullins said. "I'm standing in front of a classroom of students waiting to hear from you. They're ready for their most important lesson."

"I think it's ingenious the way you're pairing lessons with Beatles songs. I'll bet Moses wished he'd thought of it."

Skye shook her head in disbelief. The SB was cracking jokes! And corny ones to boot.

"Are you ready to hear another Beatles tune?" the SB asked.

"Yes!" answered the class in response.

"Fabulous," continued the SB. "I've got two of those cute little mop-tops with me today, John and George. The others couldn't join us because they're still alive and kicking, thank Myself for that. George brought in his guitar, and John is going to help me harmonize. I think John actually wrote the song we're about to sing. It's a marvelous tune and perfectly conveys the most important lesson to know while living on Earth. So here it goes."

Skye braced herself. If the lesson came straight from the SB, it had be extremely important.

A guitar riff served as an introduction, and the SB and John started harmonizing.

"All you need is love, love. Love is all you need."

As they sang the song, Dr. Mullins walked around the room, opening half a dozen cardboard boxes situated throughout. From each box sprang several helium heart-shaped Mylar balloons printed with the word "Love."

The class busied themselves by climbing on the top of the desks to reach for the balloons. When the song was finished, they hooted and clapped, and the SB said, "Thank you so much, John and George. I enjoyed that. Maybe in another ten or twenty years we can have a Beatles reunion."

"You'll have to have a word with my mates Paul and Ringo about that one," John said.

"Are there any questions?" the SB asked.

Silence. No one, it seemed, wanted to question her.

"Don't be shy," She coaxed.

"I have a question," Skye said. The words skidded off her tongue before she could stop them.

"Yes, Skye," the SB said brightly. "Let's hear it."

"Uh, you know my name?" Skye said in a flustered voice. She'd hoped to retain her anonymity.

"'Course I do," She said. There was a pause. "It's that whole omniscient thing. Comes in handy at social gatherings, let me tell you."

"Oh, of course, I forgot. I mean, I didn't forget. I just—"

"It's okay, Skye. Fire when ready."

"Well, your Supreme Beingness, um, I just thought...Rather, what I meant to say was...Don't you think this last lesson was a little...simplistic?"

"What did you say?"

The room fell silent. A few people nervously eyed the ceiling as if they expected it to fall in. The girl sitting next to Skye moved her desk several feet away.

"I, uh..."

"I spent a lot of time on that lesson, Skye. Eons in fact."

"Maybe 'simplistic' wasn't the right word," Skye said quickly. "I retract the question."

"Just teasing you," the SB said with a laugh, and the whole class, including Skye, breathed a collective sigh of relief. "I have a pretty thick skin and don't take offense easily. How could I with everyone and his brother yelling my name every time they stub their toes? But back to your question. You're exactly right, Skye, when you say the lesson sounds simple, but, like a whole lot of other things, it's only deceptively simple. You could live a million lives and not understand all of the nuances of this one little lesson. It's also the one from which all the others flow. The more you learn to love well, the more you will summon your own strength and godliness. Do you understand?"

"I guess," Skye said.

"Don't sweat it right now. With each lifetime, you'll comprehend it a little bit more. Loving others on Earth is the best way to illuminate the mysterious, to rouse us where we are asleep. And I know you wish you felt more awake, don't you, Skye?"

"Yes," Skye said, marveling that the SB knew the smallest details of her life.

"Oops!" the SB said abruptly. "Gotta run. Trouble in the Middle East again. Man, those folks run me ragged. *Ciao*, everybody."

"*Ciao*," the class answered back.

"Nice lady," Dr. Mullins said, handing out CDs with all the Beatles songs he'd covered in class. "A little souvenir from me to you on our last meeting. I've enjoyed teaching you. I wish for all of you to have fruitful lives on Earth. Class dismissed."

The students jostled toward the door, chattering over their encounter with the SB. Again, Professor Mullins summoned Skye to his desk.

"I hope the SB cleared that last lesson up for you, Skye," he said.

"I'll try to remember, I promise." She paused. "I don't suppose you have any idea when I'll be called down?"

He shrugged. "Whenever you're ready."

"What?"

"It's up to you entirely."

"You're kidding me."

"Not at all."

"But I don't want to go...ever. I have no desire to leave Heaven. Zip."

He gave her a queer smile. "Haven't you figured it out yet, Skye? You're the creator of all of your circumstances. You were the one who wanted to go to Earth in the first place."

"No, I didn't," Skye insisted. "I fought against going. I was told I was handpicked by the SB."

"You were," he said with a nod. "But the desire came from you first."

"I don't understand. I never asked to go to Earth. This is all very confusing to me."

"It will all be clear soon enough, Skye." He touched her gently on the shoulder. "Have a wonderful life."

Eighteen

"Please make yourself comfortable," the therapist said. She gestured toward an oversized cushioned rattan chair with a round back. Ryan hadn't seen one like it since the late seventies. In fact, the therapist's entire office was decorated in early American Earth Mother. There were hanging spider plants, hemp wall tapestries, and beeswax candles.

The therapist—her name was Jennifer Carr—looked like a relic from the Summer of Love. She wore a long flowing dress and granny glasses. Ryan could easily picture her in earlier days, perched on the shoulders of a bare-chested boyfriend, grooving to Joe Cocker at Woodstock.

The chair was surprisingly comfortable. It was so large he felt protected by it, like a snail in its shell.

Dr. Carr asked some preliminary questions, and she seemed so self-assured he gradually relaxed.

"Let's talk about your relationship with Susan before the accident," she said, pulling a pencil from her thicket of wiry gray hair. "What do you think made it so special?"

"Do you have a couple of weeks?" Ryan said with a chuckle. He sighed, and his tone grew more serious. "The relationship I had with Susan wasn't perfect, not by any stretch of the imagination, but it was unlike anything I'd ever experienced before."

"Was it common interests between the two of you that made it so exceptional? Similar backgrounds? Great sex?"

"No," Ryan said, surprised to be talking about sex so early in the game. "I mean, yes. The sex was...mind-blowing. And we did enjoy many of the same things, but it was more than that."

"I know it may be hard to put into words, but describe it for me if you can."

Ryan's expression grew thoughtful as he recalled the wonder of looking into Susan's eyes and seeing the person he was meant to spend eternity with.

"It was as if we'd been asleep all of our lives and love woke us up."

"And now?"

Ryan sighed. The difference between then and now was like comparing the ocean to a painting of the ocean.

"It's just two people going through the motions," he said.

"Maybe we should talk about the day of the accident."

Ryan startled at her statement. He hadn't discussed that day for a very long time, hadn't wanted to talk about it or even think about it.

"We had an argument," he finally managed. "It was the worst one we'd ever had. Susan thought I betrayed her."

"How?"

"By making love to another woman."

The woman in question was Tracy Stevens, the daughter of a wealthy senator. She and Ryan had slept with each other for years even when he was involved with someone else. But when he'd fallen in love with Susan, he'd quit fooling around with Tracy. She was reluctant to accept her diminished role in Ryan's life and continued to dog Ryan even after he announced his engagement to Susan, always urging him to come over for a quickie.

Tracy was a constant source of friction between Susan and Ryan. She'd often call the house and hang up when Susan answered. Since he shared a history with Tracy and still had professional ties with her father, Ryan was reluctant to be unkind to her, hoping she'd soon give up.

Ryan's stomach roiled as he remembered the terrible morning

when Susan told him she had to go to out of town for a family emergency.

"I might even have to spend the night," she'd said, hurriedly spreading marmalade on an English muffin at the breakfast table. "I'm going in to work for a few hours, but then I'm leaving straight from the office."

"What kind of family emergency?" Ryan asked. As far as he knew, Susan had no kin to speak of. Both of her parents were dead and she had no brothers or sisters.

An odd look entered her eyes. "I don't really want to talk about it. Not until I know exactly what I'm dealing with. It's just so bizarre."

"Maybe I should come with you," Ryan said. Susan had been acting distracted for the last day or so. Was this so-called emergency the reason why?

"No. I promise I'll explain everything as soon as I know what's going on. Please try to understand. This is something I have to do myself."

After she left, his mind started churning out all kinds of explanations for Susan's secretiveness. Then he did something completely out of character. He headed to the medicine cabinet and looked for her diaphragm case. He became even more agitated when he saw it was missing. The phone interrupted his thoughts. Tracy was on the other line.

"Ryan, it's a glorious day for brunch on my verandah. I'll have my cook whip up Belgian waffles for the two of us."

"Thank you, Tracy, but, as usual, I'm going to have to decline," he said distractedly. "Some people around here work, you know."

"Ryan. You forget how well I know you. It's Friday. You're *always* late going into the office on Fridays."

It was true. He worked a half day on Fridays, and Tracy frequently called Friday mornings because she knew Ryan would be home and Susan would be at her office.

"Sorry. I still can't make it. Thanks for the invite," he said, hanging up.

A half hour later the doorbell rang, and Tracy stood on his welcome mat. She wore a short Lilly Pulitzer dress and held a sterling silver chafing dish in one hand and a chilled bottle of Moet in the other.

"If Muhammad won't come to the mountain," she said with a wink.

She looked as pretty as a bouquet of fresh-cut flowers, and his stomach was growling. What the hell. He decided to let her inside. They were old friends, after all, and maybe she'd take his mind off this latest strangeness with Susan.

The two of them downed a couple of flutes of champagne, and Ryan was tipsy before he had his first bite of waffle.

"Where's Suzy Q? Off doing her Dr. Dolittle thing?" Tracy asked as they sat in the breakfast nook. She wore some kind of lotion or bronzer that made her olive skin glow seductively in the sunlight.

"No, actually," Ryan said with a sly smile. "Truth is I don't know where she is." He felt so warm inside. Warm from the maple syrup and the sunlight and the buzz of the Moet. At that moment everything seemed right, even Tracy's bare foot lightly grazing his inner thigh. Before he knew it, they'd moved from the breakfast nook and had become pleasantly entangled on the sofa.

"Why don't we take this party to the bedroom?" Tracy asked in a throaty voice.

Her request seemed so natural and normal to Ryan—he'd been with Tracy so many times it didn't even feel like cheating—that he scooped her up and carried her upstairs without a second thought.

As soon as he crossed the threshold of the bedroom, he was jarred out of his champagne haze. Susan was everywhere in the room, from her sandalwood perfume to her discarded terry-cloth robe to the Lucite framed photograph on the bureau, her trusting eyes staring at him. What had seemed harmless only moments ago now seemed like a horrendous breach of trust.

"Sorry," he said, depositing Tracy on the bed like a load of dirty laundry. "I can't do it."

"It's just sex between friends," Tracy said with a pout. "Surely you don't plan on being faithful to Susan your entire life? You aren't even married."

He couldn't look at her. Didn't want to think about how close he'd come to messing up the best relationship of his life. "Thanks for the brunch, Tracy. You better go now."

"Will do," Tracy said smoothly, as if his rejection of her was as inconsequential as a fleabite. "Just need to make a little trip to the powder room and then, poof, I'm on my way."

"You know where it is," he said, relieved she'd been so easy to get rid of.

An hour later, Ryan was running on the treadmill when he heard Liberty bark and the front door open. *Not Tracy again*, he thought as he strode down the hall to the foyer.

But it wasn't Tracy; it was Susan, and he smiled, thinking she was finally going to tell him about her mysterious errand. Instead, she barely looked at him and said, "I left my overnight bag in the bedroom."

She rushed down the hall, obviously in a hurry, and he followed behind her, hoping to get more information.

As soon as he entered the bedroom, the smell hit him. It must have reached Susan's nostrils at the same time, because she turned around and said, "What in the world?"

Ryan recognized the scent immediately. It was Joy—Tracy's perfume of choice—but the aroma of it was overwhelming, as if an entire bottle had been spilled in the bedroom. The perfume wasn't the only violation. The bed, which Susan had made earlier, was now mussed, and a pair of pink thong underwear was spread on Susan's pillow with a white envelope beside it. Susan immediately went to the bed and tore open the card, reading it aloud.

"The memory lingers on?" Susan said, her hands shaking, her face contorted in pain.

"Susan—"

"What did you do, call her as soon as you found out I was going out of town?"

"Susan, this is ridiculous. I didn't—Tracy did this. She dropped by unexpectedly and then she said she was going to the bathroom, but obviously she came in here and—"

"Do you rendezvous with her every Friday morning?" Her face was shock white and her chin trembled. "In our bedroom?"

"Of course not! Susan, if you'd just hear me out. I had nothing—"

But Susan wasn't listening. Tears coursed down her cheeks as she whipped her bag over her shoulder.

"Didn't I predict this would happen?" she spat. "I knew I never should have gotten involved with you."

"Please, Susan," Ryan said, reaching out for her, but she dodged him and dashed out the door. He followed behind her, but she was too quick for him. She had already gotten behind the wheel of her Chevrolet Tahoe, refusing to stop as he ran alongside the vehicle while she pulled out of the circular drive.

"And that was the last time you saw her before the accident?" Dr. Carr asked.

"Yes," he said, shaking away the memories of their last encounter. "It was the worst thing that could have happened."

"Did you ever learn who she was going to see that day?" Dr. Carr asked, flipping a page of her notepad.

"No," Ryan said. "I asked her, but she doesn't remember. I assume it couldn't have been very important since it's never come up again."

He'd also found her diaphragm in the drawer of their bedside table. She hadn't taken it with her. It had just been moved from its regular spot. He'd behaved like such an idiot that day.

"How did you find out about the accident?"

"I couldn't concentrate on my work because of our fight," Ryan began, hoping to make it through the story without having a breakdown. "I kept calling her cell phone, but I'd always get voicemail. Then, while I was in a meeting with a client, my secretary buzzed me. 'Susan's been in a car accident and she's badly hurt.' I wasn't even surprised. There'd been a feeling of dread hanging over me all day."

Ryan told Dr. Carr how he'd raced over to Grady Hospital and discovered Susan had been admitted to intensive care. The physician gave him a laundry list of horrors: traumatic brain injury; cerebral contusion; compound fractures of both legs; fractured ribs, cheekbones, and nose.

"I'm sorry," he said. "I don't think she'll be with us in the morning."

That night, Ryan never left her side, never took his eyes off the contraptions monitoring her vital signs and tubes that threaded through her broken body. His entire concentration was focused on the faint beating of her heart.

Morning came, and the machines were still steadily blipping with Susan's lifeblood. Her doctor was cautious but more hopeful.

"I prayed harder than I'd ever prayed my entire life," Ryan said, feeling drained from the telling. "I just knew Susan was going to live even though it took two weeks for her to regain consciousness. The doctors warned us she'd be confused when she woke up."

"And was she?" Dr. Carr asked.

Ryan sighed. He'd never forget the vacant expression on Susan's face when she first opened her eyes and looked at him. It was as if she'd never seen him before in her entire life.

"She had no idea who I was and no memory of our argument before the accident. She still has occasional memory problems. It's as if she had to learn about her life all over again."

"That must have been difficult for both of you."

"It was," Ryan said, staring into the prism in the window that was throwing off streaks of color onto the wall behind Dr. Carr. "But there were so many other issues going on that I couldn't dwell on it. She had to have surgical pins and rods placed in the bones of both of her legs to help the fractures heal, and she was forced to endure hours of physical therapy just so she'd be able to walk again. That's when I first began having my...problems."

"Yes?" Dr. Carr said, looking up at him expectantly.

"I started to see a completely unfamiliar side of Susan. There was weepiness, bouts with depression, and an extreme neediness. I knew her injuries were excruciatingly painful, and nobody could blame her for the way she was acting, cursing out doctors, screaming at nurses. But it was completely unexpected. The Susan I knew before the accident rarely raised her voice...and she was so strong."

"And the changes in her were upsetting to you," Dr. Carr said.

"Yeah." He dipped his head in shame. "Her neurologist warned me there'd be personality changes. I guess I just didn't expect them to be so drastic. I know I sound selfish. I should just be grateful she's alive. You wouldn't believe what she's been through: bone-grafting, facial surgery, liver drainage. I just..."

"Go ahead, Mr. Blaine," Dr. Carr said gently.

"She doesn't look the same. She doesn't sound the same. She doesn't eat the same foods and she doesn't even have the same sense of humor. I'm constantly having to remind myself that she's Susan, the woman I love...or the woman I *used* to love." He covered his face with his hands. "I didn't mean to say that."

"I think you did," Dr. Carr said, her gaze steady.

"But the point is I want to love her again," he said, dropping his hands from his face. "I *need* to love Susan. After all, it's my fault she's the way she is. I'm sure she wouldn't have crashed her car if we hadn't been fighting. Sometimes I even wonder if she did it on purpose. She was such a good driver and then there was no explanation..." No, he couldn't let his mind go there. The Susan he knew would never try to kill herself; he had to believe that. He swallowed and searched Dr. Carr's face. "Do you think you can do anything to help me?"

After his hour was up, he left the counselor's office and sat in the quiet of his car for a moment to regain his composure. The session had taken more out of him than he'd expected.

Dr. Carr had no magic answers, of course, but she did say that if he, indeed, wanted to love the new Susan, he would have to let go of his old version of her. He knew he was the one who had to change. He'd already been moving in that direction since he'd gotten home from the hospital.

That meant there would be no more listening to the old Allman Brothers CDs, no more long sessions of thumbing through the photo albums, and definitely no more calling Minerva.

Minerva had served her purpose as one means to help him heal. He'd been allowed to talk about the pre-accident Susan, and recall his memories of her. Of course, there was no way he could explain to Minerva and her listening audience that the girlfriend who'd "left him" actually slept in his bed and had never gone away at all. It only felt like that.

Nineteen

When Skye entered Newcomers' Quarters to pick up Chelsea, Rhianna stood waiting in the lobby, garbed in khaki clothes and a pith helmet as if ready for a safari. Skye smiled at her friend's attire, remarking, "Dr. Livingston, I presume?"

Rhianna bowed from the waist. "At your service. Here to protect you from encounters with unruly natives."

The elevator door opened, and Chelsea emerged from the car. She wore the skinny jeans she'd purchased at the mall, a tummy-skimming t-shirt, a spiked necklace, and a pair of tennis shoes as big as a circus clown's.

"You can start with this one," Skye said, tugging on the wire coming out of Chelsea's ear.

Skye made the introductions, not really sure what Chelsea and Rhianna would make of each other, but she needn't have worried.

"Those Vans are incredible," Rhianna said as she noticed Chelsea's shoes. "Can I try them on?"

"Sure," Chelsea said, slipping out of her clodhopper shoes. "Do you skate?"

"Do I skate?" Rhianna said, kicking off a pair of red crocodile cowboy boots. "Can Tony Hawk do a half-cab nose slide?" She put on the shoes and plodded happily across the marble floor of the lobby. "Want to switch shoes for the evening?"

"Okay," Chelsea said, slipping a skull-patterned-socked foot into Rhianna's boots.

The three made their way to the transportation concourse and boarded a monorail. They found seats on the padded benches running the length of the cars just before the pneumatic doors slid shut with a soft swishing sound.

"Welcome. I'm Velma, your electronic tour guide," said a disembodied velvet-voiced female. "You are now leaving ND quarters. This train makes a tour of the Supreme Being Sector. Feel free to exit at any point of interest."

The monorail whooshed down the tracks leading out of the ND atrium and into the sunlight.

"Straight ahead are the famed Pearly Gates," continued the tour guide. "Will Saint Peter open them for us? We shall see."

The word "Heaven" was spelled out with thousands of pearls across the gleaming golden gate. At the last possible moment, a bearded gentleman in a white robe gave a thumbs-up and inserted oversized gold keys into the gate. It swung open, allowing the monorail entry. A sigh of relief passed through the car. The majority of the passengers were the newly deceased. Skye rolled her eyes at the cheesy tourist attraction. It got them every time.

"We are now entering the Supreme Being Sector, called Mount Zion by many of its residents," continued the guide. "As we crest this hill, you'll be able to see the Capitol building on your right, headquarters for the Supreme Being and Her cabinet."

The golden-domed Capitol sparkled in the distance framed by a double rainbow. It took only moments for them to reach the tunnel, which plowed straight through the building. The passageway was painted a warm pinkish red, meant to resemble the interior of a human heart, and the sound of thousands of angels singing a single clear note of praise filled the car as they soared through. Some of the passengers wiped tears of joy from their eyes or wore expressions of complete and utter rapture.

As they exited the building, the tour guide said, "Next stop, Sacred Creation of New Souls."

"Let's get off here," Skye said, rising from her seat and pressing a hand against the wall of the car to steady herself. "I want Chelsea to see this."

"I don't know," Chelsea said, her mouth twisting with distaste. "My dog Gypsy had puppies once, and it was pretty disgusting."

"There's nothing disgusting about this," Skye said. "It's the most beautiful and moving thing I've ever seen."

"It reminds me of Frankenstein's lab," Rhianna said, stiffening her arms and legs. "It's alive. It's alive!"

The monorail came to a stop, and the trio filed out of the car and followed a pathway that led to an in-the-round outdoor amphitheater. A sign outside read, "Next birth in five minutes." They took seats on the stone benches, which were swiftly filling to capacity. The Sacred Creation of New Souls was one of the most popular attractions in the Supreme Being Sector.

In the middle of the amphitheater was a small oval pool filled with a gleaming silver fluid that looked like liquid mercury. Thunder rumbled in the distance, and an angel emerged from an arched opening and stood beside the pool. The thunder grew louder and was accompanied by pale threads of lightning, which scratched the sky. The heavens were bloated with blue-black clouds, and the air jittered with electricity.

Lightning struck in the middle of the pool, momentarily washing the audience's faces in an icy blue light. The pool, which had been placid only moments ago, now boiled with hundreds of silver bubbles. In the midst of the flurry was one oversized bubble. After a moment it became clear the large bubble was actually the head of a new soul, slowly emerging from the pool. Soon shoulders, a torso, and legs could be discerned, all covered in the silver sluice of the liquid.

The audience watched in silent wonder as the new soul rose to its full height and climbed the rounded steps leading out of the pool. As soon as the newly created being reached the stone tiles surrounding the pool, the silver coating slid to the ground like a discarded garment, and the soul, a female, stood naked, her flawless skin luminescent in the fading lightning.

Skye ventured a glance at Chelsea. Even the teenager was mesmerized, her mouth wide with wonder. The angel approached the new soul and gently slipped a white garment over her head. Then she embraced the newly created woman and led her through the arched opening. The heavy clouds receded and the pool grew still once again. There was a momentary hush over the audience just before they broke into enthusiastic applause.

Chelsea let out a low whistle once the clapping died down. "So every single soul in the universe came out of that pool? Even me?"

"Even you," Skye said with a nod.

"I don't remember it," Chelsea said.

"You've lived too many lives since then to remember," Rhianna said, getting up from the stone bench. "But for me it was only a year ago. I remember it perfectly."

"Rhianna," Skye said. "Don't tease her."

"What?" Rhianna said, a bewildered look on her face. "I'm not teasing. You remember it, don't you?"

"No," Skye said, suddenly perplexed. "Nobody remembers it." She paused. "Do they?"

"I do," Rhianna insisted, her expression earnest. "And why wouldn't I? I was fully conscious when it happened. If you don't remember being created, what is your first memory?"

"Waking up in the New Soul Compound," Skye said. The New Soul Compound was a large dormitory where all new beings spent their first week of existence. There they received their duty assignments and were oriented into Heaven.

"I've always assumed new souls were in some sort of twilight sleep when they were created," Skye said. "I didn't think *anyone* remembered it."

"I'm not the only one," Rhianna said. "I've talked to Joy and a couple of the other girls in Hospitality about it, and they all remember."

"Maybe there was some kind of trauma when you were created, and it got purged from your mind," Chelsea offered. "When I was born, I came out butt first and got stuck in the birth canal."

"Maybe," Skye said, although she'd never heard of mishaps occurring during the creation process.

Rhianna slung an arm around Skye's shoulders. "I wouldn't worry about it. It wasn't such a big deal. You climb out of the pool and all these strangers are ogling your naked backside. What's memorable about that?"

"Can we go to the amusement park next?" Chelsea asked.

"I'd like to go to the Nocturnal Theater first," Skye said quickly.

"I *love* that place," Rhianna exclaimed. "I have the most extraordinary dreams. Let's go."

They caught the next monorail, passing by some of the SB Sector's kitschier attractions such as Hall of Saints (much like Disney's Hall of Presidents), Garden of Eden Water Park, Noah's Ark River Cruises, and Wrath of God Miniature Golf. (The holes had wind, flooding, and locust hazards.)

"Next up," said the electronic tour guide, "the Nocturnal Theater, where you play the starring role in your dreams."

"What if your dreams are kind of, um, embarrassing?" Chelsea asked as the three females exited the monorail after it came to a stop.

"Nobody sees them but you." Rhianna skipped along the sidewalk leading to the Nocturnal Theater. "Everyone has their own viewing booth, just like the peep shows in adult bookstores." She gave Chelsea a playful pinch on the arm. "What kind of embarrassing dreams?"

"The kind where you go out in public wearing only your underwear," Chelsea said. "Or dreams where kissing is going on."

"Tell!" Rhianna demanded. "Who would you kiss if you could kiss anyone in the whole universe?"

"Living or dead?" Chelsea asked.

"Either."

"I'll answer that question if you answer it first," Chelsea said.

"I'll answer it if Skye answers it," Rhianna said with a wag of her brows.

"Pooh," Chelsea said with an indifferent toss of her hair. "I already know who Skye would kiss."

"Me too," Rhianna said. "Mr. Newscaster himself."

"No," Chelsea said with a shake of her head. "It's someone else. Skye is in love with—"

"Chelsea!" Skye said.

"You're not stopping now," Rhianna said, her eyes practically popping out of her head. "Who could it be? Don't tell me. It's your Earth professor. You're hot for your teacher. How tragically quaint."

"Wrong," Chelsea said, bouncing triumphantly on the heels of her shoes. "It's Ryan Blaine."

"Who?" Rhianna said.

"The Earthly Pleasures guy," Chelsea said.

"Oh, yeah, Ryan. The ex-president's son," Rhianna said, smacking her forehead with the palm of her hand. "He is *so* last season, Skye. Get with the program. Ryan's out; Lars is in."

"No," Chelsea said. "Skye's still crazy for Ryan. She was watching him the other night."

"What are you, the town crier?" Skye said. She gave Rhianna a sheepish smile. "Ryan Blaine had a motorcycle accident and was my client for about ten minutes until he returned to his body. Yes, he was quite the tasty dish, but he and I can't ever be together. End of story. Pass the tissues."

"She can't stop thinking about him," Chelsea said, clearly relishing her role as magpie.

"Wait a minute," Rhianna said, grasping Skye's shoulders. "Look at me, Skye Sebring. Don't tell me *you* have actually fallen in love?"

"Admittedly, I'm intrigued by him. But how can I fall in love with someone I met once? It doesn't make any sense."

"Love isn't meant to make sense, silly," Rhianna said.

"I'm not even in the same dimension as Ryan," Skye said. "My love for him is a waste."

"Love is never a waste," Rhianna said, green eyes flashing. "What about the medieval troubadours who cultivated love for its own sake, never expecting its return? Love is an end in itself, igniting the senses, flowering the soul. Have you ever felt more alive?"

"Wow," Chelsea said with a sigh. "I wish I was in love."

"I should have guessed," Rhianna said, tossing Skye a sly look. "You look more present than usual. Love wakes us up."

"Maybe that's why I've been so tired lately," Skye said. "Not only is it waking me up, it's keeping me up all night."

"You know what I'm saying," Rhianna said.

Skye didn't respond, but she didn't protest either. Things *had* been different for her ever since she'd met Ryan Blaine. Her trouble-free world no longer existed, and yet she didn't necessarily mourn it.

The trio entered the Nocturnal Theater, a narrow room with a half-dozen curtained enclosures that looked like voting booths. The receptionist greeted them and explained how dream-viewing worked. Each of them would have her own private screening station, complete with a set of electrodes that would easily attach to the temples. The electrodes would retrieve recent dreams and project them onto the screen in front of them.

"Each dream lasts about ten minutes," said the receptionist. "And you can choose the number you'd like to watch by adjusting a dial on the screen."

"If we want to go to the amusement park, we'd better limit ourselves to three dreams apiece," Skye said.

The receptionist directed them to empty viewing booths, and Skye pulled back the curtain and sat on the stool in front of a screen the size of a computer monitor.

"Here goes nothing," she said, wondering if she would see anything at all as she attached the electrodes according to the directions inside the booth. She touched the start sign on the screen, the device whirred to life, and the words "Retrieving data" appeared.

After a moment the screen darkened, and Skye frowned. The machine didn't seem to be working. Skye was about to summon the receptionist when she heard the soft sound of someone singing. She turned the volume button a couple of millimeters to the right until she could discern the words of the song.

"Inky Dinky *parlez vous.*"

She had to turn the contrast button all the way up before she could make out a couple of shadowy images on the screen. In the dim light she saw an unfamiliar elderly black woman rocking in a chair as she sang.

The woman crooned several songs in an off-key voice that should have been grating but was actually pleasant. Who was this person, and why was Skye dreaming about her? Had she been a client? Possibly. The only old people she ever saw in Heaven were the newly deceased who arrived in her office. Still, even though Skye had dealt with hundreds of clients during her tenure at the Hospitality Sector, she felt certain she would have remembered this particular woman.

"I think it's time to hit the hay, Sleeping Beauty," the woman said, startling Skye. For a second, she thought the woman was actually addressing her. But no; as she looked at the screen more closely, she saw a bed with a railing in the background. The woman was talking to someone lying in a hospital bed.

How curious. There was no need for hospital beds in Heaven. Why would she be dreaming about a place she'd never been to? Was all of this somehow related to her recent viewings of Earthly Pleasures?

The screen went blank before Skye could consider the implications of her dream. As the device called up another one, Skye hoped this dream would make more sense. But when the next image appeared on the screen, it looked identical to the first. Same dark room, same old woman. This time the woman was crying; her tears cut silver trails on her leathery cheeks.

Skye felt unexpectedly moved by the woman's sobs, as if they were her own tears being shed. She wanted to enfold the woman's bony shoulders into her arms and comfort her, even though Skye had no idea why she was crying.

Perhaps the person on the bed had died, the one the woman

had been singing to. Skye squinted at the screen. There was a vague shape in the background, but the lighting was dim and the grieving woman was blocking much of the view.

What could it mean? The device began to retrieve the final dream, and Skye had the urge to rip the electrodes from her temples. *Get up and leave. This is a lot of nonsense.* But she couldn't. The previous two dreams, though disquieting, had captivated her.

When the last dream came on the screen, it was obvious she was seeing the same room she'd seen in the first dream. This time the room was flooded with moonlight that reached the foot of the hospital bed and illuminated the white of the sheets. Skye's eyes followed the light as it spilled over the bed and revealed the other person in the room.

The pale face, much younger than the black woman's, was distorted with pain. The eyes were swollen slits, the mouth a misshapen pink wound. Skye watched speechless, not believing her eyes as the young woman continued to sob and cried out, "Call Lynn," the very same words Chelsea said she'd been calling out the night before. But then, almost as if she sensed she was being watched, the woman's eyes widened and stared out at Skye, with a pleading gaze.

"It's just a dream," Skye whispered. "It's just a dream." Then the world as she knew it fell away.

Twenty

It was ten minutes before her night shift began at Magnolia Manor, and Lydia Chance was trying to dislodge a popcorn kernel from between her teeth with the tip of her tongue when she heard the scream. She wasn't particularly alarmed. Residents in the Verandah Wing were known to cry out in their sleep now and again.

She left the break room and jogged down the hall, trying to figure out who was making such a racket. When the sound rang out again, Lydia could tell the ruckus was coming from Mrs. Kale's room.

She was surprised. Old lady Kale could spit up a monsoon, but Lydia assumed it was her only trick. She hoped that she wasn't adding hollering to her repertoire. Lydia opened the door and saw a terrified-looking Mrs. Kale sitting up in bed with her fingers stuck in her ears.

She blinked. *What in the world?* Her glance immediately went to Emily's bed. The young woman was staring at the same water spot on the ceiling, but her mouth was opened into a wide O and she was shrieking.

"Emily?" Lydia said, rushing to her side. She still didn't quite believe what she was seeing.

She rested a hand on the young woman's shoulder, and Emily's head slowly swung in her direction and her rubbery arm tried but failed to reach out to Lydia before it flopped uselessly against the mattress.

"Where's Colin?" she slurred.

Lydia felt a wave of dizziness, and the last thought she had before her knees gave way was, *That was no reflex!*

"Did you have any kissing dreams?" Rhianna asked. She smacked the back of her hand as Chelsea emerged from behind her curtained screening booth.

"No," Chelsea said. "But I was flying, which was very cool. What did you dream?"

"I was riding bareback on an elephant, eating kumquats from a crystal bowl," Rhianna said with a smile. "It was all very civilized." She pointed to the booth next to the one Chelsea had just come from. "Skye still in there?"

"Guess so," Chelsea said.

"We better drag her out if we're going to make it to the amusement park on time." Rhianna shook the curtain. "Hey, Dream Weaver, let's shake a leg."

There was no response.

"Skye?" she said, trying again. Rhianna shrugged. "I thought this one was hers."

"I thought so too." Chelsea drew back the curtain to reveal an empty booth. "Maybe we were wrong."

"Wait a minute," Rhianna said, sniffing the air. "I can smell her perfume. This was definitely her booth."

"I'll ask the receptionist if she's seen her." Chelsea headed in the direction of the exit.

"We're looking for our friend," Chelsea said, addressing the woman behind the desk. "Blonde hair, blue eyes. Did she leave?"

"No," the receptionist said. "I didn't see her, and I haven't moved from this spot."

"Is there another way out?"

"No. One way in, one way out."

Rhianna and Chelsea peeked under the other curtained booths and called Skye's name. After combing the entire theater, and looking into each booth twice, they had nowhere else to search.

Twenty-One

"That will be a buck fifty," Wanda Myers said, handing a sausage dog and bun over to one of her regulars, a lawyer named Ernie who had an office across the street.

She heard snickers and knew without looking it was those same two high-school girls from St. Andrews Academy who'd been teasing her for the last few days. They sat on a bench directly behind her hot-dog cart.

"It's a groovy granny," one said, shrieking with laughter.

"It's not the Mod Squad; it's the Menopause Squad," said the other.

"Twiggy wears Depends!"

Wanda chuckled to herself. *Twiggy wears Depends.* That was a new one. Those girls were nothing if not sharp, as they darn well ought to be. Their parents spent plenty of money so they could attend that fancy private school of theirs.

Wanda got teased all the time, but she never let it ruffle her tail feathers. She knew she looked like a refugee from the sixties, with her hot pants, go-go boots, and her wild yellow hair spilling out of her floppy vinyl hat. Sometimes men would see her from the back (she still had the shapely gams of a college girl, but wore fishnet panty hose to disguise her spider veins) and whistle or let out a catcall, but soon as she turned around—wow, would she give them boys a start.

"Excuse me, ma'am. I'm sorry," they'd stammer when they

realized they'd been getting all worked up over someone old enough to soak her teeth in a glass.

Wanda checked her watch. Fifteen minutes to four. Time to pack it up.

"Hey, Hot Dog Hag!" someone yelled from a car and tooted his horn. Wanda waved and blew kisses. She'd had a hot-dog cart in downtown Birmingham for going on ten years and was a fixture in the city. One of the alternative papers had dubbed her "Hot Dog Hag" a few years back and it stuck. Now and again one of the TV news stations ran a human-interest story on her. Every year a few women (and occasionally some men) dressed up as the Hot Dog Hag for Halloween. She was as much a part of Birmingham as the fifty-six-foot cast-iron statue of Vulcan that loomed over the city.

She wheeled her cart in the direction of the garage she stowed it in every day. Chub showed up to help her, just like always.

"Let me get that for you, Miss Wanda," he said, taking the cart from her. Wizened and white-haired, Chub was one of the older homeless men who hung out downtown. He had a genteel air about him even though he lived in a cardboard refrigerator box under a bridge.

"Thanks, Chub," Wanda said. "Gotta run. It's my favorite time of the day."

The girls were still sniggering as she strutted by them, wagging her long hot-pink fingernails. She ignored them, because frankly she felt perfectly comfortable in her own skin.

It was one thing if you were a weirdo and you didn't know it, like Tammy Faye Bakker when she was married to Jim. But it was another thing to work at being weird the way Wanda did. How else would a seventy-one-year-old woman get so much attention?

Wanda made it to her apartment just in time to hear the swell of the theme music. She popped open a diet A&W root beer, shooed her two ferrets off her couch, and reached for the remote. She turned the TV to *Talk to Me*, hosted by Gayle Garfield. And didn't Gayle look pretty as a picture in her tomato-red dress? Wanda thought she was a lot more fetching than people gave her credit for.

The show's title was "Getting Your Man to Commit," not a topic Wanda was particularly interested in, so she only watched with half an eyeball.

Ever since she'd gotten her heart broken, Wanda had given up on trying to figure out men. A little over a year ago she'd foolishly eloped with Harvey Hart, an out-of-work sculptor who was fifteen years her junior. Six weeks after their wedding date she caught him in their bed with another man. Now she'd sworn off men and was writing her autobiography, tentatively titled *Confessions of a Hot-Dog Hag*.

"Next up, a surprise guest," Gayle said. "Meet the woman who managed to land one of the country's most eligible bachelors."

Gayle certainly knew how to tease her audience. Wanda tried to guess who the bachelor was.

"I'd like to introduce my special guest, Susan Blaine," Gayle said after the break. "Susan, as most people know, is married to Ryan Blaine, or 'Bad-Boy Blaine' as he used to be called back in his salad days. This is her first interview after her tragic accident last year."

Susan Blaine? Wanda, like millions of gossip-loving Americans, had devoured all the details about Susan's accident and subsequent surgeries, but Wanda especially remembered her because she'd once struck up a friendship with a street person who could have been Susan's twin. What was the broad's name? Ever since she hit seventy, Wanda's mind was like the Mousetrap board game: information kicked around a maze of obstacles before it came rattling down the chute.

The street woman had loitered around Wanda's cart—a big-eyed skinny thing wearing a ragged Johnny Cash t-shirt. Wanda, who could strike up a conversation with a bale of hay, chatted up the girl and even took her out for a cup of coffee a couple of times. Judging by the mud-colored crescents under her eyes and her twitchy hands, the woman was likely a drug user. Didn't bother Wanda. When you sold hot dogs on the streets every day, you met your share of shady characters.

About a week after she'd met the street woman, Wanda had been watching Animal Planet and a woman named Susan Sims (she was not yet married to Ryan Blaine and was still a complete nobody) appeared on one of the shows as a guest animal behaviorist. Wanda couldn't get over how much Susan Sims looked like a coiffed and cleaned-up version of her street buddy.

When Wanda saw her new friend the next day hanging out in front of a pawnshop, she approached her, saying, "They say everyone has a twin walking around in this world, and, honey, I think I've found yours."

The street gal took an immediate interest, wanting to hear all the particulars. She even smiled for the first time ever, saying, "Isn't that something? Imagine someone who looks like me being on TV."

By this time Wanda had taken a shine to the pitiful alley rat. Over the next few days she went out of her way for the girl, giving her a makeup kit she'd gotten free from Estée Lauder and some old clothes from her closet. She'd even treated her to a few free hot dogs. But things had soured fast when Wanda caught the woman trying to sneak a few bucks out of her till. She cussed the little larcenist up and down, and after that day she never saw her again.

"Welcome, Susan," Gayle said to a woman with short spiky blonde hair. When Susan appeared on Animal Planet a little over a year ago, her hair had been long enough to skim her shoulders, and it hadn't been commonly known she was involved with Ryan Blaine.

As the camera panned in for a closer shot of Susan, Wanda could see how much the car accident had banged up her face. Now, instead of looking like the street woman's twin, Susan looked more like a sister or even a cousin.

"So glad to have you here," Gayle said excitedly, seizing Susan's hand as if she were her very best friend. "So tell us what every woman wants to know. What's Ryan Blaine really like?"

"A little bit clumsy. He's always tripping over his big feet or breaking things," Susan said with a laugh. "But he's such a great kisser I forgive him."

Wanda wasn't confused by what Susan was saying but by how she was saying it. She turned up the volume on the remote.

"Is he, now?" Gayle said, her mouth opened wide, looking into the camera as if sharing a private joke with the viewing audience.

"He's pretty good at most everything he does."

There it was again. "Most everything" came out "moth everything." No mistaking it. Susan lisped.

The interview continued as Wanda's mind raced. She'd nearly forgotten the street gal had lisped. Surely it had to be more than a coincidence that Susan Blaine lisped as well.

"So what do the two of you argue about?" Gayle asked. "Do you have a pet peeve when it comes to Ryan? And what does he nag you about?"

"Believe it or not, sometimes Ryan misses the hamper when he takes off his socks," Susan said. The audience clapped and laughed in recognition. "He also thinks I read too many gossip magazines," she continued. Gossip coming out as "gothip." "And he *hates* my Johnny Cash CDs. He makes me play them in my office with the door shut."

Johnny Cash? Wanda nearly choked on her soda. The street girl had also been a huge fan. What was going on? Had Susan lisped during her appearance on Animal Planet? She'd only caught the very tail end of the show, but Wanda thought she'd remember such a distinct speech impediment.

Two women who lisped. Two women who were fans of the same country singer. Two women who could pass for identical twins. When Wanda suggested to her street buddy she'd seen her "twin sister" on television, she hadn't meant it literally, but as she watched Susan Blaine on *Talk to Me* it seemed the two almost certainly had to be related.

Was she Susan Blaine's twin sister? Did Susan even know about her twin's existence, or was she a secret she'd prefer to hide, especially now that she'd married a big shot like Ryan Blaine?

Wanda's curiosity got the best of her. She decided the only way to get answers to her questions was to write Susan Blaine a letter.

Twenty-Two

Caroline was still in bed even though it was nearing lunchtime. Yesterday Ms. Waters had come into her room and issued a strong warning. Caroline was not to go into the Verandah Wing and see Emily for any reason, and if she did, the staff would consider using restraints.

"It's for *your own good*," had been the despicable woman's parting words.

Caroline refused to meet her eye or acknowledge a word Betty Boop said. This morning, at about seven a.m., during the shift change, when most of the staff was gossiping in the break area, she had crept out of her room and snuck into Emily's. She found Mrs. Kale snoring in her old bed, but Emily's was empty—the sheets and covers made up, the IV gone. There wasn't a trace of her left.

Caroline clenched her jaw. Obviously Ms. Waters had moved Emily to another room in hopes of tricking her. Well, she'd underestimated Caroline. There were twenty rooms on the Verandah Wing, and she intended to search them all.

She left her old quarters and made her way along the corridor, peeking into every room. It took her nearly an hour, but she managed to scour the entire wing.

When she came to the last room and there was still no sign of Emily, she felt like tearing her hair out. What had happened to her roommate? What had Dixie Waters done with her? Then a sobering notion occurred to her. Maybe Emily hadn't been moved. Maybe she'd left this place the way most of the residents did, on a stretcher, a sheet covering her stilled features. After all, Emily had become extremely dependent on Caroline. Maybe when the poor girl woke last night and saw she was gone, she'd lost hope.

Caroline returned to her bed and remained under the covers in one of the darkest funks of her life. She decided she would not speak, eat, or leave her bed until she found out exactly what had happened to her roommate.

Twenty-Three

Emily heard voices. People talking in low, serious tones. She heard the name "Emily" repeated several times. As soon as she opened her eyes, the room grew silent and a penlight blinded her.

"Please blink twice if you can understand me," said a male voice. She lifted a hand to her face to shield her eyes from the brightness. Her hand was so heavy it felt as if it were encased in a block of cement.

Three doctors were huddled around her bed, clipboards in hand, clinically scrutinizing her as if she were a new strain of mold growing in a petri dish.

"This is a fruitless exercise," said the female of the group. "It's highly unlikely the patient can understand—"

"I understand you just fine," she said. Her speech sounded thick and slurred to her ears, as if her tongue was too large for her mouth.

The doctors' cool appraising expressions were replaced with looks of shock when she spoke. One let out a gasp, and another dropped his penlight.

"Would you...could you...answer a few questions?" said the tallest doctor. He had a dark mustache shot with gray and a pockmarked face. His name tag identified him as Dr. Perry.

I'm the one who needs to be asking the questions, she thought. Unfortunately, she had trouble deciding where to begin. What kind of mess had she gotten herself into now?

"I'll try," she said. Remaining awake was such an effort. Sleep lapped away at the edges of her consciousness, threatening to blot her out entirely.

"Do you know your name?" he asked.

"Emily?"

She was simply repeating what the doctors had said earlier. Was Emily her name? What had happened to her?

"What year is it?" the same doctor asked.

Her head throbbed. *Stop bombarding me with questions*, she wanted to say. *I'm still trying to figure out my name.* Obviously her first name was Emily, but what was her last name? How could she not know?

"The year?" the doctor repeated.

"I'm working on it," she said. The wheels of her thoughts turned sluggishly as if coated in mud.

"What's nine times nine?" asked the female doctor, clearly eager to jump into the game.

Finally, a question she could answer. "Eighty-one," she said, triumphantly. At least some of her synapses were merrily firing, even if others were taking the day off. "And eleven times eleven is 121," she added, showing off a little. She hoped they wouldn't ask any twelves; she was rusty with those.

"What's the year?" asked the tall doctor again. She closed her eyes, valiantly trying to retrieve that slippery bit of data in the murk of her mind. The year eluded her, but other memories were rising up from the silt. There was the sound of a radio and an elderly black woman in a rocking chair. Yes! The woman's name was Caroline and she sang off-key and rubbed her legs. Or was she just part of a dream? No. She didn't think so.

"Where's Caroline? I want to speak with her, please." Caroline would help her make sense of this. The old woman had known her before she'd landed in the hospital with all these quiz-happy doctors.

"Colin?" Dr. Perry said. "I'm sorry. Who is Colin?"

"Caroline," she said, trying to improve her pronunciation. "She was with me in..." She had no idea where she used to be. A room with a bed, but not a hospital. God! Why was all of this so hard? "Wherever I was before."

"I don't know if that's possible," Dr. Perry said, flicking away her question. "Can you tell me, Emily, who is the president of the United States?"

There he went again, making like he was Alex Trebek. She pondered his face and those of his colleagues. They were practically drooling with interest in her, a very bad sign indeed. If she'd attracted the undivided attention of three doctors, she was obviously suffering from some rare and terrible medical disorder. When they finally got around to telling her what was wrong with her, she didn't want to be alone. The only person she could remember was Caroline.

"No more questions until I see her," she said, which was just as well. She no longer had the stamina to stay awake even a minute longer.

Twenty-Four

"What happened to Skye?" Chelsea wailed as she and Rhianna exited the Nocturnal Theater.

"Hey now," Rhianna said, putting a hand on the girl's shoulder. "People in Heaven don't get lost. Have you ever seen any pictures on milk cartons around here?" She withdrew a WishBerry from a fringed purse and grinned. "This baby has a people-locator function."

"Really?" Chelsea wiped away tears stained black by her eyeliner.

"It does everything," Rhianna typed in Skye's information and pointing to the blinking screen. "See, it says locating, locating, locating. It's thinking. Ah! Here we go. Skye Sebring's location is presently..." Rhianna squinted at the words. "What?"

Chelsea snatched the computer from her hand. "Skye Sebring's location is presently...unknown?" She choked on a fresh set of tears. "I knew it. Something terrible has happened to her."

"Terrible things don't happen in Heaven," Rhianna said, taking the computer from Chelsea and giving it a little shake. "There's gotta be some kind of explanation."

"What now?" Chelsea asked, nibbling on the ends of her hair.

"Hmmm. We're in the Supreme Being Sector. Let's head over to the Capitol. They're supposed to know everything around there."

The pair traveled to the Capitol building and located the administrative offices.

"May I help you?" asked the male receptionist, sitting behind an imposing desk. His slender fingers formed a triangle beneath his chin.

Rhianna described the circumstances of Skye's disappearance. "I couldn't even find her with the locator function," she said.

"Has it ever occurred to you that she doesn't want to be found?" asked the man, pursing his rubbery lips in consideration. "I had a girlfriend once, and she put me on Locator Block. I couldn't find her for anything. She could be on Pluto for all I know."

"Skye wouldn't put us on Locator Block," Chelsea said. "She just disappeared like a puff of smoke, and we're worried sick about her."

"Let me look her up in the main computer," the man said, poising his fingers on the keyboard. "What was the name?"

"Skye Sebring," Rhianna said. "We really appreciate this."

"Skye Sebring," he said, punching the data in. "Yup. Found her."

"Where is she?" Chelsea demanded.

"She's...That's peculiar." He glanced up at them. "Sorry. Can't tell you. It's classified."

"Give us a break," Rhianna said. "She's a really good friend and we just want to know—" Her beeper went off. "Darn," she said, glancing at the display number. "I've gotta get to Guardian Angel Headquarters ASAP. Looks like I have my first assignment." She touched Chelsea on the shoulder. "Can you get back to newcomers' quarters okay?"

"What about Skye?" Chelsea said. She leaned over the receptionist's desk. "Please tell us where she is."

The man stubbornly shook his head.

"Sorry. No can do."

"Chelsea, I have to go," Rhianna said.

"Take me with you. I don't want to be by myself right now."

"This is my first gig as an angel," Rhianna said. "There's rules against having people tag along."

"Skye took me to work with her," Chelsea said in a small voice, her pinky stuck in her mouth.

"Fine." Rhianna grabbed her hand and tugged her out of the office. "It's not like I've ever been a stickler for the rules."

They found a teleport kiosk in the lobby of the Capitol and boarded it. Rhianna used her computer to change into her gown. In a blink, they arrived and found themselves in front of Guardian Angel Headquarters.

"Gosh, you look so...saintly," Chelsea said.

Rhianna glanced down at her flowing white gown and frowned. "Too saintly." She pointed to the spiked choker around Chelsea's neck. "Can I borrow that thing? It's the perfect touch."

"Sure," Chelsea said, unfastening the choker and handing it to Rhianna, who clasped it around her own neck.

"That's better," she said. "Okay, let's go."

They entered Guardian Angel Headquarters, a gilded high-rise structure. The lobby had barreled vaulted ceilings embellished with frescoes of gamboling cherubs. As they hurried to the elevators, they passed a half-dozen angels gliding across the polished floors.

They traveled to Rhianna's office on the fifth floor, which was a small cubicle similar to those in the Hospitality Sector. Rhianna instructed Chelsea to sit beside her as she booted up her computer and signed in.

"Welcome, Rhianna." Michelle, her supervisor, appeared on the screen. "Are you ready for your first assignment?"

"Fire when ready," Rhianna said.

Michelle was platinum blonde, a popular hair color among guardian angels. Her creamy white skin looked as if it had never been exposed to the rays of the sun.

"I wanted to speak directly with you about this client because it's someone you know. Quite well," said Michelle.

"Are you sure?" Rhianna said. "I didn't think I knew any Earthlings, at least not personally."

"You know this one," Michelle said, her brow knitting together. "It's Skye Sebring."

"What?" Rhianna said. She exchanged a look with Chelsea, who gasped and inched her chair closer to Rhianna's.

"That's not her name on Earth, of course," Michelle said. "You have a file on your computer desktop that will tell you everything you need to know. It's a complex case."

"How is this possible? Skye wasn't due to be born on Earth yet," Rhianna said.

"She wasn't born," Michelle said. "She finally returned to her Earth body, rather abruptly."

"Returned? There's gotta be a mistake," Rhianna said. "Skye's a *new* soul. She's never been to Earth before."

"Yes, she has, Rhianna. Several times, in fact. She'd repressed her last life while she was in Heaven, primarily because she'd been deeply traumatized while on Earth."

"I don't understand," Rhianna said with a puzzled squint.

"A little over a year ago, Skye was very seriously injured, and she lapsed into a coma. In such cases, there's often a split of the soul, or what we call 'L' status, the 'L' standing for limbo. Skye arrived in Heaven, but a part of her was left behind in her body on Earth."

"How come she didn't arrive in the Hospitality Sector?" Rhianna said. "And why did she think she was a new soul all this time?"

"She did arrive in the Hospitality Sector, and was immediately sent to the Special Cases Department. Usually such situations resolve themselves in a matter of days. Either the soul allows the body to die or it returns to Earth, but Skye continued to remain in limbo, likely because of some disturbing things that happened to her before she was injured."

Rhianna cocked her head. "So she was led to believe she was a new soul by the Special Cases Department?"

"Yes," Michelle said with a nod. "It's the only solution in such instances. A limbo state needs to be resolved naturally. After she was processed by the Special Cases Department, we arranged for her to wake up in the New Soul Annex and become a greeter."

"So that's why she didn't remember being created," Rhianna said.

"And that's why the machine in the zoo printed out the details of her last life," Chelsea said. "Why did she go back?"

"Who's that with you?" asked a startled Michelle.

"I have a friend sitting next to me," Rhianna said. "Her name's Chelsea, and she was a client of Skye's."

"More than a client," Chelsea said. "She was like a big sister to me."

"I'm sorry, Chelsea," Michelle said, her eyes filling with sympathy. "Skye's obviously been conflicted about which dimension she wanted to exist in, and she finally made the choice to return to her body."

"You still haven't told us why she went back," Chelsea said.

"It's in the file," Michelle said. "But it's for guardian angels' eyes only. Skye is a really unusual case. We don't often have people in limbo for such a long period of time. She'll need your help, Rhianna. There are difficult times ahead for her on Earth."

"I'll do my best," Rhianna said.

Michelle smiled. "That's why we chose you to be her guardian angel. The two of you were so close. That can make a difference when you try to influence her on Earth."

"I was close to her too," Chelsea said. "I want to know what happened to her."

"It's against regulations," Michelle said. "And Rhianna's a brand-new angel."

"Please," Chelsea insisted. "She means so much to me."

"I'm not much for regulations, Michelle," Rhianna said, tugging on her spike collar. "Back when I was a greeter, I used my *Hospitality Handbook* as a doorstop."

"Civilians are not supposed to be privy to guardian angel records," Michelle said.

"This is a special circumstance," Rhianna said.

Michele sighed. "Okay. She can look at Skye's records, but then you must send her on her way. Good luck, Rhianna."

After she signed off, Rhianna put her mouse over Skye's file. "Let's see what's going on with Skye. I wonder why she finally felt compelled to go back to Earth. She never seemed remotely interested in the place."

"Maybe it was that guy, Ryan Blaine," Chelsea said in a wistful voice.

Rhianna printed out the files, making copies for both of them. After studying Skye's background for a few minutes, Chelsea let out a high-pitched cry.

"I can't believe what she's been through," she said, holding her stomach. "No wonder she didn't want to return to Earth. This is the worst thing I've ever heard."

Twenty-Five

"Something's rotten in Denmark," Wanda whispered to herself as she paced her living room, going over the telephone conversation she'd had only an hour earlier. She'd mailed Ryan Blaine's wife a letter two weeks ago and had almost given up on hearing back from her when she finally called.

"Hello. This is Susan Blaine."

Wanda got starstruck when she heard Susan's voice. Since her *Talk to Me* appearance, she had been on the cover of every celebrity magazine printed.

"Is this a good time to talk?" Susan asked cautiously.

It wasn't. Wanda had been soaking in the tub when the phone rang, and her machine had already picked up when she'd seized the receiver. It let out an earsplitting squeal, and Wanda fumbled to turn down the volume.

"It's the perfect time to talk," she said, even though she was dripping water all over her linoleum floor in the kitchen. Susan was a very important lady, and Wanda didn't want to put her off.

"Thank you for your letter," Susan said. "I can understand why you wrote it. It's strange, isn't it? I couldn't believe it myself."

Susan went on to explain that a little over a year ago, a woman named Emily called her veterinarian office, claiming to be her twin sister.

"I was in shock. I didn't know I had a sister, and certainly not a twin. I was adopted and knew nothing about my birth family's background."

"I saw you on Animal Planet about that same time," Wanda said excitedly. "Emily! That's her name. I remember now. As I said in the letter, I knew your sister and told her how much the two of you resembled each other. I'm sure that's why she got in touch with you."

"That must be it," Susan said. "Naturally, I wasn't sure what her game was, but I agreed to meet her in Birmingham. It's only two hours away from Atlanta. When I saw her, I was amazed at how much we looked alike. This was before my accident. Emily was run-down from living on the streets, but there was no doubt she was my twin sister. We'd both been adopted, and, as you said in your letter, we both lisped. Our similarities, from our taste in food to our love for Johnny Cash, were uncanny."

"That's not as nutty as you would think," Wanda exclaimed. "After I saw you on *Talk to Me*, I did a little research on identical twins. I read about a pair of male twins who were also separated at birth. Even though they lived miles apart, both had wives named Betty; both had dogs named Toy; both worked as sheriff deputies. It bowled me over."

"Yes, yes," Susan said, sounding a little impatient with Wanda's litany on twins. "Unfortunately I didn't get to learn much more about Emily." Her voice hitched slightly. "She died the day after our meeting."

"What?" Wanda said, dropping into a chair. "She'd quit coming around my hot-dog cart, but I assumed she was afraid I'd sic the cops on her for trying to steal my money. I had no idea she passed away. I'm so sorry."

"Thank you. It was really sad and I blame myself."

"You? Why do you say that?"

"I didn't want her wandering the streets anymore, so I paid for a very fancy hotel room in downtown Birmingham. I also gave her some money for meals, promising I'd return the next day. I didn't know for sure, but I guessed she was involved in drugs, and I was going to look into a rehab program for her. I'd hoped to talk her into cleaning up her act. When I came back, the hotel management told me a maid had found her dead on the floor of the bathroom."

"What happened?"

"She binged on crack and had a heart attack. She probably bought the drugs with the money I'd given her for food." Susan let out a faint moan. "I shouldn't have left her alone. It was all my fault."

"Don't blame yourself," Wanda said. "Emily probably had a long history of drug abuse. I see people like her all the time. It's a real pity."

"I'm sure it is." An unexpected cold note entered Susan's voice. "Of course, it's your word against mine that I even have a sister. So if you're thinking of blackmailing me, you won't get very far."

"Blackmail?" Wanda said, moving the receiver an inch farther away from her ear as if she couldn't believe what she was being accused of. "Who do you take me for?"

"I have no idea how to take you. I've never heard of you until today."

"I was just curious after seeing you on *Talk to Me*," Wanda stammered. "I wasn't sure you even knew about Emily."

"Well, I do, and it's a very private matter. As you know, I'm married to Ryan Blaine, and this is the sort of thing tabloids can't get enough of. So if you were planning to sell the story—"

"Not on your life!" Wanda stood up so fast she almost lost her towel. "I wouldn't dream of it."

"I'm glad to hear that, Mrs. Hart," Susan said, her tone pleasant once again. "I didn't meant to be ugly, but there are so many wackos out there."

Wanda could not stop thinking about her phone conversation with Susan Blaine. She could hardly blame the lady for her blackmail concerns. She supposed all variety of shysters tried to prey on celebrities, and Susan was just being protective. Still, there was something else about their conversation that continued to nag at her.

Wanda had gone into the kitchen to toss a pizza in the oven when out of the corner of her eye she noticed her answering machine blinking on the phone table, indicating she had one message. She pushed the button and heard Susan's voice saying, "Hello, this is Susan Blaine."

She was momentarily bewildered, but then she remembered she'd answered the phone after her outgoing message had begun, so the machine had recorded their entire conversation.

Wanda listened to it again, hoping she could discover what was bothering her about their chat. When she found nothing unusual, she cut the shrink wrap from her pizza but stopped just before she opened the oven door. "Once more," she said as she pushed the play button again. She listened intently, not really expecting to hear anything different, but at the end of the tape, Susan said something that made Wanda drop the pizza on her foot.

"God Almighty," she said, staring at the answering machine as if it were a coiled cobra. A half-dozen questions with no reasonable answers ripped through her mind. She knew only one thing for certain: Susan Blaine was a big fat liar.

Twenty-Six

"Ms. Brodie? It's Mona. Are you awake?"

Caroline heard the nursing home director, but instead of answering, she buried her face deeper into her pillow. She liked Mona well enough, but she also felt betrayed by her for leaving that hellcat Ms. Waters in charge while she'd been gone.

Mona gently shook her shoulder. "It's Emily, Mrs. Brodie. She's awake now, and she's been asking for you."

Instantly, Caroline was alert. She flopped on her back to face Mona. "Emily?"

Mona nodded. "You were right all along. Emily came out of her coma."

Caroline batted away her bedcovers. "Where is she?"

"University Hospital. She was transferred there this morning. She wants to see you. I'll take you there myself."

"Hallelujah!" Caroline said, bounding out of bed with the spryness of a cheerleader. "I knew she'd come around."

"I'll wait for you in the office while you get ready." Mona paused for a moment, toying with the buttons of her cardigan. "By the way," she added in a soft voice, "Ms. Waters is no longer with us at Magnolia Manor. I'm sorry she was unkind to you. She's my niece, you see, and I thought I'd give her a chance, but—" She shrugged her shoulders. "She made some very bad decisions while I was gone."

"Good riddance to bad rubbish. I'm just glad you're back,"

Caroline said, grinning as she grabbed her toilet kit from the top of the dresser.

She took a steaming hot shower and the water felt like a thousand warm fingers on her back. After toweling off, she flung open her closet and withdrew her Sunday finest, a purple linen dress with a matching feathered straw hat and dotted veil.

"That's what I call hat-titude," Caroline said with a cackle as she perched the hat on her head. This was an auspicious occasion, and she wanted to be dressed to the nines.

"Look at you," Mona said, clapping her hands together when Caroline stepped over the threshold of the office, holding a beaded clutch. "Won't Emily be pleased."

As they rode to the hospital in Miss Mona's Buick Regal, Caroline got a case of the butterflies. What would their first meeting be like? She didn't really know her roommate; all of their conversations had been completely one-sided. Was Caroline just enamored with the fairy-tale version of Emily she'd created in her mind? Maybe Emily would curse, and talk about turning tricks and drugs. Maybe Caroline wouldn't want anything to do with her.

Put a lid on it, she chided. She had a feeling about the young woman. Yes, it was true Emily had stumbled on hard times. Didn't everyone do that now and again? Hadn't she had her own dark night of the soul fifty-odd years ago when her husband was running around on her? Obviously, Emily had temporarily lost her way, and she'd gotten a wake-up call. And yes, it was one hell of a wake-up call, but Caroline knew some people required more than just a tap on the shoulder.

She and Mona arrived at the hospital and were directed to Emily's floor. A burly security guard stood outside her room, clipboard in hand.

"Name?" he said.

"Caroline Brodie and Miss Mona Scales." Caroline frowned. "Is anything wrong?"

"Just trying to keep out curiosity-seekers," the security guard said. "I got a Caroline Brodie on this list, but no Mona Scales."

"I'll wait out here," Mona said, touching Caroline's elbow. "You go ahead, dear. And good luck with our Emily."

Caroline nodded and adjusted the angle of her hat. Just as she approached the door, it swung open and three doctors emerged, two males and one female.

"It's impossible to keep this kind of news under wraps," the female doctor said. She was a wisp of a thing haloed by a cloud of dark hair. "The local television station's already called, but I think her recovery will attract national—"

The male doctor looked up and noticed Caroline standing outside the door.

"Please tell me you're Mrs. Brodie. I'm Dr. Perry," he said, extending a hand.

"Is Emily in there?" Caroline tried to peer over the doctor's shoulder.

"Yes, she is, and she's anxious to see you," Dr. Perry said. "Thank you so much for coming."

"A den of grizzly bears couldn't keep me away. So is she..."

"Completely conscious, although she drifts in and out of sleep," Dr. Perry said. "The only person she wants to talk to is you."

"And I can't wait to speak with her."

"I'm sure you can't. But before you do, there are a couple of things you should know. First, Emily has no idea how long she's been in a vegetative state. It's best if you avoid discussing particulars with her while she's in such a frail condition."

"Yes," Caroline said.

"Secondly, although it's a miracle that Emily has regained consciousness, there's no telling how long she'll be with us." His voice became solemn. "It could be for a very brief time. The last person on record who came out of a lengthy vegetative state spoke with family members for several hours and then died the next day of a stroke. We don't know what we can expect from Emily, but in cases like hers, it's prudent to prepare for the worst."

"I'll prepare myself for the best, Dr. Perry, thank you very much, and you should too. If the man upstairs brought her this far,

He can surely bring her a tad further." She smoothed the pleats of her dress. "Can I please go in and see Emily now?"

"Be my guest," Dr. Perry said.

Caroline tiptoed into the room, just in case Emily was sleeping, although how anyone could catch even a single "z" in such a brightly lit room was another matter altogether.

Emily was laid out on the bed, flat on her back as usual, but for the first time ever, her eyes were closed. She was so motionless Caroline felt a flutter of panic in her throat. Was the girl still alive?

"Emily," Caroline called out, surprised by the roughness of her voice. She cleared her throat to chase away the frogs. "Emily," she said, this time much louder and clearer.

The young woman was an expanse of immobile cotton. Caroline was about to reach out and touch her cheek when she remembered how she'd always roused Emily in the past.

"Inky Dinky *parlez vous*," she sang.

Emily's body twitched several times. Caroline kept singing, this time a little louder, until ever so slowly the young woman opened her eyes.

"Caroline? Caroline, is that you?" she slurred. Emily's face broke into a weak smile, showing a row of strong healthy teeth, just as Caroline had imagined in her dreams.

"Yes, Sleeping Beauty, it's me," Caroline said, a quaver in her voice as she rushed to the bedside to grasp Emily's hand. "I'm here now. Don't fret."

"Thank God," Emily said. "I was afraid you were just part of my dreams. But you're real."

"Realer than most folks, I can promise you that." Caroline scrambled in her pocketbook for a tissue. It was as if the girl had reached inside her ribcage and given her heart a little pinch.

"There's so much I want to say."

Caroline patted her hand. "Don't be straining yourself now. There'll be plenty of time for that."

"Can you come see me again?"

"'Course I can."

Caroline didn't know how she'd make it back to the hospital, but she would get there, come hell or hurricane.

"Caroline." He voice was as faint as a fly under glass. "Please don't leave me again. I don't know these people. You're all I have."

"I'm sure that's not true," Caroline fibbed. As far as she knew, the girl had no people to speak of. Certainly none dropped in during the time they were roommates. "But I promise, I won't leave you."

"Caroline, never leave me," Emily said again, stretching out the syllables of Caroline's name as if she loved the sound of it on her lips. How silly she'd been to fret over Emily's past. There wasn't a lick of toughness in her expression. The hard-edged street woman had been worn smooth by the coma, leaving a girl as innocent as a newborn chick.

"And next time you come, bring the radio. I missed *Minerva* last night."

"Will do, lamb. I missed it myself."

Emily's head lolled to her side. Caroline could tell she was struggling to stay awake for her benefit. "How long have I been away, Caroline?"

She'd asked the one question Caroline wasn't allowed to answer. Thankfully, before she could decide on a reply, Emily had fallen asleep again.

When Emily woke up the next morning, Caroline was no longer in the chair beside her. She was about to call out for a nurse when she heard a man talking just outside her room.

"You know I'm not supposed to take phone calls at work...Just call the plumber. I think we used A-Rite last time. Look in the phone book...I'm pulling the same duty as yesterday...I told you about it last night, the woman who's been in a coma for over a year."

Emily's limbs stiffened. So that's why she had a parade of doctors in her room. How could she have lost an entire year? Christmas, Easter, Arbor Day...It was incomprehensible. What in God's name had happened to her? Her mind whirled as she tried to process the news. It was far too much for her to absorb in her weakened state, and her consciousness started to ebb until she passed out completely.

When she woke up, Dr. Perry and his staff were in her room. "Emily," Dr. Perry said. "Are you awake? I'd like to speak to you."

She didn't reply. The truth weighed upon like a load of bricks; she could scarcely breathe. Emily didn't want to talk with these people. She needed Caroline. She longed to hear her sing and to feel the calming touch of her hand. Where'd she gone? Hadn't she promised she wouldn't leave?

"Caroline," she said in a plaintive voice, her eyes filling with tears. "I want to see her. Bring her back to me."

Dr. Perry exchanged an uneasy glance with his colleagues and fidgeted with the band of his steel wristwatch.

"I'm afraid that's not possible."

Not possible! Why was he being so contrary? Wasn't it bad enough that she'd lost a year of her life? That she was a medical anomaly? Couldn't he grant her this smallest of wishes?

"I want Caroline," she said petulantly. Their trained seal would not perform until she came back. "Did you send her away?"

"Of course not, Emily. Please look at me. There's something I need to tell you," Dr. Perry said. His voice was apologetic, tinged with pity. "It's bad news, I'm afraid."

Over forty years ago Caroline had lost her only child, a stillborn baby boy named Russell. Now she was getting a second chance. She felt as if she'd birthed Emily and coaxed her back into the world. Certainly the young woman would need Caroline as she found her way in life again. Dr. Perry seemed to agree. After Emily had fallen asleep, he'd entered the hospital room with Miss Mona and asked her to step outside.

"Would you consider staying here in Emily's room for a while?" he said to Caroline. "We'll bring in a portable bed. I believe she'll have a much better chance for recovery if you're near."

Miss Mona assured her that her spot at Magnolia Manor would stay open as long as she needed it. Dr. Perry said she could take her meals free in the cafeteria. They'd both had pleading basset-hound eyes. As if staying with Emily was something she needed to be talked into! Of course she'd do it. For the first time in years, her heart felt as light as a puff of smoke. Truth was, in some ways she needed Emily more than Emily needed her.

"What about my things?" Caroline asked. "I need someone to fetch them for me, especially my radio. I promised Emily I wouldn't leave her again." Miss Mona assured her she'd have someone bring everything over that afternoon. She and Emily would listen to *Minerva* together tonight. It was like old home week.

"De Camptown ladies sing this song, doo dah," Caroline sang as she went back inside the hospital room and sank into the beige armchair beside Emily. "Too bad there's no rocking chair," she remarked.

"I'll have one brought over from the nursery," said Dr. Perry.

"That would be right decent of you."

"Thank you, Mrs. Brodie," Dr. Perry said. "I'm sure Emily will be thrilled to see you when she wakes up."

"I'm not moving a muscle," Caroline said. "I'll be right here like I said." She paused and put a hand to her temple. Her eyes felt loose in their sockets, as if something in her head had short-circuited.

"Mrs. Brodie, are you all right?"

"I'm fine," she lied, reaching an arm out as if to steady herself. "I just need to..." Her vision blurred, and the words she wanted to speak swam away from her like minnows in a pond. Her chin fell to her chest, and she slid from her chair and collapsed on the floor.

"Mrs. Brodie!" Dr. Perry shouted.

They were the last words Caroline would ever hear on Earth. The pain in her temple was so sharp, it felt as if it were slicing her skull into two pieces. Just when she thought she'd go mad from the ceaseless burning in her brain, the pain receded. It was replaced with a peace that wrapped itself around her like a downy cocoon.

She was suspended in her cozy chrysalis, traveling toward a yellow disc of light in the distance. It looked comforting and welcoming, like the light spilling from a cottage window in a dense black forest, and she was drawn to it. As she drifted in the direction of the light, she remembered a movie she'd seen on late-night television about ghosts. "Go into the light, children," said one of the characters, coaxing troubled souls to cross over to the other side. Lord have mercy. It was her time to cross. She was one of those who'd left her body. She was dying. No! She couldn't go. Not now.

No matter how enticing the light, she refused to leave Emily behind. She would renounce the light. Kick and curse her way back into her body. Wasn't that how it was done in the movies? She tried it, but the cocoon cushioned her jabs and muffled her cries and she continued to be propelled toward the light until she was engulfed in it. Caroline didn't know who would be waiting for her in the sweet by-and-by—her late husband, Max, her dear-departed mother, Baby Russell, or the Devil himself—but instead she saw the face of a woman in a navy-blue suit and white knee socks who said, "Welcome to the Hospitality Sector of Heaven. My name is Joy, and I'm your greeter."

"Heaven?" Caroline's eyes adjusted to all the brightness and she found herself standing in a small cubicle, like something you'd see in an insurance office. "Missy, send me right back where I came from. There's someone on Earth who needs me."

"Yes, she does, Mrs. Brodie," said another voice. A woman with a corona of fiery red curls stepped out from behind the first lady. She wore a long white gown and a black spiked collar around her neck.

"Who are you?" Caroline asked. "A Hell's Angel? Don't matter to me. I can't let Emily down."

"And you won't," said the redhead. "You can still help Emily from here. You have my word on it."

Caroline whimpered, desperately wishing she could return. She'd only had one visit with Emily. It wasn't fair to leave her so soon. But as much as she wanted to go back to Earth, there would be no reprieve, at least not according to the redheaded woman with the spiked collar. A weakness in a blood vessel of her brain had caused an aneurysm. Although Dr. Perry had rushed her into surgery only minutes after she'd collapsed, she could not be resuscitated. Her body was creaky and worn out, and it was her time to leave the Earth.

Twenty-Seven

"Look at her," Rhianna said, staring at Emily's blank expression on the computer monitor in her cubicle. "She's giving up. Ever since you died, she hasn't said a word to anyone. All she does is sleep, and she's refusing physical therapy."

"I get by with a little help from my friends," Caroline sang into the hands-free mouthpiece. Dr. Mullins had emailed his syllabus to Rhianna, so she and Caroline were familiar with every lesson Skye had learned during her Earth classes.

"We've both been singing nonstop for nearly a week," Rhianna said.

Caroline, who had spent the last week in ND quarters getting oriented, had been given special permission to join Rhianna in her quest to help Emily. Since she'd arrived in Heaven the network of lines in her forehead had smoothed out; the once loose skin at her neck was tight and firm, and her steel-wool hair had darkened to charcoal.

"Sleeping Beauty, it's Caroline. Open those baby blues."

Emily's expression on the monitor remained unchanged, like one of those grim statues in Stonehenge. Caroline flinched and looked away. "I'm not getting through to her. Why can't she hear us?"

"She's surrounded by a wall of discouragement," Rhianna said. "She doesn't think anyone cares about her. The voice of her self-pity is louder than we are. It's drowning us out."

"I care about you," Caroline said, blowing a kiss in the

direction of the computer screen. "Please snap out of this, sugar pie."

"This just isn't working. We're going to have to try something else," Rhianna said. "Emily's counselor is coming in to visit her in a half hour. I have another idea, but it's going to take some teamwork."

Belinda Hobbs clip-clopped her way into Emily's room in her dangerously high heels, leaving a mist of honeysuckle perfume in her wake. She'd come to visit every day since Caroline died.

"Hi there. How you doing today?" Belinda said brightly. She said the same thing each day as if she expected Emily to answer. Her bracelets clinked together as she arranged herself on the chair beside the bed. Her physique was a study in roundness; she looked as if she were smuggling a collection of melons under her snug-fitting suit.

Emily didn't speak or meet her eyes. She'd gone back to staring at the ceiling, hoping that if she stayed still and silent long enough, she could will herself back into her coma.

Keys jingled and a heavy purse was dropped to the ground. "I haven't seen you cry yet, Emily." Paper crinkled. Belinda moved her chair closer to the bed and Emily could smell the cool puff of peppermint on her breath. "Crying might help. Doesn't Caroline deserve a few tears?"

Caroline deserved a swimming pool full of tears, but Emily couldn't cry them for her. She was numb to her own pain; her tear ducts were paralyzed.

"I know you and Caroline were very close, but there are others who care for you. Me, for instance, as well as Dr. Perry, and the hospital staff."

People who are paid to care, Emily thought dully. If there was anyone else in this world who loved her, where was he or she? No one had come to see her—not a solitary soul. What kind of person had she been that no one cared if she lived or died? Even her beloved Caroline had only known her in her coma. Maybe the old woman wouldn't have loved her if she'd known the real Emily.

"I'm here for you, Emily," Belinda said. "We're all rooting for you."

The words were meaningless to Emily. Belinda might as well have been reading a grocery list. *Move along, Dr. Phil,* Emily thought. *You're getting nothing from me.*

Perpetua, Belinda's guardian angel, sat in front of the computer monitor, observing her charge. "Belinda loves to sing, although she's not especially gifted at it."

Rhianna was looking over Perpetua's shoulder. "This isn't *American Idol.* I don't care how well she sings, just so long as she gets through to Emily."

"Unfortunately, Belinda's been depressed for weeks and hasn't felt like singing much," Perpetua said, distractedly patting the severe bun on the back of her hair. "It's been much harder to communicate with her lately. Her dark thoughts are deafening. I can barely get a word in edgewise."

Rhianna's fists curled in frustration. "Don't I know it?"

"I had no idea how loud a person's thoughts can be," Caroline said, gazing sadly at Emily.

"I'll do my best to give Belinda the suggestion," Perpetua said. "I am encouraged that she wanted to help this young woman. It's an excellent sign. Before Emily came along, there were days when she could barely drag herself out of bed."

As Emily drifted off to sleep she heard the first note come out of Belinda's mouth. It sounded like the last honk of a dying mallard. The notes that followed were equally mournful. What was she doing? Why wouldn't she just go away?

"I get by with a little help from my friends," she sang.

It was an old Beatles song. Emily had no choice but to listen to one clunker note after another. The mangled melody was almost unrecognizable, but the words were familiar and for some odd reason, they started to move Emily. Each time she heard the word "friend" it was like a shovel breaking through her defenses and letting in veins of light.

"Stop," Emily said softly after several stanzas.

"What?" Belinda's purse tumbled off her lap. A cell phone and a collection of cosmetics rained down on the floor.

"You're singing," Emily said.

"Was I singing? I guess I didn't realize it. You know how you get a song in your head and it just takes hold? But never mind that. Listen to you, you're finally talking to me."

"You sing even worse than Caroline," Emily said in a near whisper. "And that's quite a feat."

"Oh God, I know...My ex-husband would always change the station when I'd sing along to the radio in the car." She smiled. "I can't believe you're talking...finally! Thank God."

Emily pressed a hand between her breasts. "It was too hard to talk. It hurts here...so badly."

"Of course it does, Emily." Belinda shot up from her chair and stood by her bed. "I heard Caroline was an incredible woman. And she loved you."

"I couldn't even go to her funeral," Emily said. Her chest heaved and shook.

Belinda hovered over her, touching her hair, saying, "I'm sorry. I know she meant a lot to you."

Emily cried for Caroline and Belinda stayed near, holding tissues to her nose and talking softly into her ear. Her ministrations to Emily didn't feel bought and paid for; they felt sincere and empathetic, as if Belinda understood a thing or two about pain.

For the first time since Caroline's death, Emily didn't feel as if she'd been abandoned by the entire world.

Twenty-Eight

I can't understand why you aren't answering my letters. This isn't a prank. There's something urgent I must tell you about your wife.

Wanda signed her name to the letter and stuffed it into an envelope.

How many letters had she written so far? Wanda was beginning to lose count, but she was going to keep churning them out until she got what she was after.

Four months ago, Wanda had sent Ryan Blaine a registered letter discussing her suspicions about Susan. When she didn't immediately hear back from him, she guessed she'd been written off as some kind of nutcase. Who could blame the man? He probably received all sorts of strange mail. And she didn't want to get into the specifics about his wife in case someone else read his letters, maybe even Susan herself. Still, she kept writing, a few notes every month, until two weeks ago she'd started to write Ryan Blaine every day, hoping her persistence would pay off.

This nastiness with Susan Blaine plagued every moment of Wanda's life. She played the recorded answering-machine conversation with Susan several times a day and spent all of her free time scouring newsstands and the internet at the library, looking for any mention of Ryan and his wife.

Any sane person probably would have given up by now, but Wanda had never considered herself close to normal. If what she believed about Susan Blaine were true, it'd be a mortal sin for her not to try to alert Ryan Blaine. She was the only person in the world who knew what his wife had done, and Wanda was partially to blame. How could she live with herself if she didn't bust her tail to expose Susan's secret?

As she sealed the envelope, the phone rang and a curt male voice asked for her by name.

"Speaking," she said.

"This is Gordon Hoyle, calling on the behalf of Ryan Blaine."

Wanda let the letter float to her bedroom rug. "It's about time," she said with a relieved sigh. She sat down on her twin bed. "I thought I'd never hear back. I've written so many letters my hand's about to fall off—"

"Yes, you have," Mr. Hoyle said, his voice an angry staccato. "And I'm calling to ask you to stop. You're not the only woman writing letters condemning Ms. Blaine, but you've certainly been the most persistent."

"Other people have been writing Ryan Blaine about his wife? I don't get you."

"Letters from heartbroken women, just like yourself, who are upset that Mr. Blaine is married."

"Heartbroken?" She knew her voice sounded screechy, but she couldn't help it. "You don't understand. I'm seventy-one years old. I'm not—"

"I recognize obsessive behavior when I see it," Mr. Hoyle interrupted. "You've been classified as a security risk by my office."

"I'm not a security risk, I tell you. I'm just trying to help. This is a very serious—" She paused, weariness settling heavily on her shoulders. "Has Ryan Blaine even read my letters?"

"Look, lady, I'm trying to do you a favor. Stop writing letters and this will go no further. But if you continue—"

"He needs to read my letters!" Wanda shouted. "Better yet, put him on the line. Is he there? It will only take a minute of his time. I have proof of—"

Mr. Hoyle wasn't listening. He continued to drone on as if reading from a script. It was exasperating. "If you continue, legal actions will have to be taken. I'm sure neither of us wants that."

"Let me speak with Ryan Blaine! It's urgent. I'm not some nut ball, I tell ya. I've been on the six o'clock news. In my hometown I'm known as the Hot-dog Hag. Won't somebody listen to me?"

Twenty-Nine

Several days after she'd squeezed out her very first tears over Caroline, Emily was moved to a private rehabilitation hospital paid for by an anonymous donor who'd read about her plight. Word had leaked out to several newspapers about her miraculous awakening, but on the same day her story became known, a commercial jet went down in the Allegheny Mountains, killing all two hundred and fifty passengers on board. The crash dominated the media for days, and Emily's news was buried in the back pages.

No one bothered to revive the story, likely because of Emily's former station in life. If she'd been a teacher or a nurse, surrounded by loving family members, her miraculous recovery would have been a more popular human interest story. But because of her unsavory past, Emily didn't make a very heartwarming subject.

Belinda eventually told her about the circumstances that had led to her yearlong stay in Magnolia Manor. How she'd been assaulted in a deserted alley. How she'd been nude and left for dead. How it was believed that she'd been a homeless crack user and had no family members, at least none that had come forward during the year she'd been in her vegetative state.

"We don't even know your last name, Emily," Belinda said, twisting her small pale hands on her lap as she sat beside Emily's bed. "But the doctors are pretty sure your memories will gradually return. At least most of them. Thank God, you probably won't remember the assault itself."

Emily should have been devastated upon hearing the details of her past life, but for some reason she was unmoved. Belinda could have been reciting the plot points of a Lifetime movie; she felt no sense of identification or shame when it came to the actions of the pre-coma Emily. Maybe, when her memories started to filter back, regret and self-loathing would set in, but for now she was indifferent. It was as if she were lugging around a bag of someone else's dirty laundry. The only thing she cared about was regaining her independence, which meant learning how to walk again.

At the rehabilitation hospital Emily threw herself into a regimen of physical therapy so grueling it would make an Olympic athlete weep. Because her muscles had been inactive for so long, her orthopedist was doubtful she'd ever be able to walk again. But Emily ignored his pessimistic predictions and labored each day until sweat beaded on every surface of her body and she was limp from exhaustion. She endured several hours of daily exercises with elastic bands to increase her range of motion, choking back tears and persevering even when the pain was so severe she felt she might black out.

After only a few weeks of being strapped onto a tilt table, a padded device with a footboard intended to strengthen her emaciated muscles, she astounded the medical staff by forcing her withered chicken legs into a standing position.

After the tilt table, she graduated to the parallel bars and was determined to take her first step. Her doctors thought the swift recovery of her bones and muscles bordered on the miraculous. Emily credited Caroline's nightly massages. The love had flowed from the old woman's fingers to Emily's limbs, keeping them from complete atrophy.

Throughout her recovery, Belinda was there for her, spending every minute of her free time at Emily's bedside.

"Don't you have a life?" Emily teased when Belinda bustled into the hospital room loaded down with cartons from the Chinese restaurant.

"What I *have* is tofu and broccoli, no MSG," said Belinda, who always changed the subject when Emily touched on personal matters. She knew something was troubling her counselor. Whenever she thought Emily was sleeping, Belinda listened to music on her iPhone, crying silent tears. Now and then, Emily heard traces of the music and was surprised by how jarring and dissonant it was. It wasn't the kind of music she would have expected Belinda to enjoy.

"I don't why anyone in their right mind would eat tofu," Belinda teased. "It looks like brown Jell-O."

"Mmmm," Emily said as Belinda spooned a few tablespoons of tofu and broccoli out onto a plate and placed it on her tray. "Smells good. I think I may have been on a macrobiotic diet at some point in my life."

"Macrobiotic?" Belinda said. The counselor was a devoted carnivore and was at that moment tucking into some barbecued spare ribs and shrimp toast. "What's that?"

"Mostly whole grains and sea vegetables. I have memories of eating lots of bowls of miso soup. Wouldn't that be novel? A crack whore on a macrobiotic diet."

Belinda flinched as she looked up from her meal. "Hush your mouth."

"I'm sorry, crack ho."

"Emily!"

"It's hard for me to imagine doing anything so unhealthy. I really hate the smell of smoke. One of the orderlies snuck a cigarette and came into my room smelling to high heaven." Emily pinched a piece of tofu with her chopstick and popped it in her mouth, chewing thoughtfully. "Maybe I smoked organic crack."

"It's my guess that you'd been doing drugs for only a short while," Belinda said, dabbing at her mouth with a napkin. Emily could tell Belinda was uncomfortable discussing her checkered past. "I imagine you had a whole different kind of life before it took a wrong turn."

"I'm pretty sure I worked with animals at one time," Emily said. "I have all these memories of handling dogs and cats."

"That's terrific," Belinda said, clapping her hands. She

continually gushed over Emily's accomplishments like a young mother swooning over her preschooler's refrigerator art. "Just give it some time, and most everything will come back to you."

Emily wasn't in a big rush to retrieve her memories. She feared they'd distract her from her path to wellness. Still, snatches of her past kept returning to her: a first Communion, a Valentine's Day party, maneuvering a small sailboat as the wind whistled in her ears. None of her recollections, however, provided any concrete clues to her identity.

Her strength was returning more quickly than her memories. After four months of aggressive therapy, she took her first tentative step using a walker. A few days later, Belinda picked her up from the hospital to celebrate.

"It's girls' day out," she said with a playful smile. "And we won't be coming back until the cows come home."

Her friend wore a pair of blue jeans—Emily had never seen her in slacks before—and a red scoop-neck top. The outfit accentuated all her round curves, reminding Emily of a vine-ripe tomato.

Belinda whisked Emily off to a manicurist, and before she knew it, all twenty of her nails were buffed, filed, and polished with a coat of bright red called "Too Darn Hot." Afterward, the two women lunched at a small austere Japanese restaurant. Emily took slow, mincing steps with her walker, but Belinda was infinitely patient.

Once they were seated and served, Belinda leaned across the blond wood table to reach for the ceramic container of soy sauce. Emily noticed her fingernails were painted a sparkly blue color, an odd choice for a woman who typically dressed in conservative tailored suits.

"Did you also get a manicure this week?" Emily asked, pointing at Belinda's hand.

"I meant to take this off," Belinda said, cutting her eyes to her plate. She was suddenly very busy mixing soy sauce with stiff dabs of wasabi.

"It's an interesting color choice. Youthful."

"Yes, I guess it is," Belinda said quickly. "You know, they serve green-tea ice cream here. It sounds revolting, but it's actually quite good."

Clearly the nail polish was a sore subject. "Sorry. I didn't mean to say something I shouldn't have."

Belinda didn't reply. Instead she chased a sliver of ginger around her plate.

Later, after they'd left the restaurant and were on the expressway driving to the mall, Belinda abruptly turned to Emily.

"I didn't mean to be so evasive when you asked about my nail polish. I wear it because it reminds me of someone. I hope you don't mind, but I can't talk about it just yet. The pain's too fresh."

"I'm sorry," Emily said. "I shouldn't have said anything."

"It's been a rough few months for me," Belinda said, pulling down the rearview mirror to check her lipstick. "You're the first client I've had since my...loss. I'd intended to take a lot more time off, or even quit counseling altogether. But when I heard about you from some of my coworkers at the hospital, I asked to be assigned to your case. I'd developed a really dark view of the world, and then you came along...a bona fide miracle."

Emily nodded. There were some days her awakening felt more like a curse than a miracle, but she was glad she'd indirectly helped lift Belinda out of her doldrums.

"I also have a confession to make. I'm undergoing grief counseling with the pastor of a nondenominational church in town." She laughed softly. "Probably sounds like the blind leading the blind."

"No. Asking for outside help when you're a counselor yourself seems like a brave thing to do."

"I had to see someone. I was drinking a bottle of white wine every night, sleeping twelve hours at a stretch—anything to numb the pain. I had to snap out of it for the sake of my son."

"I didn't know you had a child."

"An eight-year-old. You'll meet him one day. No husband though. We're divorced."

"So what kind of advice does your pastor give you?"

"Right now, he's teaching me to put my life in the hands of an HP," Belinda said, switching on the windshield wipers. A desultory drizzle had begun. "Surrender, he keeps saying to me."

"HP?"

"Higher power. God, I suppose. Sometimes it's hard for me to believe there's anyone up there, much less someone keeping tabs on what Belinda Hobbs is up to on a daily basis."

After Caroline had died, Emily, too, had been doubtful of God's existence, but now she just wasn't sure. She figured she hadn't been very religious before the coma. How many prostitutes/druggies, after all, were devout churchgoers?

"Surrendering to an invisible HP seemed to me about as smart as handing over the keys of a Rolls-Royce to a tipsy valet. But my pastor asked me to suspend disbelief. He told me to start by trusting my HP with something simple. Something I didn't care too much about. Like parking spaces."

"Parking spaces?"

"Yup," Belinda said. "So a week ago I told my HP, get me some kick-butt parking spots, and maybe then I'll let you handle the more important stuff in my life."

In the crowded lot, she turned in to a space that was only steps away from the entrance. "You want to know the crazy thing?" She rested her arms on the steering wheel and shrugged. "I haven't had a lousy parking spot since."

"Parking spots?" Emily said in an amused voice. "You'd think a higher power would have better things to do, like maybe tackling the problems in Syria for starters."

"Not according to my pastor. 'No job too small for the HP' is what he always says."

Two days later Belinda left town for a training seminar, and for the first time since she'd arrived at the rehabilitation hospital, Emily was left to her own devices. She decided to take a long stroll around the grounds of the hospital with her walker. Maybe if she really pushed herself, she would surprise Belinda by being able to walk on her own when she got back. Fall was breezing into Birmingham, and the leaves chased one another across the yellowing grass. Emily made jerky progress along the sidewalks surrounding the hospital. Several joggers and dog walkers were also out, enjoying the celebratory flavor of the crisp air.

Emily spied a nest in a low-hanging branch of a dogwood tree and left the sidewalk to investigate its contents. Big mistake. The grass was slick from the sprinkler system, and she took a misstep with the walker and slipped and fell, a sharp pain slicing through her right leg.

She was spotted by a groundsman who was trimming crepe myrtle trees for the coming winter. He summoned staff members to carry her back to her room. Her orthopedist sent her to X-ray, and after he saw the results, he delivered some truly discouraging news. Her tibia was fractured, and the break required the surgical insertion of a titanium nail and screws.

Emily felt like throwing her water pitcher against the ugly yellow-green wall of her hospital room. Every ounce of her energy had been focused on learning how to walk unaided so she could eventually be discharged from the hospital. Belinda had offered her a room in her home until she was ready to be on her own. She'd been itching to begin a new life—perhaps in a vet's office—but now all plans would be delayed.

It was noon, two days after her spill, and Emily was recovering from the agonizing surgery and nursing a nasty cold. As usual, she was listening to Caroline's clock radio, which Mona had kindly brought her as a memento. The only time she turned it off was when Belinda came by for her visits, and she never, ever missed the *Minerva* show.

The deejay on the oldies lunch hour kept saying, "What a bee-you-tifil day," and outside her window she had a view of a row of Bradford pear trees blazing with golden foliage. The hospital staff seemed intoxicated by the tart autumn temperatures, their cheeks as ruddy Gala apples, their laughs and smiles more frequent than usual. Emily couldn't stand being cooped up in her room. She was so sick of being bedridden. She was also desperate for a conversation with Belinda, but her friend was at a team-building retreat in the wilderness, swinging from ropes and scaling walls. She'd be out of touch for at least a week.

Emily blew her nose. Her bed sheets were a field of balled-up tissues, and her pajamas, which had been changed just this morning, already had a grubby feel as if she'd perspired in them for days.

She clicked through a parade of evangelists and infomercials on television and finally turned it off. For the first time since Belinda had come into her life, she felt the acute ache of loneliness.

The next day Emily's cold settled into her chest, and her mood shriveled to black. Her melancholy was fast and unexpected, sinking into her bones and settling over her like a blanket of soot. Not even the thought of Belinda cheered her.

She'd been socked in by the same sort of despair just after Caroline's death. Was she the kind of person who was susceptible to dark moods? Maybe in the past she'd used drugs and sex to outrun her demons. Well, she wasn't outrunning them now. She was so disheartened, she'd invited depression to her table and was feeding it heaping helpings of self-pity.

Every once in a while she'd hear a wee faint voice in her mind saying, "You giving up after you've come this far?"

You betcha, she'd answer. *Life's a bitch and then you die.* Her chest was so congested she was tired of breathing.

"It's Beatlemania weekend, and we're taking you way back to 1967," said the disc jockey through a flurry of interference.

Where's an HP when you need one? she thought, remembering her earlier conversation with Belinda.

Could there really be someone up there looking after her? Where was He, after all, when she'd lapsed into her coma in the first place? Maybe He was just too busy finding parking spots for people.

"Help!" the Beatles sang in urgent voices. The volume on the radio seemed to get louder. "I need somebody."

Emily's mouth opened to call out for the nurse, but her words were lost in a gurgle of fluids. Was she drowning in her own mucus? Maybe she was getting pneumonia. If she died, who would miss her? Belinda? Maybe a couple of the nurses? But after a few months they'd forget she ever existed.

"No job too small," Belinda's words repeated in her mind.

Okay, Emily thought, *I'll go ahead and ask for help.* She'd gotten too weak to speak, so she shaped the words in her mind.

Help me. Please. Whoever is out there. She waited. Her lungs were expanding in her chest cavity like wet sponges, but other than that, nothing happened. What had she expected? Bluebirds nipping at the corners of her sheets? Rainbows spilling in through the windows?

Disappointment cut through her like a knife. Obviously she'd wanted to believe but had refused to admit it, even to herself. Where was her so-called help? She'd asked for it. She needed it.

Suddenly her chest tightened and a cough jettisoned from her lungs. Emily jerked her head up from the pillow.

"So you're up. I just got here," Belinda said, sitting beside her bed. She laid a cool hand on Emily's cheek. "Dang. You're burning up. I better call the nurse in."

"Belinda," she croaked. "How did you—" Emily was too spent to finish the sentence.

"I left the training session early. I just had this strong feeling you needed me. What in the world happened to your leg?"

Emily's cold had edged dangerously close to pneumonia, and she spent the next few days coughing up thick globs of phlegm and soiling her bed sheets with sweat. She still struggled with depression, but it was like a gray cat she could shoo away if she tried.

Belinda visited daily, bringing a bounty of goodies like white chocolate Lindor truffles, glossy fashion magazines, and strawberry smoothies, which Emily sipped through a bendable straw.

She hadn't forgotten her feverish half-awake plea to the Heavens. Nor was she sure what to make of Belinda's sudden appearance. Was it an answered prayer, or just dumb luck? Over the next few days she conducted a series of tests. She'd silently ask for the nurse to find a good vein on the first try or request an undisturbed night's sleep. So far, if there was indeed someone watching over her, he or she was doing a decent job.

Thirty

"Who's designing Susan's wedding gown?" demanded a bone-thin woman in the second row of the auditorium, her elbow thrust out from her hip in a defiant stance.

Ryan's neck prickled with annoyance at her query, but he refused to let it show on his face. He'd just finished delivering a speech to a local Rotary Club when he opened the floor for questions. Obviously a reporter had crashed the gathering. There had just been a story in *People* entitled "Ryan and Susan to Renew Vows in Wedding of the Year."

"What does that have to do with the recent legislative changes in Georgia?" he said with a good-natured smile, referring to the topic of his speech.

"Rumors say it's Christian Dior," said the woman. Her lipstick was a bright shade of crimson.

"Anything else?" Ryan gave the reporter a warning glance. "On the issues I've raised today?"

He addressed a handful of questions, which thankfully didn't involve Susan or his upcoming nuptials, and then he thanked his audience and stepped down from the podium.

"Let's hustle you through the back exit, sir," said Gordon Hoyle, the security person he'd been forced to hire. "There's a media mob out front."

Ryan sighed and picked up his briefcase. Ever since Susan's appearance on *Talk to Me*, the press had trailed the two of them like a pack of hyenas. It was worse than when he lived in New York. The paparazzi had gotten far bolder over the years, shoving cameras inches from his face, booing him when he refused to give them the shots they craved.

Initially he'd been furious with Susan. Why would she want to jeopardize their hard-won privacy by appearing on national television?

Darcy, on the other hand, had sided with Susan. She reminded him how he used to bask in the media attention during his bachelor days.

"Do you expect Susan to be so different from you?" Darcy had said. "She's not a saint, you know."

His sister's comments humbled him. It was unfair to expect more from Susan than he had from himself. The pre-accident Susan would likely have shunned a *Talk to Me* appearance, but he was slowly learning to quit making those kinds of comparisons. Every week he had an hour-long session with his counselor, Jennifer Carr, and she was helping him to accept Susan as she was. He'd put all his and Susan's pre-accident memorabilia into a box and stored them in the attic, and he'd stopped calling Minerva.

Gordon gestured it was time to leave, and he and Ryan ducked behind the stage and made their way through a series of hallways until they reached a metal exit door.

"Let me make sure this area is secure," Gordon said. The security guard was a densely muscled bald man with a pulsing blue vein on the side of his skull. He cracked open the door and peered outside for a few moments, and then motioned for Ryan to follow as he walked across a small asphalt loading area.

"I told your driver to meet us here," Gordon said. Just as his Lincoln Town Car pulled up, an old woman wearing hot pants and white vinyl boots sprang out from behind the Dempsey Dumpster.

"Mr. Blaine, I need to speak with you."

"Stay back, ma'am," Gordon said, blocking her path with his broad form. "Get in the car, sir," he ordered Ryan. "I'll handle this."

"Please, Mr. Blaine," the woman pleaded, frantically trying to get past Gordon. "I've written. I've tried to call. I even went to your house."

So this was the woman he'd been warned about. Last week she was caught hiding among the hedges near his front door and was charged with trespassing. A judge issued a restraining order against her, but apparently she'd chosen to ignore it.

"It's about Susan," the woman continued as Gordon grasped her slight shoulders. Ryan's driver was standing by the passenger door, waiting for Ryan to get in the car so he could shut it behind him.

"She's not who you think she is," the woman said. "Please, Mr. Blaine. You gotta be able to sense it. It isn't just your imagination. It's real!"

Despite her strange getup, the woman had a sharp look of intelligence in her gray eyes. *Would it hurt to hear what she had to say?*

"Wait," he said to the driver. "Gordon, let the lady talk."

Thirty-One

"You don't look like a Mortimer," Belinda said.

Mortimer Stiles, the anonymous donor who'd been paying Emily's bills for the last several months, had stopped by the rehabilitation hospital for a surprise visit after hearing about her recent leg surgery.

"What *does* a Mortimer look like?" Mr. Stiles asked with a slight French accent.

"I don't know," Belinda said, cheeks flaring pink. "Bald, pince-nez, an ascot?"

Mortimer Stiles had a full head of chestnut-colored hair, bushy dark eyebrows showcasing a pair of vibrant green eyes, and broad shoulders that tested the limits of his gray wool pullover. He reminded Emily of Michael Landon during the *Bonanza* years.

"Sorry to disappoint," Mr. Stiles said.

"Oh, you're not a disappointment," Belinda said. "Not at all. I mean...We're so glad you're here."

"Emily, when I was told about your awakening, I was so deeply affected I wanted to do something for you," Mortimer said.

"That's very kind of you," Emily said.

"Not at all. You don't know it, but you've done me a great favor." He paused, rubbing the knuckles of his left hand. Emily noticed the absence of a wedding ring. "Your story made me feel hope again after a long period of not being able to feel anything."

"Really?" Belinda said, studying him with greater interest.

"Yes," he said, meeting her gaze. A shadow crossed his face as he continued in a faltering voice. "I experienced a terrible loss recently. My son John was in a water-skiing accident last year and he lapsed into a coma for over three months. Unlike Emily, he never came out of it. He was only fifteen when he died."

Belinda, who was already quite fair, turned as pale as bread dough.

"I'm so sorry, Mr. Stiles," Emily said.

"Call me Mortimer. Please," he replied.

Emily glanced at Belinda, who hadn't said a word and seemed to be mulling something over.

"I didn't want to live anymore," Mortimer continued. "I used to be such a positive person, but John's death changed my view of the world. I didn't understand the point of existing in a place that allows children to die. But..." He smiled down at Emily. "When I heard about you, Emily, something inside of me shifted. For the first time in weeks, I allowed myself to believe in—"

"Hope," Belinda said softly.

"Yes, exactly," Mortimer said with a nod. "I didn't mean to go on about my own losses. I just wanted you to know why I feel so—"

"I know exactly how you feel," Belinda said. She looked startled by her sudden announcement, as if she hadn't meant to speak so boldly, and her voice grew more hesitant. "What I mean is...I was also drawn to Emily...for a similar reason."

Both Emily and Mortimer were silent and alert, waiting for her to continue.

"I had a loss as well. My child." Belinda shrank into her chair. "She was just...thirteen." Belinda leveled her gaze at Emily. "It's her music I've been listening to and her nail polish I've been wearing, but I've never been able to say the words before. My little girl, my sweet daughter...Chelsea...she..." Her whole body shook as if disgorging something deep from inside. "She died."

"Belinda," Emily said, fervently wishing she could jump out of the hospital bed and come to her friend's comfort. Darn her useless legs. She glanced at Mortimer, who read the helplessness in her eyes.

"Chelsea. That's a beautiful name," he said softly, rising from his chair. Then he gently took Belinda in his arms and held her. Rather than resisting him, Belinda melted against his chest, where she cried softly.

After a few moments, Belinda pulled away from Mortimer somewhat reluctantly. "I'm sorry. I don't know why I told you about my daughter. We don't even know each other."

"You confided in me because you knew I'd understand," Mortimer said.

"Thank you," she said, and her glance drifted to Emily. "I'm so sorry, Emily. I didn't mean to cause a scene. You're convalescing; you don't need—"

"Yes, I do," Emily quickly replied, her eyes filling with tears for her friend's heartbreak. The loss of a child. Life's worst tragedy. Yet Belinda had still managed to give Emily so much comfort. What a precious gift she had in her friend. "Thank you so much for telling me about Chelsea. And now would you please come over here so I can hug you too?"

Belinda hurried to Emily's bedside, and the two women rocked back and forth in an embrace. "I want to know everything about your little girl," Emily whispered to her friend. "Whenever you're ready to talk about her."

Belinda nodded and hugged Emily even closer. "Would you like to see a picture?"

"I'd love to."

She picked up her purse and produced her wallet. "This is her seventh-grade picture."

Emily glanced down at the smiling blonde. "Oh my gosh. Is this your daughter?" Emily smiled as an extremely vivid image of a young girl wearing big tennis shoes and sparkly blue nail polish flashed in her mind. "Snap! I bet she'd get a kick out of you wearing her nail polish."

Belinda shot Emily a stunned look. "You just said 'snap.' You've never said that before. What made you say it?"

"I don't know," Emily said. She looked again at the photo but didn't get any more feelings of déjà vu. "I guess I must have heard the expression somewhere before."

"Chelsea used to always say 'snap,'" Belinda said, shaking her head. "I got the oddest feeling when you said it. It was almost as if Chelsea had popped in for a split second just to say hello."

Mortimer rose from his chair. "I should be leaving. I'll let the two of you—"

"Mortimer, I can't tell you how much I appreciate what you've done for me," Emily said to him.

"It was my pleasure." He picked up his satchel and withdrew a bulky manila envelope. "I almost forgot. Before I leave, there's something I want you to have. To give you a start on your new life."

Emily took the envelope and pulled apart the brass clasp. She gasped. The envelope was stuffed with hundred-dollar bills.

"There's twenty thousand dollars in there," he said. "I'd have written you a check, but I understand you still don't remember your last name."

Emily nodded, still speechless over the contents of the envelope.

"I've spoken with the nurse, and she says she'll store it in the hospital's safe until you're discharged," Mortimer said.

"Mortimer," Belinda said, grazing her hand on his forearm. The effect of her touch immediately registered in Mortimer's eyes; they glowed even greener. "That's so generous. Isn't that generous, Emily?"

"Yes," Emily said in a faint voice. All the excitement of the afternoon had exhausted her. "Thank you so much."

Belinda and Mortimer appeared to be contained in their own private bubble and she didn't think either of them had heard her.

As she watched the two of them together, an unfamiliar longing stirred inside her.

Had there ever been someone in her life who could cut through all her barriers with a simple touch or a few words? And if so, where was he now?

Thirty-Two

Ryan tried to keep his voice calm, a superhuman effort after what he'd just learned. "Susan," he called out, the tread of his feet as loud as shotgun reports on the tiled flooring of his foyer.

In his hand, he clutched the envelope that contained the tape from Wanda's answering machine. He kept squeezing it in an effort to keep his hands under control. How could she possibly explain herself?

He prowled through the hall, glancing into each room, but the house had an empty feel. Likely she was keeping one of her weekly beauty appointments. There were so many since her television appearance—manicures, massages, waxings. Last week he'd paid a bill from an esthetician. He didn't even know what an esthetician did.

Ryan entered her dressing room. Susan wasn't in her usual spot, sitting on a padded chair in front of her vanity, rubbing into her pores some high-priced cream made from a baby's foreskin. He scanned the top of her vanity, looking for her engagement calendar, when his hand knocked against her dental mold case. Recently she'd started to bleach her teeth to such a blinding whiteness he felt like shading his eyes every time she smiled.

He turned to leave the dressing room, but after a spark of inspiration, instead seized the case that held the mold and pocketed it. Then he trotted out to the garage, flung open the door of his Mercedes, and called his dentist on his cell phone.

"Hi, Lucy, this is Ryan Blaine," he said to the receptionist as he dug in his trouser pockets for his car keys. "I have an emergency on my hands. Could you look and see if you still have some of Susan's old records?"

As he waited for her to check, he was so distracted he backed the car out of the garage and almost broadsided a trash can.

"You have them? Good. I'm on my way. And will you tell Bob I'm coming? I'll need five minutes of his time."

When Susan first moved to Atlanta, she'd gone to Ryan's dentist, Dr. Robert Stalling. Dr. Stalling was an old buddy and had been the family dentist since Ryan lost his first baby teeth. After her accident, Susan never returned to Dr. Stalling. Instead she'd started seeing a cosmetic dentist in Buckhead. Ryan hadn't thought much of it at the time, but in light of what he now knew, her decision to find a new dentist seemed far from innocent.

After a few minutes, he arrived at the dental office and charged into the reception area.

"Hi, Lucy," he said to the pale redhead behind the desk. "Did you speak with Bob? I just need a few—"

"Hello, Ryan. This is a treat." Dr. Stalling ambled into the waiting room. He was a small dapper man with round oversized spectacles. "Of course I can spare a few minutes for one of my best—" He glanced at Ryan's face and his brow furrowed. "Are you all right? You look like you're about to lose your lunch. Let's go into my office," he said, crossing to Ryan and putting a guiding hand on his shoulder. "I've got the records you wanted on my desk."

Ryan dropped into a leather wing chair and placed the box with the mold on the dentist's desk.

"This is a mold of Susan's teeth. Will you take a look at it? See how it compares to her previous records? I realize these things are usually confidential, but I still have medical power of attorney over Susan."

Dr. Stalling wore a quizzical expression, but he did as Ryan asked, picking up the mold and examining it. Then he looked inside a file folder on his desk. He squinted, and the vertical groove between his eyes deepened.

"I'm getting a little slower in my old age, Ryan. Who did you say this mold belonged to?"

"It's Susan's. Her new dentist cast it."

Dr. Stalling glanced down at the mold, twisting it in his hand. "Then there must have been some kind of mix-up. This can't possibly be Susan's."

"Are you sure?"

"Absolutely. Teeth marks are as individual as fingerprints."

"Even with identical twins?"

"Yes. They're completely different."

The impact of Bob's words made Ryan so woozy he grabbed the arms of the chair to keep from passing out. There was no denying the truth. With the dental mold and the tape...Ryan's hand automatically went to his pocket. The envelope containing the tape was missing. He must have left it on Susan's vanity when he picked up the mold.

Ryan bolted up from his chair so fast a stitch pierced his side. "Thanks so much for your help, Bob," he said, holding his abdomen. "Sorry to be in such a rush, but I need to get going."

Dr. Stalling shook his head. "I can't imagine a dentist making this sort of error. Are you sure everything is okay? Why don't you sit for a while?"

"I need to get home immediately. I'll call you later and explain everything."

Susan walked up the flagstone pathway leading to her front door, fluffing her newly streaked hair. She'd gone to Elton Sutherland, Atlanta's top stylist, and he and his staff had whisked her off to a private area of the salon and kept her happy with cucumber sandwiches and glasses of Chardonnay. Best of all, when it came time to pay, Elton refused his $250 fee.

"Having you as a client is honor enough," he'd said, hoping no doubt she'd drop his name in the right circles.

She stood unsteadily on the threshold of her doorway (Jimmy

Choos were a pain to walk in, especially when she had a buzz) and waved goodbye to her driver, Roland, as he pulled away. Then she headed into her dressing room to check out her hair under the recently installed pink light bulbs. She knew she spent too much time in front of the mirror, but who cared? She was looking fabulous so she might as well enjoy it. She'd gone to a makeup artist who had shown her all kinds of ways to cover up the scars on her face and taught her how to apply her makeup like a pro. Now if she could only talk Ryan into paying for a boob job. Her breasts were itsy-bitsy—like two halved lemons clinging to her chest.

Her dressing-room lights were on; she must have forgotten to turn them off before she left. On her vanity there was a long white business envelope. She was pleased to see her name printed on the front, and she eagerly tore it open. The envelope contained an undersized cassette tape, but there was no note or any clue as to where it came from.

Looks like an answering-machine tape, Susan thought. Maybe it was a sweet-nothing message from Ryan. Lately he'd been so anxious to please her. This morning he'd prepared a tray with coffee, croissants, and a vase with a single red rose and brought it into the bedroom.

He should treat me nice, she thought with a thrust of her chin. Finally she was getting to live the life she deserved.

"Let's see what we got here," she mused, carrying the tape into the bedroom so she could listen to it on the answering machine. Her machine blinked with several messages. Not surprising. She was such a popular girl these days.

She pressed the button to listen to the first message and heard an unfamiliar female voice on the line.

"Hello, Mr. Blaine. This is Lucy from Dr. Stalling's office. I don't know if you realized it, but you were in such a hurry you left the mold for your wife's teeth here. Please give our office a call when you get in. Doc Bob is really concerned about you."

Her teeth mold? Surely this Lucy person had to be mixed up. Her mold was on her vanity, right where she left it this morning.

Wasn't it? Susan returned to her dressing room, but the familiar blue case was nowhere in sight. *Why would Ryan take her dental mold to Dr. Stalling's office?*

Had something happened in the last few hours to make Ryan suspicious of her? She glanced at the tape she still held in her hand.

Could the tape have anything to do with it? There was only one way to find out.

Ryan's Mercedes was just one car in an endless string stuck on 1-285. A traffic copter circled and sputtered overhead, and he'd inched past the same paneled station wagon at least ten times.

A gap-toothed boy in the backseat squashed his lips against the car window. To his left, a woman had her sunroof open and held a square of silver reflective board beneath her chin, trying to catch some rays.

"A list of pile ups includes 1-75 west outside of Morrow, and 1-285 east, which is backed up for over ten miles," said the radio announcer. "Expect delays of nearly an hour."

Ryan snapped the radio off so hard he nearly yanked out the button. He was so pumped up with adrenaline he felt like abandoning his car and sprinting all the way home.

"Please don't let her find it," he whispered. What an idiot. He'd left it in the worst possible place in the house. Lately, Susan spent hours in her dressing area, primping and preening in front of the mirror. If she spotted the envelope, she'd certainly play the tape, which would be disastrous. He needed time to calm down, to decide how to handle the situation and whether or not he should get the police involved.

His mind returned once again to his conversation with the woman who'd accosted him earlier. When he invited his "stalker" into his car, relief had flooded her weathered face.

"I've been living with this information for way too long," she said. "It's been clawing at my insides. I can't sleep or eat."

Gordon had sat beside her, vigilant of any abrupt moves as she began her story. "Have you ever had the feeling that your wife was someone else entirely?" she said. "That she was a complete stranger?"

"Mr. Blaine," Gordon said. "I think this has gone far enough. It's not a good idea to encourage—"

"No, Gordon," Ryan said firmly. "I want to hear what she has to say. In private, please."

"But, Mr. Blaine—"

"It'll be okay."

After the security guard and driver left the car, the woman's eyes, vivid with blue shadow, locked with Ryan's.

"My name is Wanda, and I have a hot-dog cart in Birmingham, Alabama. In order for you to understand what I'm about to say, I have to tell you about a homeless gal I once met named Emily."

She described how she'd struck up a friendship with Emily, and remarked on her resemblance to the guest animal behaviorist on Animal Planet.

"I didn't give our conversation a second thought until I saw your wife on *Talk to Me*," she continued.

Wanda recounted her surprise upon hearing Susan's lisp and her love for Johnny Cash. To her, it was obvious that Susan and the street woman were twin sisters, but she didn't know if Susan knew Emily existed.

"Curiosity was killing me, so I wrote Susan a letter, and she called me a few months ago. I accidentally taped the call. It tells the tale much better than I can," Wanda said.

She'd copied the tape to a standard-sized cassette. She gave the copy and the original to Ryan, who leaned over the backseat and slid it into the player up front.

His shock mounted as he listened to Susan speak of an identical twin sister whom she had visited and who'd died of a heart attack after smoking crack cocaine.

"When I saw her I was amazed at how much we resembled each other," Susan's voice said on the tape. "Of course, Emily looked terribly run-down. As you said, she'd been living on the streets. Once I spoke with her it was clear she was my twin sister. We'd both been adopted; we both had lisps..."

After the tape finished playing, Ryan leaned his head back against the seat, his thoughts swirling as he tried to make sense of what he'd just heard. It was as if he'd been given the sharp, jagged pieces of a glass puzzle. There were so many things wrong with their conversation. Susan had *never* lisped before her accident. Nor was she a Johnny Cash fan. Her obsession with the country singer also came after her collision. And the idea that she met her twin sister and had kept it from him was incredible. Ryan took slow deep breaths, because he was on the verge of hyperventilating.

"I knew something was fishy," Wanda said. "And it took me a listen or two to figure it out. On the tape, you hear Susan call me Mrs. Hart."

"I don't understand," Ryan said in a weak voice.

"It's not my name anymore," Wanda said. "A little over a year ago, I was married, but the bum cheated on me and I kicked him to the curb after only six weeks. When I met Emily, she was one of the few people who knew me as Mrs. Hart. I used to joke with her, saying, 'My husband's name is Hart and he stole my mine.' A little while afterward, I went back to my maiden name and never used the surname Hart again. The letter I wrote Susan was signed Wanda Myers. Susan slipped up on the phone and called me Mrs. Hart. That's when I knew I had to speak with you."

Ryan pressed his cheek against the cool window of the car as his stomach lurched. "Are you saying you think this street person is posing as Susan?" he asked in a ragged whisper.

"Looks that way to me."

"Then where, for God's sakes, is the real Susan?"

Wanda nervously pulled on the loose skin of her neck.

"I'm real sorry, Mr. Blaine, but I'm afraid she might be dead."

The words Susan had spoken on the tape echoed in Ryan's ears. "She's dead and it's all my fault."

Could it be true? He'd kissed this woman's lips, sat at her bedside for hours, made love to her, married her. Had she murdered Susan? There didn't seem to be any doubt. He stumbled out of the car and retched strings of saliva beside the back tire.

Now, nearly two hours later, Ryan looked at the hundreds of idling cars stretching in front of him and leaned on the horn, even though he knew it would do no good. He had to retrieve the tape before that impostor, whoever she was, got her hands on it. How could he have been so stupid as to leave the original on the vanity?

Thirty-Three

Susan tossed clothes into an overnight bag, her heart beating as fiercely as if she'd just sucked on a crack pipe. So it was that nosy Hot-dog Hag who'd somehow figured her out. She must have gotten in touch with Ryan and spilled her guts. It had been a mistake to call the crazy old woman, but what choice did she have? Wanda had figured out the whole twin-sister thing, and Susan needed to know what she'd planned to do with that information.

The question was, how much did Ryan know? Too much, she was sure, particularly if he'd gotten Dr. Stalling to check out her dental mold. It was all he needed to prove she wasn't Susan, and when he found out what really happened to his precious girlfriend, she'd be facing a life in prison or the death penalty. She had no choice but to haul butt out of Atlanta and disappear. Not that it would be easy. Her face was smiling out from the cover of every mainstream magazine from *Redbook* to *People*. How was she supposed to hide when almost everyone knew who she was?

She snatched a set of car keys from the hook in the kitchen and dashed to the garage, her bag banging against her thigh. After her accident, she'd sworn she'd never drive again, but she wasn't going to get very far on foot.

Shoot! Ryan had taken the Mercedes, leaving only his Porsche. How was she going to drive a car with a stick shift when she could barely handle an automatic? No time to think about that. She opened the trunk, tossed her bag inside, and jammed the keys into the ignition. The car stalled and rocked, but she managed to jerk the Porsche out of the garage. If she could just get the car on the highway, she wouldn't have to change gears very much.

As she turned out of her drive in front of the house, Ryan's Mercedes rounded the corner. He came to an abrupt halt when he spotted her behind the wheel of his Porsche.

She screamed, trying to decide on her next move. The Porsche was faster than the Mercedes; she could probably outrun him. But he'd most likely call the police on his cell phone and have them chase her.

The automatic window came down, and the hard look in Ryan's eyes told Susan everything she needed to know.

"Where is she?" he shouted, in a voice so full of poison she feared he was going to come over and wring her neck.

I gotta get out of here, she thought, panicking. She stomped on the accelerator, and her tires squealed as she veered down the road with Ryan following on her tail. When she got to the intersection leading out of their gated community, the traffic light turned red and she had to stop. Ryan's car door slammed. He got of the car and was coming after her. *Oh God.*

"I'll just have to take my chances," she said, closing her eyes as she floored the engine and shot out into the intersection.

Chance, however, was not kind to the woman who'd been posing as Susan Sims for over a year. A tractor-trailer truck carrying a load of gravel was rumbling down the road, and she drove directly into its path.

Thirty-Four

Emily was finally scheduled to go home in the morning. Well, not home exactly; she still didn't know where "home" was. She was, however, finally leaving the rehabilitation hospital to move in with Belinda. After hobbling on crutches for six weeks, she was now able to get around with the aid of a cane. Her orthopedist predicted she'd probably be walking on her own within a month. She decided to take one last stroll around the hospital grounds, and as she walked she recalled a conversation she'd had with Belinda two weeks earlier.

"What color do you want your room to be?" Belinda had asked. "Maybe a restful blue?"

"I've done enough resting for a lifetime," Emily said with a laugh. "Leave it the way it is."

"I can't do that. The room is a god-awful shade of purple."

"Purple? Why would you have a purple room? Oh," Emily said, finally understanding. "Are you giving me Chelsea's old room?"

Belinda nodded.

"Are you sure? I could get my own apartment, you know. Thanks to Mortimer, I have the funds."

"Absolutely not. You're staying with me. At least for a while. And I want to do whatever I can to make you feel comfortable in the room."

"Good. Then leave it purple. I never mentioned this before, but I think purple is a fantastic color."

She also assured Belinda that she found Billy Corgan of

Smashing Pumpkins to be cute, not creepy, and didn't mind his visage leering down from the wall.

It wasn't as if she were going to be staying at her friend's house forever, only until she found work and became accustomed to living outside the hospital walls. Besides, Emily had a strong suspicion her friend's life would be changing in a significant way soon.

It had been a little over a month since Mortimer Stiles had made his appearance in Emily's hospital room, and he and Belinda had become what Belinda called an "instant couple." (Just add some heavy groping and stir. No heating necessary, Belinda joked.) They engaged in the kind of intense phone conversations only new lovers have, private talks that stretched into the wee hours of night. When her son, Andy, stayed with his father, Mortimer would usually sleep over at Belinda's house.

"Don't worry. I'll cut out the adult slumber parties as soon as you move in," Belinda said with a wink.

"I don't want you to change your habits just because I'm moving in," Emily protested.

"It's fine. Helping you get your life in order is my main priority," Belinda insisted, but Emily still worried she was going to be in the way.

The air outside was more biting than crisp, and Emily ducked her head against the wind. Winter, with its watery gray skies and straw-colored lawns, seemed to have trundled into Alabama overnight.

As she haltingly made her way across the leaf-strewn grounds, the smell of wood smoke spiraled into her nostrils, awakening memories of velvety hot chocolate, scratchy wool sweaters, popping fires, and something else: a voice. It was dusk, and a mother called her daughter into the house.

Emily stopped walking and stood motionless, aching to hear the voice again. "Susan!" This time the voice was more insistent, and she envisioned a young child running up a winding path toward a small white clapboard house. The window panes blazed with the promise of hot soup, a lit hearth, and the comforting clatter of dishes. She wanted nothing more than to burst into the toasty house, shuck off her shoes, and walk stocking-foot into the kitchen, where she'd peer into pots and snitch a curl of carrot from the cutting board.

"Coming, Mother," she whispered.

Even though it was seven a.m., it was still dark out when Emily took a final tour of her hospital room, looking for any personal effects she might have forgotten to pack. Yesterday, after her walk, she'd retrieved her money from the hospital safe, and now it lined the bottom of her oversized purse. A sealed envelope addressed to Belinda was on the chair beside the bed. She closed her mind to her friend's reaction when she found the letter.

"You're doing the right thing," she whispered to herself, satisfied she hadn't forgotten anything. When she closed the door and stepped into the hall, she almost ran into a new nurse named Laura, who was pushing a breakfast cart.

"Careful," Laura said with a smile, her auburn ponytail bobbing behind her. "Or you really will have egg on your face." Her glance registered the tied-up pillowcase Emily was carrying, bulging with her meager belongings.

"Running away from home?" she asked.

"I'm meeting Belinda downstairs," Emily said in explanation, even though it was a lie. Belinda wasn't due to pick her up for at least two more hours.

"Don't be a stranger," the nurse said cheerily as Emily headed toward the bank of elevators down the hall.

Emily nervously exited the building, half expecting someone to stop her. The taxi she'd ordered was idling outside under the pale yellow glare of a streetlight, the smoke from its exhaust mingling with the diminishing darkness. She hobbled to the cab, cane in hand, and asked to be driven to the bus station. With no identification, it was the only form of transportation she could use.

The cab felt like a safe cozy cave, lit by the numbers on the meter and the green phosphorescence of the dash. A barely audible strain of music droned from an easy-listening station on the radio, and the interior smelled like sausage biscuits, likely from the cabbie's breakfast. Condensation had formed on the window, and she traced her real name in the scrim of fog:

Susan.

She no longer wanted to be connected with the drug user and prostitute named Emily. She still didn't remember that period in her life—a time when she'd been so disconnected from her true nature she'd used a false name—nor did she ever want to remember.

"I'm so sorry, Belinda," she whispered as the cab bumped through the downtown streets of Birmingham.

Her friend would certainly search for her at the bus station, but with Emily's two-hour head start, it would be impossible for Belinda to know which of the five morning buses she'd boarded since she was now traveling under her real name.

She hated to cause Belinda worry, but now that most of her memories had returned, she wanted to put her horrific past behind her. She would have preferred a proper goodbye, but she knew Belinda would try to talk her out of leaving.

The longer she stayed in Birmingham, the more likely her bad memories would leap out of the bushes like the bogeyman. She had no desire to recall the events that led up to her coma. Ever.

Thirty-Five

All of the major newspapers carried the details of Susan's accident on their front pages, and CNN featured updates of the story every half hour. Not that there was a lot to report. Susan was unconscious and not expected to ever wake, and Ryan refused to speak to the press. The only people Ryan had seen since Susan's collision with the gravel truck were his sister and Wanda Myers.

The three of them had congregated in the small gloomy chapel attached to the hospital. Darcy's face was slack, and she kept clutching the side of the carved wooden pew to steady herself. She was still reeling from hearing the truth about Susan, and was clearly doped up on all kind of meds.

"I swear on my mother's grave that your family's secret will die with me," Wanda said in a shaky voice, holding up her hand as if making a pledge.

"Thank you, Wanda," Ryan said. His eyes were swollen from crying—not for the woman who was barely alive in the hospital, but for *his* Susan. She was completely lost to him, and the only person who knew exactly what happened to her couldn't speak.

Ryan returned home from the hospital with a single mission in mind: to eradicate any trace of Susan's imposter. He tackled the closets, stuffing newly bought dresses and shoes into twenty-five-gallon garbage bags. The colors were garish, the detailing flashy—every outfit the woman had ever purchased screamed, "Look at me!" How could he ever have believed that monster was Susan?

In the very back of the closet, puddled on the floor, was a

sleeveless blue sheath, the dress Susan had worn the night they'd first made love. Most of her old clothes had been relegated to the attic by the imposter; she must have overlooked this piece. He dropped to his knees and brought the fabric to his face. "Oh, Susan," he whispered, rocking back and forth on his heels. "What did she do to you, sweetheart?"

The phone interrupted his reverie. He crawled to the bedside table and consulted the caller ID. It was Susan's physician on the other end.

"I'm calling about your wife," the doctor said. "She's regained consciousness and wants to see you."

Thirty-Six

Emily, a.k.a. Susan Sims, alighted from the Trailways bus, her butt aching from too much sitting, and arrived at the last place she'd remembered living, Devon's Island, South Carolina.

"Susan Sims, this is your life," she whispered to herself as she entered a bus station, which smelled of dirty feet and was the size of the average person's living room.

It was misting outside, and the windows of the station clouded up as she slipped some quarters into the slot of a pay phone to call a cab.

A yellow-and-black checkered car arrived and took her to the Winchester Hotel on Bay Street. As she paid the driver, she spied the green-and-white striped awning of the coffee shop two blocks from the hotel. On nice days she'd sat outside under one of the umbrellas with an iced coffee sniffing the sea air. Three doors down from the coffee shop was the dusty and narrow antiquarian bookstore where she'd stocked up on battered editions of Jane Austen novels.

She entered the lobby of the turn-of-the-century hotel and waited at an imposing carved-oak check-in desk, which had real keys on brass tags hanging on the back wall. If it weren't for the blue glow of the clerk's computer, Susan could have sworn she'd time-traveled back to the late 1800s.

The clerk asked for a credit card, and Susan fibbed and told him her wallet had been stolen. She paid for the room charges in cash and was asked to leave a hundred-dollar deposit for incidentals. Then she went into the gift shop to purchase something to read. The magazines in the rack out front all looked several weeks out of date, so she chose a Sue Grafton mystery instead.

If the lobby was circa 1898, her room was pure seventies, with squat lamps, green shag carpet, and a crudely rendered seagull print hanging above the bed.

She dropped her bundle of belongings on the burnished orange bedspread and glanced out the window. The drizzle had stopped, so she descended the twisting staircase back to the lobby and walked seven blocks until she came to a brick office building with a sign out front that read "For rent or sale."

She peered through the smudged windows. There wasn't a trace left of her veterinary practice—just a few empty cardboard boxes. Everything had been sold or discarded, but what did she expect after so much time?

She perched on the stoop outside the front of the building, trying to decide on her next plan of action. She didn't know why she'd come to Devon's Island other than that it was the last place she remembered as being home. She'd only moved to South Carolina to be near her grandmother, and Lois had been dead for almost two years.

She finally had the answers to many of the questions about her life before the coma. She'd been adopted when she was less than a week old. Her father abandoned the family when Susan was eight. They'd been living in Asheville, North Carolina at the time, and her mother, Barbara, who used to baked cookies once a week and make shadow puppets on the wall, took to her bedroom every night with a bottle of gin. Susan was expected to take on a lot of responsibility at a young age. By the time she turned nine, she was in charge of most of the household chores, from standing on a step stool, stirring the orange powder from boxed macaroni and cheese into cooked noodles, to stuffing heavy heaps of wet bed sheets into the dryer.

As a kid, Susan had precious little free time and few friends. Her companions were her pets. Barbara, perhaps out of guilt for being such a lackadaisical mother, allowed her daughter as many animals as she wanted as long as she took full responsibility for them, including buying their food and paying for their shots. Susan's love of pets eventually led to a post-grad degree in veterinary medicine. She'd intended to set up a practice in Asheville, but her plans changed when her mother died of cirrhosis of the liver two months after Susan had earned her diploma.

"I don't know what it is with the women in this family, but we have lousy luck with men," said her grandmother Lois, whose husband had also left her for another woman. Susan made a promise to herself that she'd never be like her mother.

After Barbara's funeral, Lois begged Susan to move to South Carolina. As an incentive, she offered to financially back her practice. Her grandmother was her only living family member, so Susan agreed to make the move.

Susan settled into her grandmother's house intending to stay only until she could find an apartment of her own, but she quickly grew to cherish the first taste of family life she'd experienced since her father had left. She and Lois had homemade banana nut muffins and strong black coffee each morning, chatting over the daily paper and watching the birds and squirrels squabble over the feeders on the back porch. Susan lived with Lois for three years, until her grandmother died in her sleep.

One of her last recollections was meeting in the lawyers' office for the closing on Lois's house. She'd already moved into a rental home with her dog, Mutsy, and had planned to continue to work until the end of the summer. That was where her memories stopped. Where was Mutsy? And how had she ended up roaming the streets of Birmingham, Alabama? She knew her grandmother had left her some money, but obviously she'd run through it, or she wouldn't have been trading sex for drug money.

You might never recover the memories of the year before you were assaulted.

Those were Dr. Perry's exact words. Susan had lost a little more than a year.

"Susan, is that you?" She nearly toppled off the stoop of the building at the sound of her name.

"It's me, Rochelle." A puffy-faced woman with choppy bangs lumbered up the sidewalk. *Rochelle Jenkins.* She worked as a receptionist in the doctor's office next door to Susan's practice. Sometimes she and Susan strolled to the coffee shop and grabbed a pimiento-cheese sandwich together. "Gosh, it's been ages."

"Rochelle," Susan said softly, trying to find her voice. "Great to see you."

Rochelle reached the stoop and stared down at Susan. She had to be nearing thirty but looked far younger, with a round face and sulky oversized lips.

"Good golly, you're thin. Have you been doing Paleo?"

"Paleo?"

"The diet?"

Susan wasn't familiar with the Paleo Diet, but she knew it couldn't be nearly as effective as the IV diet she'd been on for so long.

"I've been sick," Susan said, touching her cane. "But I'm better now."

"Checking out your old stomping grounds, I see," Rochelle said, looking the building up and down. "Thinking about setting up shop again? You'll have some competition. There's a new vet on Broad Street."

"Really? I hadn't actually decided—"

Rochelle grinned, revealing a bit of salad wedged between her front teeth. "Did you bring your fellow with you? I'd love to meet him."

"Fellow?" Susan flinched.

"The guy you moved away for. You were so *mysterious* about him at the time."

Susan stood silent for a moment, her lips slightly parted as if she were about to speak. So there had been a man in her life after all, and she'd moved to Birmingham to be near him. Obviously the relationship had gone horribly wrong.

"We broke up," Susan said quickly. "It's just me now."

"That's too bad," Rochelle said. "You were over the moon for him. Didn't seem like you at all, you picky thing. Are you moving back to Devon's Island?"

"I don't think so."

Rochelle was right. It sounded out of character for her to pick up and run off with a man. She'd always been so cautious when it came to romance. Who was the guy? Had her love for him led to drug abuse? Had she ended up repeating the mistakes of her mother after all?

Rochelle glanced at her watch. "I gotta get back to work. How long are you going to be around? We could have lunch. Just like old times."

"Maybe we'll do that," Susan said.

After Rochelle left, Susan caught a cab out to her grandmother's house just outside town. From the window of the car, she stared at the old Victorian structure with its steeply pitched roof and spindly gingerbread porch. The last happy moments she could remember had been spent within those walls. She dabbed at her eyes as she asked the cabbie to move on.

Susan returned to her room and dialed the number of vital records in North Carolina, arranging to have her birth certificate sent to the hotel so she could start the process of rebuilding her identity. She had no idea what kind of shape her driving record was in and whether or not she'd had run-ins with the police. Likely her credit rating was shot. There were so many things she dreaded finding out about herself.

Later that evening, she set out for the nearby coffee shop to get a bite. A cold wind blew in from the ocean two blocks over, and the light jacket purchased for her by Belinda in Birmingham didn't ward off the chill. She hugged her arms and walked through the steam of her own breath as she passed a restaurant with a blue neon sign outside identifying it as Crabby Abby's. A male patron in a long dark overcoat emerged, and the first few lines of the Beatles song "Let It Be" floated through the open door.

"Let it be..." Susan found herself whistling the tune as she leaned her cane against the building and knelt to tie the laces of her tennis shoe. A bank of clouds shifted in the heavens and one star gave a weak wink before the haze swallowed it up.

As she limped along the sidewalk, the song played over and over in her head like a warped CD. Susan had no idea what she was going to do in the next weeks, months, and years. What did people do when they had to start their lives from scratch?

They surrender. She could almost hear Belinda's voice in her ear, just like the "whispered words of wisdom" in the Beatles song. Could Susan surrender? Could she really trust an HP to give her life direction?

You don't really have anything to lose. No direction, no friends, no family. No compass to help her find her true north.

The star had escaped the gauze of clouds. Susan imagined it to be the twinkle in the eye of an unseen angel. She wasn't sure she could completely surrender, but at the very least, she could ask a question.

"Why did I wake up from my coma?" she whispered. "There must be some reason. It's not as if the world has even noticed I was missing from it for a year. Why am I still here?"

Thirty-Seven

"I'm frankly amazed she can speak, in her condition," the doctor said, rubbing his bristly chin as he stood in the ICU waiting room.

"May I see her now?" Ryan said.

"Yes. Go in immediately." He grasped Ryan's shoulder in a gesture of sympathy. "I don't know how long you'll have."

Ryan entered the ICU and his gaze swung to the bedridden figure on the left-hand side of the room. "Susan" looked the same as when he'd left her last, motionless and battered, as if she'd been savagely beaten with a baseball bat. He'd been told her internal injuries were even worse and it was a miracle she could still draw a breath.

"Ryan. Is that you?" The eyelids fluttered; the voice was weak but audible.

So she *could* speak.

"May we have some privacy?" Ryan said to the attending nurse. He grasped his wife's hand in a show of being a dutiful husband. As soon as the nurse disappeared behind the curtains, he dropped it like a stone.

"Where is she? Just tell me that. You killed her, didn't you?"

There was no response, just the steady wheeze from her respirator. It was not lost on him that over a year ago he had been standing in this very room, begging God to save the woman he'd believed to be Susan.

"Tell me," he demanded.

He assumed Susan's imposter lost consciousness again until

her chest made a rattling sound and she gasped out a sentence.

"Susan always had it so much better than me, you know," she said. "I was the one who was abandoned."

"What happened to Susan?" Ryan asked as he hovered over her, hands clenched at his side.

"You hear it all. Or you hear nothing." The voice from the bed was unwavering and surprisingly strong.

He had the urge to shake the answer out of her but resisted.

"Sit," she ordered. "Listen. This may take a while." She closed her eyes as if summoning the energy for what was coming up next. "As I'm sure you already know, I'm not Susan. My name is Emily Hewitt, and I'm Susan's identical twin sister."

Ryan nodded, bracing himself to hear her story.

She and Susan had been born to a teenage mother who gave them both up at birth. Susan had been adopted, but Emily, being the smaller twin, had a host of health problems and ended up in the foster care system. She briefly described a bleak childhood that led her to a life of drugs and prostitution. Ryan was impatient with her backstory. He just wanted to know what had happened to Susan.

The imposter also explained how she'd learned of Susan's existence through a hot-dog vendor named Wanda. Suspecting Susan might be her lost twin, she called her at her office and convinced Susan to meet her in a diner in downtown Birmingham.

"That was the mysterious family errand Susan went on just before her accident," Ryan said, more to himself than the woman lying on the bed. "I shouldn't have let her go alone."

Emily ignored his comment and continued her ragged monologue. When they were at the diner, Emily had told her twin sister her sob story, hoping Susan would offer her money, but instead Susan insisted on taking her home with her. Emily was desperate for drugs and didn't want to go anywhere with her sister.

"I lured her into an alley, telling her I had some of my stuff hidden there," Emily said. "With Susan hovering over me, I reached behind a trash can for a two-by-four. It took one whack on the head to knock her out cold. She went limp and I snatched her purse from her arm and dumped its contents on the ground, searching for her wallet. I found credit cards but no cash. Susan wasn't wearing jewelry, and there was nothing in her purse worth pawning. I had the keys to her Chevrolet Tahoe parked in front of the diner, but I doubted my dealer would trade rock for a stolen SUV."

"So the blow to the head killed her?" Ryan said. Every cell in his body jumped with the urge to throttle her.

"No," she said flatly, as if his concern for Susan was inconsequential. "She was still alive, moaning. I was furious. Why did she get to have pretty clothes and a pricey SUV while I walked the streets? I decided the very least I was going to get out of the deal was her suit and shoes. As soon as I put them on, I felt completely different, way more powerful. 'How does it feel to be lying naked in an alley?' I shouted in her face. 'How does it feel to be me?'"

Ryan tried to block out the lurid image of Susan lying helpless in a filthy alley. "But she was still alive?"

Emily's eyes flickered, signifying a dismissal of his question. "Suddenly an idea occurred to me. I could drive the Tahoe to her house, steal her blind, and no one would be the wiser. It was the perfect plan, except for one small detail." She made a noise that sounded like a cough, but Ryan wondered if it was meant to be a laugh. "I'd never learned to drive. Let me tell you something, it's a stupid idea trying to learn to drive in Atlanta traffic. The next thing I knew I woke up in the hospital, and you were was standing over my bed calling out Susan's name. You thought I was her, and I wasn't in any position to argue with you, Ryan."

Ryan hated hearing his name in her mouth, hated that he hadn't known immediately that Emily wasn't Susan.

"What happened to Susan? You have to tell me."

Emily gasped for air, the effort of speech obviously draining her. Ryan's muscles were tensed. Would she be able to finish her story without losing consciousness?

Finally her breathing evened out and she motioned with her head for Ryan to come closer.

"She was alive," she said in a feeble whisper, "but I couldn't risk her waking up and reporting her car missing. Just before I left the alley I gave her one more final whack on the head. I don't know if I finished her off or not, but she did stop moaning."

"Nurse!" he shouted, grabbing the sides of his chair and squeezing so hard a sharp pain shot through his wrist. He needed someone in the room to prevent him from reaching over and snapping Emily's neck into several pieces.

The nurse drew back the curtain, and a buzzer sounded. Emily's eyes closed; her features were blank. It was that quick and quiet, almost as if he'd killed her with his rage.

"I'm sorry. It's over," the nurse said. Ryan got up from his chair and wordlessly left the room with only one thought in his mind. He wanted to find Susan's body and bring her home.

Thirty-Eight

It wasn't as easy to locate Susan's remains as Ryan thought it would be. He assumed she was buried in a paupers' field somewhere in Alabama, but when he visited the archives of the *Birmingham News* searching for murder victims, he found no homicides involving a woman of Susan's description. Without giving away any specific details, he also enlisted the help of Gordon, his security person, who had some connections in the homicide division of the Birmingham Police Department.

Ryan didn't know what else to do. Had Emily lied? Maybe the murder hadn't actually taken place in Birmingham. Or had she omitted details of what she'd done with Susan's remains? Ryan couldn't imagine why there was no record of the death. Surely Susan's body had been found. It couldn't still be in that alley.

Ryan was seated at his computer, trying to think about his next plan of action, when the phone rang.

"Mr. Blaine," Gordon said. "I heard back from one of my buddies in Homicide."

"And?"

"The detective called me 'cause he remembered a case similar to the one you'd described. He didn't work on it, but a buddy of his did. A young woman was beaten in an alley, just like you said."

"Yes?"

"The reason he had no record of it was because his division didn't handle it."

"Why?"

"Because it wasn't a homicide." Gordon paused. "The woman didn't die from her assault. She survived it."

As soon as he hung up the phone, Ryan clicked to the 2016 archives of the Birmingham newspaper, this time typing "assault" in the search box instead of "murder." Immediately he found what he was looking for:

ASSAULT VICTIM HAS YET TO BE IDENTIFIED

An unidentified woman was found Tuesday in an alley just off Third Street. She was beaten with a wooden board found nearby and remains in critical condition at University Hospital. The woman is blonde and blue-eyed and believed to be in her mid-twenties, and may go by the name of Emily. Anyone having information about her identity is asked to call the Birmingham Police Department.

Ryan seized the phone and dialed directory assistance for University Hospital. When he was connected to the hospital operator, he said, "Yes. I'd like to see if I could find some information on a patient admitted in June of 2016."

He was passed around to several different people, and when he finally got an admissions clerk, she told him patient records were confidential and refused to help.

Ryan never played the fame card, but in this case he was willing to make an exception.

"This is Ryan Blaine. Son of former president Richard Blaine. I hate to be a pain, but I really need your help."

After an excited squeal, the admission's clerk said, "I was so sorry to hear about your wife." In minutes she gave him what he was after.

"The patient, known only as Emily, was discharged on November seventh and admitted to Magnolia Manor, a long-term care facility," she said. "That's all I have."

"A long-term care facility? You mean a—"

"A nursing home," the clerk said.

Ryan hung up the phone. A nursing home? An image of Susan among the elderly and infirm flashed through his mind.

She was alive but, as he feared, completely incapacitated.

His breathing quickened as he punched in the number for Magnolia Manor, asking for the director.

"Mona Scales. May I help you?" said a pleasant voice.

Ryan introduced himself and told her he was looking for a young woman named Emily.

"What a thrill to hear from you, Mr. Blaine," Mona said. "I wish I could help you. I'm afraid Emily's not with us anymore."

Ryan swallowed. "Was she transferred to another nursing home?"

"No." Mona clucked her tongue. "I'm sorry to say no one knows where she is."

"I...I don't understand. How could she be missing? It's not like she could get up and walk out of there on her own."

"That's exactly what she did, Mr. Blaine," Mona said patiently. "I don't mean she walked out of Magnolia Manor, but last week she left the rehabilitation facility where she was being treated. Unfortunately, she didn't tell anyone where she was going."

Ryan couldn't keep his voice from cracking. "Are you telling me that Susan, er, rather, Emily, can walk?"

"Yes," Mona said. "It took nearly six months for her to learn again, but now she gets along quite well."

"She can walk," he repeated dumbly.

"And talk. Since waking from her coma, she's almost good as new."

"Almost?"

"She still has memory problems. Her past has been coming back to her in fits and starts, and when she left, there were still so many holes." Mona paused. "You're the first person, besides a couple of reporters, who has ever asked after her. Did you know Emily?"

"I would rather not discuss it over the phone," Ryan said, his heart leaping with hope. "Please. Can I come there to see you?"

Thirty-Nine

"This is Belinda," Mona said, ushering Ryan into her office at Magnolia Manor. "I asked her here today because she knows Emily better than anyone else. I'll give the two of you some privacy." The nursing home director shut the door, leaving Ryan and Belinda sitting across from each other.

Belinda, a woman with a lush figure and dark expressive eyes, spoke first.

"I've been beside myself over Emily," she said, pulling a tissue from a box on the desk. "I've tried everything under the sun to find her. I went to the bus station, and I even hired a private detective, but it's like she's fallen off the side of the Earth."

"I understand you were her best friend," Ryan said, trying to keep the urgency out of his voice. "How much of her life does she remember?"

"She left me a letter in her hospital room saying she'd recovered her memory until a year before her coma." Belinda said, twisting a gold hoop earring. "She doesn't remember anything about her life in Birmingham before the accident. She said she couldn't bear to recall all those horrible times when she was a drug addict, and that's why she was moving on."

She doesn't remember because it never happened, Ryan almost said. Belinda seemed like a sincere person, and she'd obviously cared about Emily. Could he trust her?

"She never called herself Emily, and she never lived in Birmingham," Ryan said quickly, before he could change his mind.

Then he told Belinda the entire story, from the day her twin sister assaulted her to her imposter's recent death.

Belinda blanched as Ryan spoke, as if she couldn't believe what she was hearing.

"She didn't seem like a person who was capable of throwing her life away," she said, shaking her head. "It didn't fit her. She seemed so together. You should have see her going through recovery; that lady was a bulldog."

"Yes," Ryan said with a chuckle. "That sounds like my Susan."

"I just knew she had to belong to somebody." Belinda crushed her tissue in her hand so it looked like a pale pink flower. "That someone loved her to pieces."

He stared down at the pleats of his wool trousers, not daring to catch her eye for fear he might lose control altogether. "Susan doesn't know someone loves her. She obviously doesn't remember me."

"Her neurologist says she may never recover memories that occurred the year before her accident."

Ryan nodded. A month before Susan had her fateful encounter with her twin sister in the alley, Ryan and she had opened a bottle of champagne and she'd proposed a toast.

"To the best year ever," she'd said. "One year ago today you bulldozed your way into my life. Thank God you didn't give up." According to Belinda, their whole time together could have been wiped from Susan's mind as if it never existed.

"But you know what, Ryan?" Belinda said softly. "I think she will remember you, eventually. I don't think it's possible to forget the greatest love of your life. I once read a book on soul mates and the author claimed the memory of the people we love deeply is never erased, even over several lifetimes."

"I hope you're right." Ryan pinched the skin between his eyes. "I can't imagine ever forgetting Susan. Now I hope I can find her. I'm going to drive to Devon's Island, South Carolina in the morning. It's the place we met. Maybe she went back there."

"It's so ironic. To finally discover Susan's alive and not be able to find her," Belinda said. "It reminds me a little bit of those sad love stories you hear on—" She snapped her fingers and grinned. "Wait a minute. I know how to find Susan."

"How?"

"The radio show," Belinda said. "You have to call *Minerva*. Have you ever heard of her?"

Ryan startled at the name. He hadn't called the program in months. "What do you mean? Why should I call Minerva?"

"Because Susan listens to it every night without fail."

Forty

Susan reclined in the movie theater watching a late-night showing of *Casablanca*. It was Saturday night, and she hadn't felt like spending the evening in the confines of her hotel room.

Her birth certificate had finally arrived at the hotel, and today she'd visited the Department of Motor Vehicles and obtained a new driver's license. She was catching an early-morning bus out of Devon's Island. The town could support only one veterinarian, so there was no point in sticking around. She had plans to go to Columbia to check into opening a practice there.

The theater was empty, save for a patron sitting two rows behind her. The woman had made a raid on the concession stand. Susan kept hearing the rustling of candy wrappers, the rattling of ice in her soda, and the sound of her hand rooting around in her popcorn tub.

Susan glanced at the glowing dial of her watch. It was fifteen minutes before midnight. If she stayed for the rest of the film, she'd miss *Minerva*. The radio show was one of her few reminders of Caroline. When Susan closed her eyes during *Minerva*, she swore she could hear the creak of Caroline's rocking chair and her mutterings to the show's callers.

It won't hurt to miss Minerva one night, Susan thought, leaning back even farther into her seat. Elsa was asking a reluctant Sam to play "As Time Goes By." As soon as Sam started playing the song on the piano, the woman behind her stopped her grazing and began to sing along.

It was Susan's favorite scene and the woman was spoiling it. Even when Rick stopped Sam from playing and spied Elsa sitting beside him, the woman continued to vocalize loudly.

Susan was about to turn around and shush her, when she realized the woman wasn't singing "As Time Goes By." She was warbling a Beatles song instead.

"Listen, do you want to know a secret?" she sang.

At that moment, a wave of longing for Caroline passed through Susan, almost as if the old woman were there, her voice in Susan's ear, her warm hand on her own. She quickly rose from her seat. She didn't want to skip the radio show, not even for one night.

"Gee, sorry," said the woman behind her when she spied Susan hurrying down the aisle. "I thought I was alone in the theater. I'll stop singing. Isn't it nutty how certain songs get stuck in your head? Although I don't know how come I was singing that particular song; I hadn't heard it in a while."

"It's okay," Susan said. "I just realized there's something I need to do."

She hustled back to the hotel, flew up the stairs, and switched on the radio. The program had just begun. A young woman was talking about her boyfriend, who'd recently dumped her. "I'm going loco, Minerva. I keep driving by his house and calling him on his cell. He's like heroin."

Susan nodded in recognition as she climbed up on the sunken mattress. She turned off the lamp and clutched the hotel's foam pillow to her stomach. Her mother had been obsessed with her father, letting his memory eat away at her liver and her life. And what had Susan done to herself because of her own addiction to her fiancé?

That's one dark alley in my mind I hope I never have to visit, she thought. She listened to several more sob stories and their accompanying love songs. Someone had requested a Kenny G number, and the soft droning of the saxophone worked on her like a glass of warm milk. She was nearly asleep when someone screamed, "No money down with three percent financing! You heard me right. No money down." Susan startled awake. The clock radio's reception was poor, and sometimes other stations would bleed over into the *Minerva* show. The car commercial faded and was replaced by Minerva's silky voice.

"I have Alone in Atlanta on the phone," Minerva said. "Hello, Alone. It's been such a long time. We've missed you."

"Thank you, Minerva. It's nice to be back."

Alone in Atlanta? Susan propped herself up on her elbow. She'd heard that name before; she was certain of it.

"I hope you're calling to tell us your girlfriend came back."

"I wish that were true," said the caller. His voice was a rich baritone and it caused an unexpected shiver to pass through Susan's torso. "I'm calling because I have reason to believe she might be listening to the show this very minute."

"That's wonderful, Alone. What would you like to say to her? Her name was Susan, wasn't it?"

"Yes." A pause. "She's an animal behaviorist, and her favorite candy is Hershey's Kisses."

"Oh my God," Susan said, sitting upright. Who *was* this caller?

"Okay," Minerva said. "What's your message to Susan?"

"I failed her," he said in a halting voice. "She was a sleeping beauty for a very long time. I should have been there to give her an awakening kiss."

Susan gasped. He was talking about *her*. He sounded so genuine, and his voice was so familiar and dear, like a song on the tip of her tongue. Warmth rushed through her. She belonged to someone!

"I hope Susan hears you," Minerva said.

"Or Emily," replied the caller. "She might still be going by that name."

Susan's jaw hardened. Obviously the caller had known her in Birmingham. Was he the reason she'd turned to drugs? And why hadn't he ever visited her?

"That's very romantic, Alone," Minerva said. "Do you have a song you want me to play for her?"

"How about 'Somewhere Out There'?"

Fear rippled through Susan's body. This man was part of her past—unspeakable parts she never wanted to recall. *Turn off the radio and forget you ever heard his voice*, she thought. Obviously he still had some residual power over her, or her heart wouldn't have leaped at the sound of his voice. Something awful had happened between them. Something she didn't want to know. She reached across the lamp table.

"You got it," Minerva said.

Her hand fumbled for the off button, but she couldn't find it in the dark. She located the cord trailing out of the back and was about to give it a yank when Minerva said, "Wait!"

Susan's fingers froze on the cord. It was almost as if the radio host was addressing her.

"Every once in a while I get this little voice in my head that tells me what to do," Minerva said. "And sometimes I even listen. My voice is telling me that's the wrong song for you, Alone. I've got something better."

"Whatever you think is best, Minerva," the caller said softly. "I trust you."

"Good," Minerva said. "This is for you, Susan or Emily or whoever you are. I hope you're listening. And if you are, call the show at 1-800-OURLOVE and we'll help you to get in touch with Alone in Atlanta."

Susan tensed her back muscles, waiting for the song, although she didn't know why. It hardly mattered what song Minerva chose; she was never getting in touch with Alone in Atlanta.

"All you is need love" flowed from the radio, loud and clear, without a hint of static. "Love is all you need."

Her entire body trembled as she listened to the song in its entirety. Slowly, her fears, which had hung in her mind heavy and thick as thunderclouds, were pushed aside by a voice whispering in her ear, "Don't you worry, lamb. He's safe. Call him. He loves you as much as I do."

Caroline! She could feel her presence in the room, smell the sharp astringency of her witch hazel, hear the steady creak of her rocker. It was as if she'd crossed over from the sweet everlasting to deliver her message.

"Go on, Sleeping Beauty. It's time for you to awaken to your whole life."

Tears sprang from her eyes as she listened to Caroline's soft drawl. As soon as the song ended, she picked up the phone and dialed.

"This is Minerva," a voice said.

"This is Susan. Calling for Alone in Atlanta. Tell him that he's finally found me."

Forty-One

The next morning Susan stood outside the hotel, waiting for Ryan to arrive. He'd called her last night and Susan had hoped that when she heard his voice she would recognize him, but she did not.

He wanted to come to her that very second, but she said that she needed a good night's sleep first and urged him to wait until morning. Now that it was morning she couldn't help but wonder if she'd made a mistake in contacting him. Yes, they have been in love at one time, but now he was a stranger to her. Who knew how she would feel when she saw him?

She watched the streets; Devon's Island was sleepy this time of year and there was little traffic. So far she'd only seen a handful of cars.

A convertible turned on to the street, a man and two dogs inside. The radio was playing and the deejay was talking about the good weather. The man slowed and parked in front of the hotel. The man opened the passenger side door and the dogs bounded in her direction. They both jumped on her and nearly knocked her over with their exuberance.

"Liberty! Mutsy!" the man called out.

The dogs were licking her face. A rush of memories washed over her. "Lib? Mutsy? Oh my God!"

The dogs continued to lap at her face, as if they could not get enough of the taste of her skin. She sensed the man standing over them. Susan felt shy and was afraid to look up at him.

"Hello, Susan," he said softly.

Her eyes met his, and when he smiled it was like the sun peeking through a bank of dark clouds. Memories, warm and poignant, came flooding back. So many wonderful memories.

And love, she thought. *You love this man. Ever since the moment you met him.*

"Ryan? Is that you?"

He nodded, tears filling his eyes.

She approached him and touched his cheek as if she had to confirm that he was real. "It's really you. I thought I'd lost for you forever."

"I've missed you so much," he said, his voice thick with emotion.

Susan leaned in to kiss him, his lips so soft and familiar. She felt as if she could get lost in that kiss. Except for Liberty and Mutsy, they were completely alone on the street, and yet she felt like she was being watched by unseen eyes. She glanced up at the sky. A single heart-shaped cloud floated above, and the smell of Caroline's witch hazel filled her nostrils.

A song reached her ears from the radio in the car. One of her favorites: "Heaven is Place on Earth" by Belinda Carlisle. It was an apt song, because at that moment she genuinely felt like she was in heaven now that she was back in Ryan's arms again.

"Please, let's not ever be apart again," Ryan said, holding her close.

"No," she said breathlessly, tears pricking at her eyes. "Never, ever again."

A deep knowing filled her body. Even if they were inadvertently to part again, she suspected they would always find themselves back with each other.

Their love would always find a way.

Karin Gillespie

Karin Gillespie is national bestselling author of five novels and a humor columnist for *Augusta* Magazine. Her nonfiction writing had been in the *New York Times*, *The Writer* and *Romantic Times*. She maintains a website and blog at Karingillespie.net. Sign up for her newsletter on her website, follow her on Twitter or connect with her on Facebook.

Books by Karin Gillespie

GIRL MEETS CLASS
LOVE LITERARY STYLE
DIVINELY YOURS

The Bottom Dollar Series

BET YOUR BOTTOM DOLLAR (#1)
A DOLLAR SHORT (#2)
DOLLAR DAZE (#3)

Henery Press Books

And finally, before you go...
Here are a few other books
you might enjoy:

LOVE LITERARY STYLE

Karin Gillespie

(from the Henery Press Chick Lit Collection)

They say opposites attract, and what could be more opposite than a stuffy literary writer falling for a self-published romance writer?

Novelist Aaron Mite meets Laurie Lee at a writers' colony and mistakenly believes her to be a renowned writer of important fiction. When he discovers she's a self-published romance author, he's already fallen in love with her.

Aaron thinks genre fiction is an affront to the fiction-writing craft. He often quotes the essayist, Arthur Krystal who says literary fiction "melts the frozen sea inside of us." Ironically Aaron doesn't seem to realize that he's emotionally frozen. The vivacious Laurie, lover of flamingo-patterned attire and all things hot pink, is the one person who might be capable of melting him.

In the tradition of *The Rosie Project*, *Love Literary Style* is a sparkling romantic comedy which pokes fun at the divide between low and high brow fiction.

Available at booksellers nationwide and online

Visit www.henerypress.com for details

HOW DO YOU KNOW?

Meredith Schorr

(from the Henery Press Chick Lit Collection)

Life doesn't happen on a schedule, there are no deadlines in love, and age is just a number.

On the eve of her thirty-ninth birthday, Maggie Piper doesn't look, act, or feel much different than she did at twenty-eight, but with her fortieth birthday speeding toward her like a freight train, she wonders if she should. The fear of a slowing metabolism, wrinkling of her skin, and the ticking of her biological clock leaves Maggie torn between a desire to settle down like most of her similarly-aged peers and concern that all is not perfect in her existing relationship. When a spontaneous request for a temporary break from her live-in boyfriend results in a breakup, Maggie finds herself single once again and only twelve months from the big 4.0.

As Maggie reenters the New York City dating jungle, suitors present themselves quickly, but who is "The One?" Is he a sexy coworker, one of many bachelors at a speed-dating event, or is he the man she already set free? How do you know? Her fun-loving friends and supportive family, including meddlesome "no-filter" Aunt Helen, eagerly share their (often unsolicited) opinions, but Maggie is determined to find her own way, even if she falls on her face—repeatedly.

Available at booksellers nationwide and online

Visit www.henerypress.com for details

WAKE-UP CALL

Amy Avanzino

The Wake-Up Series (#1)

(From the Henery Press Chick Lit Collection)

Sarah Winslow wakes up with a terrible hangover... and a kid in her boyfriend's bed. She makes the horrifying discovery that, due to a head injury, it's not a hangover. She's got memory loss. Overnight, five years have disappeared, and she's no longer the hard-living, fast-track, ad executive party girl she thinks she is. Now, she's the unemployed, pudgy, married, stay-at-home-mom of three kids under five, including twins.

As she slowly pieces together the mystery of how her dreams and aspirations could have disintegrated so completely in five short years, she finds herself utterly failing to manage this life she can't imagine choosing. When Sarah meets the man of her dreams, she realizes she's got to make a choice: Does she follow her bliss and "do-over" her life? Or does the Sarah she's forgotten hold the answers to how she got here... and how she can stay?

Available at booksellers nationwide and online

Visit www.henerypress.com for details

THE BREAKUP DOCTOR

Phoebe Fox

The Breakup Doctor Series (#1)

(From the Henery Press Chick Lit Collection)

Call Brook Ogden a matchmaker-in-reverse. Let others bring people together; Brook, licensed mental health counselor, picks up the pieces after things come apart. When her own therapy practice collapses, she maintains perfect control: landing on her feet with a weekly advice-to-the-lovelorn column and a successful consulting service as the Breakup Doctor: on call to help you shape up after you breakup.

Then her relationship suddenly crumbles and Brook finds herself engaging in almost every bad-breakup behavior she preaches against. And worse, she starts a rebound relationship with the most inappropriate of men: a dangerously sexy bartender with anger-management issues—who also happens to be a former patient.

As her increasingly out-of-control behavior lands her at rock-bottom, Brook realizes you can't always handle a messy breakup neatly—and that sometimes you can't pull yourself together until you let yourself fall apart.

Available at booksellers nationwide and online

Visit www.henerypress.com for details

Lightning Source UK Ltd.
Milton Keynes UK
UKOW01n1930310817
308365UK00001B/2/P